## "Humanism" and the Domestic Political Situation

The general impression of this anti-magic cult is that it is an offshoot of Christianity (some would say a heretical one), which espouses the belief that everyone should "live with no more power than what is appropriate for human beings." It is also a movement that aims to expel magicians from the nation under that pretext. Their dogma can be summarized as follows: Miracles are a domain that belongs solely to God. For any other than God to twist His divine creation is an act of evil. Humans must live with no more than the power they have been granted.

It is currently February 2097. There has been a large-scale terrorist attack targeting magicians in attendance at the Master Clans Council in Hakone. Insisting that sectarian violence within the magician community is the root cause of this attack, humanist agitators have intensified their efforts to expel magicians from Japan, claiming that they willfully left ordinary people to die in the attack. The leaders of the Ten Master Clans are hard-pressed to present a convincing response.

## The "Hlidskjalf" Hacking System

Hlidskjalf is a system hidden within another system—the USNA military's global communications interception apparatus, Echelon III. The Seven Sages are seven individuals who have operator privileges on the Hlidskjalf platform and are thus able to access whatever data they wish from the vast seas of the world's communications networks. The Hlidskjalf terminal is a VR headset that accepts the user's input via a combination of brain waves and physical gestures. It detects hand movements with inside-out cameras and reproduces those movements in a virtual environment. Floating in this simulated space, the operator defines search parameters using glowing, hovering text, with selection and confirmation commands for the results being input via brain wave assistance. It is the world's most advanced wiretapping system.

However, of the seven operators using the Hlidskjalf system, only one uses the Seven Sages moniker—Hlidskjalf's administrator and the only person directly connected to the system, Raymond S. Clark.

## Who is Gu Jie?

Gide Hague, also known as Gu Jie, was attached to Dahan's magician development facility, the Kunlun Institute. Gu Jie researched immortality magic there, and his motivations for targeting the Japanese magic community—and the Yotsuba family in particular—are currently unknown. (He himself may not even know, depending on what sort of psychological mechanisms are at play.)

Gu Jie is ninety-seven years old, but his appearance is that of a man in his fifties. While Gongjin Zhou was his apprentice, Gu Jie himself possesses comparatively low combat ability. He is a user of ancient magic, and his methods usually aren't well-suited for direct action. He specializes in techniques like Sorcery Booster, which turns humans into magical components, and Generator, which turns humans into tools and reanimates corpses, as seen during the recent terrorist attack.

Additionally, as one of the Seven Sages, Gu Jie is a major figure in the underworld who holds sway over a variety of criminal organizations, including the international anti-magic political action group, Blanche, and the crime syndicate, No-Head Dragon. However, these groups have already been destroyed.

And Gu Jie is running out of time.

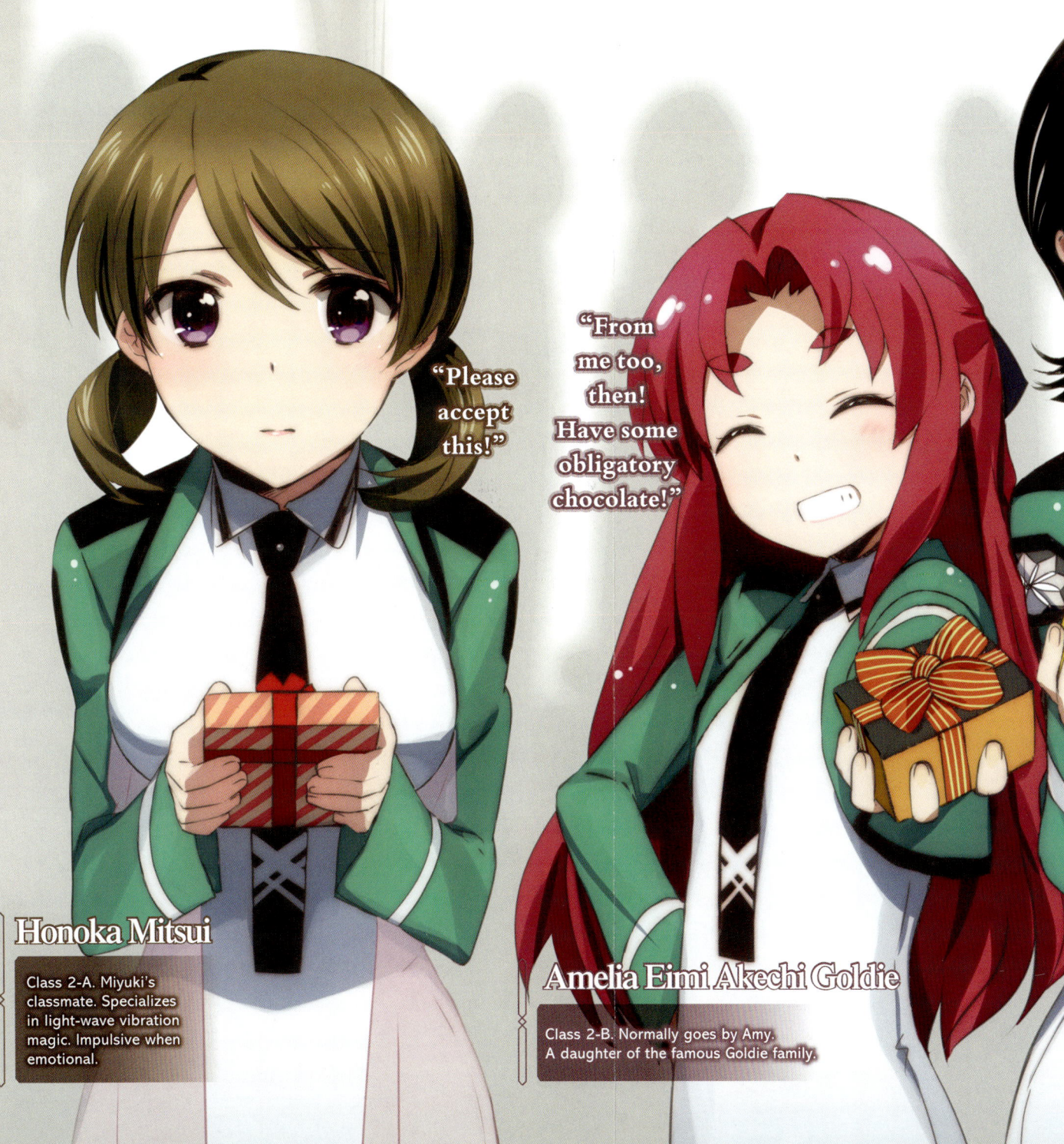

"I'm Masaki Ichijou from Third High School. I appreciate the kindness you're all showing me by allowing me to study with you. It may not be a very long time, but I look forward to the coming month."

**Masaki Ichijou**

A junior at Third High. Participated in the Nine School Competition this year as well. Next leader of the Ichijou family, one of the Ten Master Clans. Has formally proposed an engagement to Miyuki.

**Miyuki Shiba**

Class 2-A. Tatsuya's younger sister. Honor student who is currently president of the student council. Specializes in cooling magic. Has an extreme brother complex.

# The Irregular at Magic High School

## MASTER CLANS COUNCIL ARC (II)

## 18

Tsutomu Sato

Illustration Kana Ishida

NEW YORK

THE IRREGULAR AT MAGIC HIGH SCHOOL
TSUTOMU SATO

Translation by Paul Starr
Cover art by Kana Ishida

This book is a work of fiction. Names, characters, places, and incidents are the product of the author's imagination or are used fictitiously. Any resemblance to actual events, locales, or persons, living or dead, is coincidental.

MAHOUKA KOUKOU NO RETTOUSEI Vol. 18
© Tsutomu Sato 2015
Edited by Dengeki Bunko
First published in Japan in 2015 by KADOKAWA CORPORATION, Tokyo.
English translation rights arranged with KADOKAWA CORPORATION, Tokyo, through Tuttle-Mori Agency, Inc., Tokyo.

English translation © 2022 by Yen Press, LLC

Yen Press, LLC supports the right to free expression and the value of copyright. The purpose of copyright is to encourage writers and artists to produce the creative works that enrich our culture.

The scanning, uploading, and distribution of this book without permission is a theft of the author's intellectual property. If you would like permission to use material from the book (other than for review purposes), please contact the publisher. Thank you for your support of the author's rights.

Yen On
150 West 30th Street, 19th Floor
New York, NY 10001

Visit us at yenpress.com
facebook.com/yenpress
twitter.com/yenpress
yenpress.tumblr.com
instagram.com/yenpress

First Yen On Edition: January 2022

Yen On is an imprint of Yen Press, LLC.
The Yen On name and logo are trademarks of Yen Press, LLC.

The publisher is not responsible for websites (or their content) that are not owned by the publisher.

Library of Congress Cataloging-in-Publication Data
Names: Satou, Tsutomu. | Ishida, Kana, illustrator.
Title: The irregular at Magic High School / Tsutomu Satou ; Illustrations by Kana Ishida.
Other titles: Mahōka kōkō no rettosei. English
Description: First Yen On edition. | New York, NY : Yen On, 2016–
Identifiers: LCCN 2015042401 | ISBN 9780316348805 (v 1 : pbk.) | ISBN 9780316390293 (v. 2 : pbk.) | ISBN 9780316390309 (v. 3 : pbk.) | ISBN 9780316390316 (v. 4 : pbk.) | ISBN 9780316390323 (v. 5 : pbk.) | ISBN 9780316390330 (v. 6 : pbk.) | ISBN 9781975300074 (v. 7 : pbk.) | ISBN 9781975327125 (v. 8 : pbk.) | ISBN 9781975327149 (v. 9 : pbk.) | ISBN 9781975327163 (v. 10 : pbk.) | ISBN 9781975327187 (v. 11 : pbk.) | ISBN 9781975327200 (v. 12 : pbk.) | ISBN 9781975332327 (v. 13 : pbk.) | ISBN 9781975332471 (v. 14 : pbk.) | ISBN 9781975332495 (v. 15 : pbk.) | ISBN 9781975332518 (v. 16 : pbk.) | ISBN 9781975332532 (v. 17 : pbk.) | ISBN 9781975332556 (v. 18 : pbk.)
Subjects: CYAC: Brothers and sisters—Fiction. | Magic—Fiction. | High schools—Fiction. | Schools—Fiction. | Japan—Fiction. | Science fiction.
Classification: LCC PZ7.1.S265 Ir 2016 | DDC [Fic]—dc23
LC record available at http://lccn.loc.gov/2015042401

ISBNs: 978-1-9753-3255-6 (paperback)
        978-1-9753-3256-3 (ebook)

10 9 8 7 6 5 4 3 2 1

LSC-C

Printed in the United States of America

# The Irregular at Magic High School

## MASTER CLANS COUNCIL ARC (II)

*An irregular older brother with a certain flaw.*
*An honor roll younger sister who is perfectly flawless.*

When the two siblings enrolled in Magic High School,
a dramatic life unfolded—

# Character

## Tatsuya Shiba

Class 2-E. Advanced to the newly established magic engineering course. Approaches everything in a detached manner. His sister Miyuki's Guardian.

## Miyuki Shiba

Class 2-A. Tatsuya's younger sister; enrolled as the top student last year. Specializes in freezing magic. Dotes on her older brother.

## Leonhard Saijou

Class 2-F. Tatsuya's friend. Course 2 student. Specializes in hardening magic. Has a bright personality.

## Erika Chiba

Class 2-F. Tatsuya's friend. Course 2 student. A charming troublemaker.

## Mizuki Shibata

Class 2-E. In Tatsuya's class again this year. Has pushion radiation sensitivity. Serious and a bit of an airhead.

## Mikihiko Yoshida

Class 2-B. This year he became a Course 1 student. From a famous family that uses ancient magic. Has known Erika since they were children.

## Honoka Mitsui

Class 2-A. Miyuki's classmate. Specializes in light-wave vibration magic. Impulsive when emotional.

## Shizuku Kitayama

Class 2-A. Miyuki's classmate. Specializes in vibration and acceleration magic. Doesn't show emotional ups and downs very much.

### Subaru Satomi
Class 2-D. Frequently mistaken for a pretty boy. Cheerful and easy to get along with.

### Eimi Akechi
Class 2-B. A quarter-blood. Almost everyone calls her "Amy." Daughter of the notable Goldie family.

### Akaha Sakurakouji
Class 2-B. Friends with Subaru and Amy. Wears gothic lolita clothes and loves theme parks.

### Shun Morisaki
Class 2-A. Miyuki's classmate. Specializes in CAD quick-draw. Takes great pride in being a Course 1 student.

### Hagane Tomitsuka
Class 2-E. A magic martial arts user with the nickname "Range Zero." Uses magic martial arts.

### Mayumi Saegusa
An alum. College student at the Magic University. Has a devilish personality but weak when on the defensive.

### Azusa Nakajou
A senior. Former student council president. Shy and has trouble expressing herself.

### Suzune Ichihara
An alum. College student at the Magic University. Calm, collected, and book smart.

### Hanzou Gyoubu-Shoujou Hattori
A senior. Former head of the club committee. Gifted but can be too serious at times.

### Mari Watanabe
An alum. Mayumi's good friend. Well-rounded and often sporting for a fight.

### Katsuto Juumonji
An alum and former head of the club committee. Has advanced to Magic University. "A boulder-like person," according to Tatsuya.

### Koutarou Tatsumi

An alum and former member of the disciplinary committee. Has a heroic and dynamic personality.

### Midori Sawaki

A senior. Member of the disciplinary committee. Has a complex about his girlish name.

### Isao Sekimoto

An alum and former member of the disciplinary committee. Lost the school election. Committed acts of spying.

### Kei Isori

A senior. Former student council treasurer. Excels in magical theory. Engaged to Kanon.

### Takeaki Kirihara

A senior. Member of the *kenjutsu* club. Junior High Kanto Kenjutsu Tournament champion.

### Kanon Chiyoda

A senior. Former chairwoman of the disciplinary committee. As confrontational as her predecessor, Mari.

### Sayaka Mibu

A senior. Member of the kendo club. Placed second in the nation at the girl's junior high kendo tournament.

### Takuma Shippou

The head of this year's new students. Course 1. Eldest son of the Shippou, one of the Eighteen, families with excellent magicians.

### Kasumi Saegusa

A new student who enrolled at Magic High School this year. Mayumi Saegusa's younger sister.

### Minami Sakurai

A new student who enrolled at Magic High School this year. Presents herself as Tatsuya and Miyuki's cousin. A Guardian candidate for Miyuki.

### Izumi Saegusa

A new student who enrolled at Magic High School this year. Mayumi Saegusa's younger sister. Kasumi's younger twin sister. Meek and gentle personality.

### Kento Sumisu

Class 1-G. A Caucasian boy whose parents are naturalized Japanese citizens from the USNA.

## Koharu Hirakawa

An alum and engineer during the Nine School Competition last year. Withdrew from the Thesis Competition.

## Chiaki Hirakawa

Class 2-E. Holds enmity toward Tatsuya.

## Tomoko Chikura

A senior. Competitor in the women's solo Shields Down, an event at the Nines.

## Tsugumi Igarashi

An alum.
Former biathlon club president.

## Yousuke Igarashi

A junior. Tsugumi's younger brother. Has a somewhat reserved personality.

## Kerry Minakami

A senior. Male representative for the main Monolith Code event at the Nines.

## Kanda

A young politician affiliated with the Civil Rights Party. Supporter of civil rights in opposition to the military. Also anti-magician.

## Satomi Asuka

First High nurse. Gentle, calm, and warm. Smile popular among male students.

## Kazuo Tsuzura

First High teacher. Main field is magic geometry. Manager of the Thesis Competition team.

## Jennifer Smith

A Caucasian naturalized as a Japanese citizen. Instructor for Tatsuya's class and for magic engineering classes.

## Haruka Ono

A general counselor of First High. Tends to get bullied but has another side to her personality.

## Yakumo Kokonoe

A user of an ancient magic called *ninjutsu*. Tatsuya's martial arts master.

## Kouzuke

A young Tokyo-based politician in the ruling party. Known as a legislator with favorable views toward magicians.

 ### Masaki Ichijou
A junior at Third High. Participating in the Nine School Competition this year as well. Direct heir to the Ichijou family, one of the Ten Master Clans.

### Gouki Ichijou
Masaki's father. Current head of the Ichijou, one of the Ten Master Clans.

 ### Shinkurou Kichijouji
A junior at Third High. Participating in the Nine School Competition this year as well. Also known as Cardinal George.

### Midori Ichijou
Masaki's mother. Warm and good at cooking.

### Akane Ichijou
Eldest daughter of the Ichijou. Masaki's younger sister. Enrolled in an elite private middle school this year. Likes Shinkurou.

### Ushio Kitayama
Shizuku's father. Big-shot in the business world. His business name is Ushio Kitagata.

### Ruri Ichijou
Second daughter of the Ichijou. Masaki's younger sister. Stable and does things her own way.

### Benio Kitayama
Shizuku's mother. An A-rank magician who was once renowned for her vibration magic.

 ### Wataru Kitayama
Shizuku's younger brother. Sixth grade. Dearly loves his older sister. Aims to be a magic engineer.

### Harumi Naruse
Shizuku's older cousin. Student at National Magic University Fourth Affiliated High School.

### Pixie
A home helper robot belonging to Magic High School. Official name 3H (Humanoid Home Helper: a human-shaped chore-assisting robot) Type P94.

### Ushiyama
Manager of Four Leaves. Technology's CAD R & D Section 3. A person in whom Tatsuya places his trust.

### Toshikazu Chiba
Erika Chiba's oldest brother. Has a career in the Ministry of Police. A playboy at first glance.

### Ernst Rosen
A prominent CAD manufacturer. President of Rosen Magicraft's Japanese branch.

### Naotsugu Chiba
Erika Chiba's second-oldest brother. Mari's lover. Possesses full mastery of the Chiba (thousand blades) style of kenjutsu. Nicknamed "Kirin Child of the Chiba."

### Retsu Kudou
Renowned as the strongest magician in the world. Given the honorary title of Sage.

### Inagaki
An inspector with the Ministry of Police. Toshikazu Chiba's subordinate.

### Makoto Kudou
Son of Retsu Kudou, elder of Japan's magic world, and current head of the Kudou family.

### Anna Rosen Katori
Erika's mother. Half Japanese and half German, was the mistress of Erika's father, the current leader of the Chiba.

### Minoru Kudou
Makoto's son. Freshman at National Magic University Second Affiliated High School, but hardly attends due to frequent illness. Also Kyouko Fujibayashi's younger brother by a different father.

### Mamoru Kuki
One of the Eighteen Support Clans. Follows the Kudou family. Calls Retsu Kudou "Sensei" out of respect.

### Maki Sawamura
An actress who has been nominated for best leading actress by distinguished movie awards. Acknowledged not only for her beauty but also her acting skills.

### Harunobu Kazama

Commanding officer of the 101st Brigade's Independent Magic Battalion. Ranked major.

### Shigeru Sanada

Executive officer of the 101st Brigade's Independent Magic Battalion. Ranked captain.

### Kyouko Fujibayashi

Female officer serving as Kazama's aide. Ranked second lieutenant.

### Hiromi Saeki

Brigadier general of the Japan Ground Defense Force's 101st Brigade. Ranked major general. Superior officer to Harunobu Kazama, commanding officer of the Independent Magic Battalion. Due to her appearance, she is also known as the Silver Fox.

### Muraji Yanagi

Executive officer of the 101st Brigade's Independent Magic Battalion. Ranked captain.

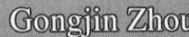

### Gongjin Zhou

A handsome young man who brought Lu and Chen to Yokohama. A mysterious figure who hangs out in Chinatown.

### Xiangshan Chen

Leader of the Great Asian Alliance Army's Special Covert Forces. Has a heartless personality.

### Ganghu Lu

The ace magician of the Great Asian Alliance Army's Special Covert Forces. Also known as the "Man-Eating Tiger."

### Rin

A girl Morisaki saved. Her full name is Meiling Sun. The new leader of the Hong Kong–based international crime syndicate No-Head Dragon.

### Kousuke Yamanaka

Executive officer of the 101st Brigade's Independent Magic Battalion. Physician ranked major. First-rate healing magician.

### Sakai

Belongs to the Japan Ground Defense Force's general headquarters. Ranked colonel. Seen as staunchly anti–Great Asian Alliance.

### Miya Shiba
Tatsuya and Miyuki's actual mother. Deceased. The only magician skilled in mental construction interference magic.

### Honami Sakurai
Miya's Guardian. Deceased. Part of the first generation of the Sakura series, engineered magicians with strengthened magical capacity through genetic modification.

### Sayuri Shiba
Tatsuya and Miyuki's stepmother. Dislikes them.

### Yuuka Tsukuba
A candidate to become the next leader of the Yotsuba clan. Twenty-two years old. Former vice president of the First High's student council. Currently a senior attending the Magic University. Strong in mental interference magic.

### Yoshimi
A Yotsuba magician related to the Kuroba. A psychometrist highly skilled in reading the psionic traces left behind in psionic information bodies. Intensely secretive.

### Maya Yotsuba
Tatsuya and Miyuki's aunt. Miya's younger twin sister. The current head of the Yotsuba.

### Hayama
An elderly butler employed by Maya.

### Katsushige Shibata
A candidate to become the next leader of the Yotsuba clan. Employed by the Ministry of Defense. An alum of Fifth High. Specializes in convergence magic.

### Kotona Tsutsumi
One of Katsushige Shibata's Guardians. A second-generation Bard series engineered magician. Specializes in sound-based magic.

### Kanata Tsutsumi
One of Katsushige Shibata's Guardians. A second-generation Bard series engineered magician. Like his older sister, Kotona, he specializes in sound-based magic.

### Angelina Kudou Shields

Commander of the USNA's magician unit, the Stars. Rank is major. Nickname is Lina. Also one of the Thirteen Apostles, strategic magicians.

### Virginia Balance

The USNA Joint Chiefs of Staff Information Bureau Internal Inspection Office's first deputy commissioner. Ranked colonel. Came to Japan in order to support Lina.

### Silvia Mercury First

A planet-class magician in the USNA's magician unit, the Stars. Rank is warrant officer. Her nickname is Silvie, and Mercury First is her codename. During their mission in Japan, she serves as Major Sirius's aide.

### Benjamin Canopus

Number two in the USNA's magician unit, the Stars. Rank is major. Takes command when Major Sirius is absent.

### Mikaela Hongou

An agent sent into Japan by the USNA (although her real job is magic scientist for the Department of Defense). Nicknamed Mia.

### Claire

Hunter Q—a female soldier in the magician unit Stardust for those who couldn't be Stars. Q refers to the 17th of the pursuit unit.

### Alfred Fomalhaut

A first-degree star magician in the USNA's magician unit, the Stars. Rank is first lieutenant. Nicknamed Freddie. Currently AWOL.

### Rachel

Hunter R—a female soldier in the magician unit Stardust for those who couldn't be Stars. R refers to the 18th of the pursuit unit.

### Charles Sullivan

A satellite-class magician in the USNA's magician unit, the Stars. Called by the codename Deimos Second. Currently AWOL.

### Raymond S. Clark

A student at the high school in Berkeley, USNA, where Shizuku studies abroad. A Caucasian boy who wastes no time making advances on Shizuku. Is secretly one of the Seven Sages.

### Gu Jie

One of the Seven Sages. Also known as Gide Hague. A survivor of a Dahanese military's mage unit.

### Mitsugu Kuroba

Miya Shiba and Maya Yotsuba's cousin. Father of Ayako and Fumiya.

### Kazukiyo Oumi

Known as the Dollmaker, a magic researcher who specializes in necromancy and a practitioner of ancient magic. Rumored to use forbidden magic to reanimate corpses.

### Ayako Kuroba

Tatsuya and Miyuki's second cousin. Has a younger twin brother named Fumiya. Student at Fourth High.

### Fumiya Kuroba

A candidate for next head of the Yotsuba. Tatsuya and Miyuki's second cousin. Has an older twin sister named Ayako. Student at Fourth High.

### Kouichi Saegusa

Mayumi's father and the current leader of the Saegusa. Also an ultra-top-class magician.

### Saburou Nakura

A powerful magician employed by the Saegusa family. Mainly serves as Mayumi's personal bodyguard.

## Mai Futatsugi

Head of the Futatsugi, one of the Ten Master Clans. Resides in Ashiya, Hyogo Prefecture. Publicly she is the majority shareholder in a variety of industrial chemical- and food-processing companies. Responsible for the Hanshin and Chugoku regions.

## Gen Mitsuya

Head of the Mitsuya, one of the Ten Master Clans. Resides in Atsugi, Kanagawa Prefecture. Whether it's public or not is a matter of some question, but in any case, he's an international small arms broker. In charge of the still-operational Lab Three.

## Isami Itsuwa

Head of the Itsuwa, one of the Ten Master Clans. Resides in Uwajima, Ehime Prefecture. Publicly the executive and owner of a marine-shipping company. Responsible for the Tokai, Gifu, and Nagano regions.

## Atsuko Mutsuzuka

Head of the Mutsuzuka, one of the Ten Master Clans. Resides in Sendai, Miyagi Prefecture. Publicly the owner of a geothermal energy exploration company. Responsible for the Tohoku region.

## Raizou Yatsushiro

Head of the Yatsushiro, one of the Ten Master Clans. Resides in Fukuoka Prefecture. Publicly a university lecturer and majority shareholder in several telecommunications companies. Responsible for the Kyushu region, except for Okinawa.

## Kazuki Juumonji

Head of the Juumonji, one of the Ten Master Clans. Resides in Tokyo. Publicly the owner of a civil engineering and construction company that primarily serves the armed forces. Shares responsibility for the Kanto region, including Izu, with the Saegusa family.

# Glossary

Course 1 student emblem

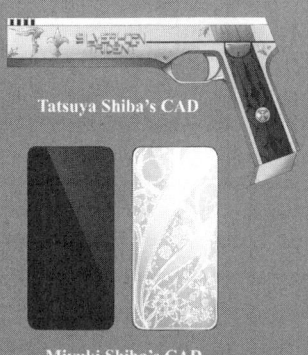

Tatsuya Shiba's CAD

Miyuki Shiba's CAD

### Magic High School
Nickname for high schools affiliated with the National Magic University. There are nine schools throughout the nation. Of them, First High through Third High each adopt a system of Course 1 and Course 2 students to split up its two hundred incoming freshmen.

### Blooms, Weeds
Slang terms used at First High to display the gap between Course 1 and Course 2 students. Course 1 student uniforms feature an eight-petaled emblem embroidered on the left breast, but Course 2 student uniforms do not.

### CAD (Casting Assistant Device)
A device that simplifies magic casting. Magical programming is recorded within. There are many types and forms, some specialized and others multipurpose.

### Four Leaves Technology (FLT)
A domestic CAD manufacturer. Originally more famous for magical-product engineering than for developing finished products, the development of the Silver model has made them much more widely known as a maker of CADs.

### Taurus Silver
A genius engineer said to have advanced specialized CAD software by a decade in just a single year.

### Eidos (individual information bodies)
Originally a term from Greek philosophy. In modern magic, *eidos* refers to the information bodies that accompany events. They form a so-called record of those events existing in the world, and can be considered the footprints of an object's state of being in the universe, be that active or passive. The definition of *magic* in its modern form is that of a technology that alters events by altering the information bodies composing them.

### Idea (information body dimension)
Originally a term from Greek philosophy; pronounced "ee-dee-ah." In modern magic, *Idea* refers to the *platform* upon which information bodies are recorded—a spell, object, or energy's *dimension*. Magic is primarily a technology that outputs a magic program (a spell sequence) to affect the Idea (the dimension), which then rewrites the eidos (the individual bodies) recorded there.

### Activation Sequence
The blueprints of magic, and the programming that constructs it. Activation sequences are stored in a compressed format in CADs. The magician sends a psionic wave into the CAD, which then expands the data and uses it to convert the activation sequence into a signal. This signal returns to the magician with the unpacked magic program.

### Psions (thought particles)
Massless particles belonging to the dimension of spirit phenomena. These information particles record awareness and thought results. Eidos are considered the theoretical basis for modern magic, while activation sequences and magic programs are the technology forming its practical basis. All of these are bodies of information made up of psions.

### Pushions (spirit particles)
Massless particles belonging to the dimension of spirit phenomena. Their existence has been confirmed, but their true form and function have yet to be elucidated. In general, magicians are only able to sense energized pushions. The technical term for them is *psycheons*.

### Magician
An abbreviation of *magic technician*. *Magic technician* is the term for those with the skills to use magic at a practical level.

### Magic program
An information body used to temporarily alter information attached to events. Constructed from psions possessed by the magician. Sometimes shortened to *magigram*.

### Magic-calculation region

A mental region that constructs magic programs. The essential core of the talent of magic. Exists within the magician's unconscious regions, and though he or she can normally consciously use the magic-calculation region, they cannot perceive the processing happening within. The magic-calculation region may be called a black box, even for the magician performing the task.

### Magic program output process

1. Transmit an activation sequence to a CAD. This is called "reading in an activation sequence."
2. Add variables to the activation sequence and send them to the magic-calculation region.
3. Construct a magic program from the activation sequence and its variables.
4. Send the constructed magic program along the "route"—between the lowest part of the conscious mind and highest part of the unconscious mind—then send it out the "gate" between conscious and unconscious, to output it onto the Idea.
5. The magic program outputted onto the Idea interferes with the eidos at designated coordinates and overwrites them.

With a single-type, single-process spell, this five-stage process can be completed in under half a second. This is the bar for practical-level use with magicians.

### Magic evaluation standards

The speed with which one constructs psionic information bodies is one's magical throughput, or processing speed. The scale and scope of the information bodies one can construct is one's magical capacity. The strength with which one can overwrite eidos with magic programs is one's influence. These three together are referred to as a person's magical power.

### Cardinal Code hypothesis

A school of thought claiming that within the four families and eight types of magic, there exist foundational plus and minus magic programs, for sixteen in all, and that by combining these sixteen, one can construct every possible typed spell.

### Typed magic

Any magic belonging to the four families and eight types.

### Exotyped magic

A term for spells that control mental phenomena rather than physical ones. Encompasses many fields, from divine magic and spirit magic—which employs spiritual presences—to mind reading, astral form separation, and consciousness control.

### Ten Master Clans

The most powerful magician organization in Japan. The ten families are chosen every four years from among twenty-eight: Ichijou, Ichinokura, Isshiki, Futatsugi, Nikaidou, Nihei, Mitsuya, Mikazuki, Yotsuba, Itsuwa, Gotou, Itsumi, Mutsuzuka, Rokkaku, Rokugou, Roppongi, Saegusa, Shippou, Tanabata, Nanase, Yatsushiro, Hassaku, Hachiman, Kudou, Kuki, Kuzumi, Juumonji, and Tooyama.

### Numbers

Just like the Ten Master Clans contain a number from one to ten in their surname, well-known families in the Hundred Families use numbers eleven or greater, such as Chiyoda (thousand), Isori (fifty), and Chiba (thousand). The value isn't an indicator of strength, but the fact that it is present in the surname is one measure to broadly judge the capacity of a magic family by their bloodline.

### Non-numbers

Also called Extra Numbers, or simply Extras. Magician families who have been stripped of their number. Once, when magicians were weapons and experimental samples, this was a stigma between the success cases, who were given numbers, and the failure cases, who didn't display good enough results.

## Various Spells

### • Cocytus
Outer magic that freezes the mind. A frozen mind cannot order the flesh to die, so anyone subject to this magic enters a state of mental stasis, causing their body to stop. Partial crystallization of the flesh is sometimes observed because of the interaction between mind and body.

### • Rumbling
An old spell that vibrates the ground as a medium for a spirit, an independent information body.

### • Program Dispersion
A spell that dismantles a magic program, the main component of a spell, into a group of psionic particles with no meaningful structure. Since magic programs affect the information bodies associated with events, it is necessary for the information structure to be exposed, leaving no way to prevent interference against the magic program itself.

### • Program Demolition
A typeless spell that rams a mass of compressed psionic particles directly into an object without going through the Idea, causing it to explode and blow away the psion information bodies recorded in magic, such as activation sequences and magic programs. It may be called magic, but because it is a psionic bullet without any structure as a magic program for altering events, it isn't affected by Information Boost or Area Interference. The pressure of the bullet itself will also repel any Cast Jamming effects. Because it has zero physical effect, no obstacle can block it.

### • Mine Origin
A magic that imparts strong vibrations to anything with a connotation of "ground"—such as dirt, crag, sand, or concrete—regardless of material.

### • Fissure
A spell that uses spirits, independent information bodies, as a medium to push a line into the ground, creating the appearance of a fissure opening in the earth.

### • Dry Blizzard
A spell that gathers carbon dioxide from the air, creates dry-ice particles, then converts the extra heat energy from the freezing process to kinetic energy to launch the dry-ice particles at a high speed.

### • Slithering Thunders
In addition to condensing the water vapor from Dry Blizzard's dry-ice evaporation and creating a highly conductive mist with the evaporated carbon dioxide in it, this spell creates static electricity with vibration-type magic and emission-type magic. A combination spell, it also fires an electric attack at an enemy using the carbon gas-filled mist and water droplets as a conductor.

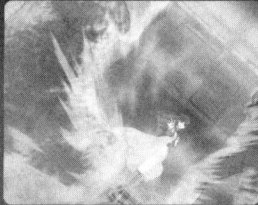

### • Niflheim
A vibration- and deceleration-type area-of-effect spell. It chills a large volume of air, then moves it to freeze a wide range. In blunt terms, it creates a super-large refrigerator. The white mist that appears upon activation is the particles of frozen ice and dry ice, but at higher levels, a mist of frozen liquid nitrogen occurs.

### • Burst
A dispersion-type spell that vaporizes the liquid inside a target object. When used on a creature, the spell will vaporize bodily fluids and cause the body to rupture. When used on a machine powered by internal combustion, the spell vaporizes the fuel and makes it explode. Fuel cells see the same result, and even if no burnable fuel is on board, there is no machine that does not contain some liquid, such as battery fluid, hydraulic fluid, coolant, or lubricant; once Burst activates, virtually any machine will be destroyed.

### • Disheveled Hair
An old spell that, instead of specifying a direction and changing the wind's direction to that, uses air current control to bring about the vague result of "tangling" it, causing currents along the ground that entangle an opponent's feet in the grass. Only usable on plains with grass of a certain height.

## Magic Swords

Aside from fighting techniques that use magic itself as a weapon, another method of magical combat involves techniques for using magic to strengthen and control weapons. The majority of these spells combine magic with projectile weapons such as guns and bows, but the art of the sword, known as *kenjutsu*, has developed in Japan as well as a way to link magic with sword techniques. This has led to magic technicians formulating personal-use magic techniques known as magic swords, which can be said to be both modern magic and old magic.

### 1. High-Frequency Blade

A spell that locally liquefies a solid body and cleaves it by causing a blade to vibrate at a high speed, then propagate the vibration that exceeds the molecular cohesive force of matter it comes in contact with. Used as a set with a spell to prevent the blade from breaking.

### 2. Pressure Cut

A spell that generates left-right perpendicular repulsive force relative to the angle of a slashing blade edge, causing the blade to force apart any object it touches and thereby cleave it. The size of the repulsive field is less than a millimeter, but it has the strength to interfere with light, so when seen from the front, the blade edge becomes a black line.

### 3. Douji-Giri (Simultaneous Cut)

An old-magic spell passed down as a secret sword art of the Genji. It is a magic sword technique wherein the user remotely manipulates two blades through a third in their hands in order to have the swords surround an opponent and slash simultaneously. *Douji* is the Japanese pronunciation for both "simultaneous" and "child," so this ambiguity was used to keep the inherited nature of the technique a secret.

### 4. Zantetsu (Iron Cleaver)

A secret sword art of the Chiba clan. Rather than defining a katana as a hulk of steel and iron, this movement spell defines it as a single concept, then the spell moves the katana along a slashing path set by the magic program. The result is that the katana is defined as a mono-molecular blade, never breaking, bending, or chipping as it slices through any objects in its path.

### 5. Jinrai Zantetsu (Lightning Iron Cleaver)

An expanded version of Zantetsu that makes use of the Ikazuchi-Maru, a personal-armament device. By defining the katana and its wielder as one collective concept, the spell executes the entire series of actions, from enemy contact to slash, incredibly quickly and with faultless precision.

### 6. Mountain Tsunami

A secret sword art of the Chiba clan that makes use of the Orochi-Maru, a giant personal weapon six feet long. The user minimizes their own inertia and that of their katana while approaching an enemy at a high speed and, at the moment of impact, adds the neutralized inertia to the blade's inertia and slams the target with it. The longer the approach run, the greater the false inertial mass, reaching a maximum of ten tons.

### 7. *Usuba Kagerou* (Antlion)

A spell that uses hardening magic to anchor a five-nanometer-thick sheet of woven carbon nanotube to a perfect surface and make it a blade. The blade that *Usuba Kagerou* creates is sharper than any sword or razor, but the spell contains no functions to support moving the blade, demanding technical sword skill and ability from the user.

# Magic Technician Development Institutes

Laboratories for the purpose of magician development that the Japanese government established one after another in response to the geopolitical climate, which had become strained prior to World War III in the 2030s. Their objectives were not to develop magic but specifically to develop magicians, researching various methods to give birth to human specimens who were most suitable for areas of magic that were considered important, including, but not limited to, genetic engineering.

Ten magic technician development institutes were established, numbered as such, and even today, five are still in operation.

The details of each institute's research are described below.

## Magic Technician Development Institute One

Established in Kanazawa in 2031. Currently shut down.

Its research focus, revolving around close combat, was the development of magic that directly manipulated biological organisms. The vaporization spell Burst is derived from this facility's research. Notably, magic that could control a human body's movements was forbidden as it enabled puppet terrorism (suicide attacks using victims that had been turned into puppets).

## Magic Technician Development Institute Two

Established on Awaji Island in 2031. Currently in operation.

Develops opposite magic to that of Lab One: magic that can manipulate inorganic objects, especially absorption-type spells related to oxidation-reduction reactions.

## Magic Technician Development Institute Three

Established in Atsugi in 2032. Currently in operation.

With its goal of developing magicians who can react to a variety of situations when operating independently, this facility is the main driver behind the research on multicasting. In particular, it tests the limits of how many spells are possible during simultaneous casting and continual casting and develops magicians who can simultaneously cast multiple spells.

## Magic Technician Development Institute Four

Details unknown. Its location is speculated to be near the old prefectural border between Tokyo and Yamanashi. Its establishment is believed to have occurred in 2033. It is assumed to be shut down, but the truth of that matter is unknown. Lab Four is rumored to be the only magic research facility that was established not only with government support but also investment from private sponsors who held strong influence over the nation; it is currently operating without government oversight and being managed directly by those sponsors. Rumors also say that those sponsors actually took over control of the facility before the 2020s.

It is said their goal is to use mental interference magic to strengthen the very wellspring of the talent called magic, which exists in a magician's unconscious—the magic calculation region itself.

## Magic Technician Development Institute Five

Established in Uwajima, Shikoku, in 2035. Currently in operation.

Researches magic that can manipulate various forms of matter. Its main focus, fluid control, is not technically difficult, but it has also succeeded in manipulating various solid forms. The fruits of its research include Bahamut, a spell jointly developed with the USNA. Along with the fluid-manipulation spell Abyss, it is known internationally as a magic research facility that developed two strategic-class spells.

## Magic Technician Development Institute Six

Established in Sendai in 2035. Currently in operation.

Researches magical heat control. Along with Lab Eight, it gives the impression of being a facility more for basic research than military purposes. However, it is said that they conducted the most genetic manipulation experiments out of all the magic technician development institutes, aside from Lab Four. (Though, of course, the full accounting of Lab Four's situation is not possible.)

## Magic Technician Development Institute Seven

Established in Tokyo in 2036. Currently shut down.

Developed magic with an emphasis on anti-group combat. It successfully created colony control magic. Contrary to Lab Six, which was largely a nonmilitary organization, Lab Seven was established as a magician development research facility that could be relied on for assistance in defending the capital in case of an emergency.

## Magic Technician Development Institute Eight

Established in Kitakyushu in 2037. Currently in operation.

Researches magical control of gravitational force, electromagnetic force, strong force, and weak force. It is a pure research institute to a greater extent than even Lab Six. However, unlike Lab Six, its relationship to the JDF is steadfast. This is because Lab Eight's research focus can be easily linked to nuclear weapons development, (though they currently avoid such connotations thanks to the JDF's seal of approval).

## Magic Technician Development Institute Nine

Established in Nara in 2037. Currently shut down.

This facility tried to solve several problems modern magic struggled with, such as fuzzy spell manipulation, through a fusion of modern and ancient magic, integrating ancient know-how into modern magic.

## Magic Technician Development Institute Ten

Established in Tokyo in 2039. Currently shut down.

Like Lab Seven, doubled as capital defense, researching area magic that could create virtual structures in space as a means of defending against high-firepower attacks. It resulted in a myriad of anti-physical barrier spells.

Lab Ten also aimed to raise magic abilities through different means from Lab Four. In precise terms, rather than enhancing the magic calculation region itself, they grappled with developing magicians who responded as needed by temporarily overclocking their magic calculation regions to use powerful magic. Whether their research was successful has not been made public.

Aside from these ten institutes, other laboratories with the goal of developing Elements were operational from the 2010s to the 2020s, but they are currently all shut down. In addition, the JDF possesses a secret research facility directly under the Ground Defense Force's General Headquarters' jurisdiction, established in 2002, which is still carrying on its research. Retsu Kudou underwent enhancement operations at this institution before moving to Lab Nine.

## Strategic Magicians: The Thirteen Apostles

Because modern magic was born into a highly technological world, only a few nations were able to develop strong magic for military purposes. As a result, only a handful were able to develop "strategic magic," which rivaled weapons of mass destruction.

However, these nations shared the magic they developed with their allies, and certain magicians of allied nations with high aptitudes for strategic magic came to be known as strategic magicians.

As of April 2095, there are thirteen magicians publicly recognized as strategic magicians by their nations. They are called the Thirteen Apostles and are seen as important factors in the world's military balance. The Thirteen Apostles' nations, names, and strategic spell names are listed below.

### USNA

Angie Sirius: Heavy Metal Burst
Elliott Miller: Leviathan
Laurent Barthes: Leviathan
* The only one belonging to the Stars is Angie Sirius. Elliott Miller is stationed at Alaska Base, and Laurent Barthes outside the country at Gibraltar Base, and for the most part, they don't move.

### New Soviet Union

Igor Andreivich Bezobrazov: Tuman Bomba
Leonid Kondratenko: Zemlja Armija
* As Kondratenko is of advanced age, he generally stays at the Black Sea Base.

### Great Asian Alliance

Yunde Liu: Pilita (Thunderclap Tower)
* Yunde Liu died in the October 31, 2095, battle against Japan.

### Indo-Persian Federation

Barat Chandra Khan: Agni Downburst

### Japan

Mio Itsuwa: Abyss

### Brazil

Miguel Diez: Synchroliner Fusion
* This magic program was named by the USNA.

### England

William MacLeod: Ozone Circle

### Germany

Karla Schmidt: Ozone Circle
* Ozone Circle is based on a spell codeveloped by nations in the EU before its split as a means to fix the hole in the ozone layer. The magic program was perfected by England and then publicized to the old EU through a convention.

### Turkey

Ali Sahin: Bahamut
* This magic program was developed in cooperation with the USNA and Japan, then provided to Turkey by Japan.

### Thailand

Somchai Bunnag: Agni Downburst
* This magic program was provided by Indo-Persia.

# The International Situation
## State of the World in 2096

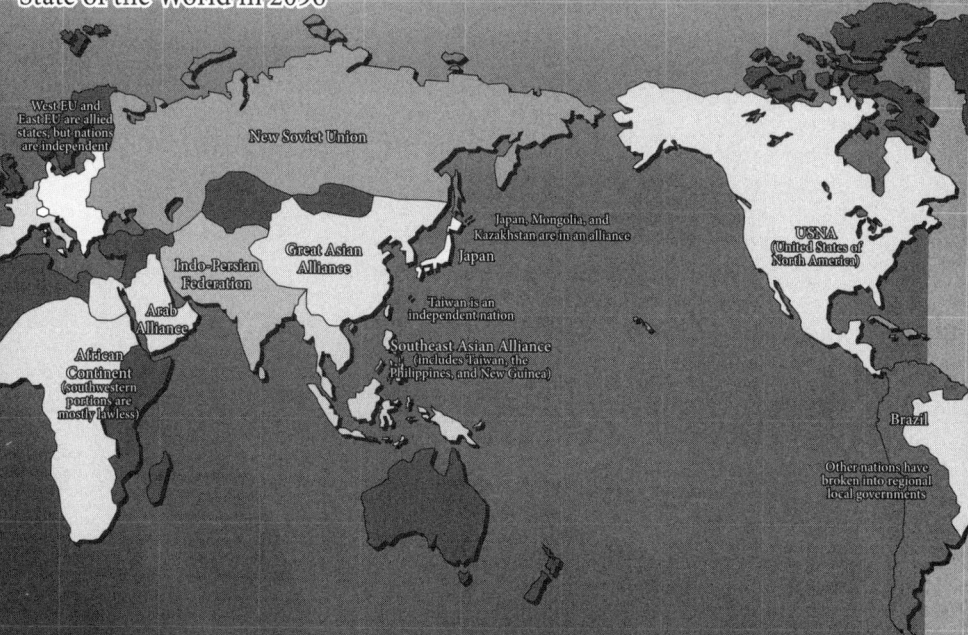

World War III, also called the Twenty Years' Global War Outbreak, was directly triggered by global cooling, and it fundamentally redrew the world map.

The USA annexed Canada and the countries from Mexico to Panama to form the United States of North America, or the USNA.

Russia reabsorbed Ukraine and Belarus to form the New Soviet Union.

China conquered northern Burma, northern Vietnam, northern Laos, and the Korean Peninsula to form the Great Asian Alliance, or GAA.

India and Iran absorbed several central Asian countries (Turkmenistan, Uzbekistan, Tajikistan, and Afghanistan) and South Asian countries (Pakistan, Nepal, Bhutan, Bangladesh, and Sri Lanka) to form the Indo-Persian Federation.

The other Asian and Arab countries formed regional military alliances to resist the three superpowers: the New Soviet Union, GAA, and the Indo-Persian Federation.

Australia chose national isolation.

The EU failed to unify and split into an eastern and a western section bordered by Germany and France. These east-west groupings also failed to form unions and now are actually weaker than they were before unification.

Africa saw half its nations destroyed altogether, with the surviving ones barely managing to retain urban control.

South America, excluding Brazil, fell into small, isolated states administered on a local government level.

## The Irregular at Magic High School

# [6]

On Tuesday, February 5, 2097, at 3:30 PM, there was a large-scale terrorist attack on a certain hotel in Hakone.

This hotel was hosting the Master Clans Council. At the time of the attack, the council had completed the selection of the next Ten Master Clans, and representatives from the Eighteen Support Clans had already left. However, all representatives from the Ten had remained to discuss the various problems facing Japan's magical society.

Six students—Tatsuya, Miyuki, Minami, Takuma, Kasumi, and Izumi—had received word of the attack while in class and immediately headed to the hotel, where they were now just arriving. The scene was still filled with cries and shouts.

The wounded and dead were being carried out of the burned-out hotel, while many others were moaning as they received first aid in the streets. The rubble's continuous rumbling made it seem like detonations were still occurring periodically. It was every bit as horrible a scene as the Yokohama Incident had been the previous fall.

Miyuki headed toward the hotel proper, intent on putting out the blaze with her magic, but Tatsuya stopped her short with a hand on her shoulder.

"Tatsuya…?" she asked, looking back at him.

He shook his head. "We should leave it to them."

The fire was well on its way to being extinguished. While the dangerous question of how many undetonated explosives might remain in the building lingered, the fire itself was being dealt with by trained professionals. Assuming that there might well be other preparations underway that weren't obvious to them, Tatsuya concluded that it was better not to recklessly get involved.

"First, I think we should try to meet up with Au— Er, Mother and the others."

He'd nearly said "Aunt" but then remembered Takuma and his other classmates were still right there. Correcting himself might have drawn more attention to the mistake, but he decided it was better to avoid saying anything that contradicted the official story.

Takumi, Izumi, and the others were constantly looking around as they spoke with Miyuki, but nonetheless it was Tatsuya who spotted the group of family heads first. "This way," he instructed.

It was something of a spectacle to see the heads of the Ten Master Clans arranged in such a tight group, but it wasn't obvious why they were still here at all. Tatsuya remained confused until he spotted people he guessed to be plainclothes detectives standing next to them.

"Father!" cried Izumi as soon as she saw him.

"Ah, wait, Izumi!" said Kasumi, following after her, likewise uninterested in anything but reuniting with her family.

"Are those…detectives?" After pausing to take in the situation, Takuma hurried after them toward his own father.

"What should we do, Tatsuya?" Miyuki asked, seeming to have realized that the ten family heads were being interviewed. Minami, too, looked to Tatsuya for answers.

"Well, we can't very well leave Izumi and the others."

All six of them had immediately rushed from school to the scene. Naturally, there had been no time to change, so all of them were still in their First High uniforms.

So if the freshmen were going to plunge headlong into a bad

situation, the older students couldn't just stand by and watch. Tatsuya gave Miyuki and Minami a helpless look, then started walking toward where Maya stood.

"Why are you questioning my father, huh?! He and the others are obviously the victims here!"

Unsurprisingly, Izumi was giving a detective a piece of her mind. In contrast to her usual ladylike demeanor, she was absolutely fearless in times like these. Her youthful idealism made it impossible for her to accept the unfairness of public authority, and her position as a daughter of the Ten made it hard for a regular public servant to defy her—especially in front of the heads of those powerful families.

*Still…why is nobody stopping her?*

None of the family heads were doing anything to hold her objections back; they were all just standing by and watching. Under normal circumstances, this outburst should have earned her a scolding from her father, Kouichi Saegusa, but far from it—he seemed to be amused. His expression was serious, but his eyes were smiling.

The only ones really taken aback were the detectives themselves, but if this went on for much longer, the reputation of the Ten Clans would suffer. It would worsen the position of both the families and the students alike, just for the sake of some mischief. And since the adults weren't making a move to stop it, Tatsuya finally decided to do it himself.

"Izumi, that's enough."

"Shiba! Why're you stopping me?" Izumi looked back at Tatsuya, who'd clapped his hand on her shoulder.

As she raised a hand to brush him off, Tatsuya grabbed her by the arm and pulled her toward him, taking advantage of her lower center of gravity. She had no time to resist—and seemingly put up no fight at all—as Tatsuya dragged her away from the detective like a dancer leading his partner across the ballroom.

"You need to cool your head. The police are only doing their job."

His words weren't directed only at Izumi; they were for Kasumi and Takuma as well. "If we get in the way, it'll only take them longer to gather the information they need." Tatsuya turned to the plainclothes detective. "My apologies," he said.

Somewhat overawed by Tatsuya's smoothly impenetrable demeanor, the detective gave a vague nod and didn't comment on the interruption.

Holding Izumi's hand and gesturing with his eyes to Kasumi and Takuma, Tatsuya moved away from the adults.

All the family heads—Maya excepted—watched him with intense curiosity.

In particular, Kouichi's and Gouki's eyes shone with keen interest.

The police interview seemed to have just started, and it went on for longer than Tatsuya expected. Eventually, the plainclothes detectives were joined by a ring of uniformed officers who essentially fenced in the group of magicians. They were almost being treated like suspects.

But that wasn't what Tatsuya was concerned about.

All that mattered to him was Maya's well-being. This would be the worst possible time for her to dismiss him and Miyuki. Now that his sister's position as the next head of the Yotsuba family was public, she and Tatsuya could no longer hide in the shadow of anonymity.

Meanwhile, their own positions were far from solidified. The only people he could be really certain were his allies were the workers at FLT R & D Section 3 from Ushiyama on down. When it came down to it, Yakumo and Kazama would probably adopt a policy of nonalignment. And he couldn't even meet any of his "sponsors" above that level.

Maya was considered one of the strongest magicians in the world, and the reputation was deserved. Few could defeat her in combat, and the number of magicians who could come away from her Meteor Line unscathed was nearly zero. Not even Tatsuya was an exception.

Tatsuya's Dismantling technique was an effective response to

Meteor Line. But Maya was not only a potent magician; her casting speed was also second to none. She had a much more diverse hand to play than Tatsuya did. Meteor Line was not her only ace in the hole, either. There was no guarantee that Tatsuya would get to make the first move. If she cast Meteor Line before he completed Dismantle, he would not escape in one piece. The only thing that would let him win was his Regeneration, but anyone without a similar anomalous ability would stand no chance against Maya, since once Meteor Line was cast, no defensive magic—not even something like the Juumonji family's Phalanx—could stop it.

But that overwhelming strength was limited to magical combat. Physically, Maya was completely average—she was a relatively delicate woman, with no particular training or conditioned strength beyond her natural beauty and health. If she was cut, she would be hurt; if shot, she would bleed.

No magician, no matter how strong, could keep a magical barrier active indefinitely. Continuous defense magic had yet to be perfected—even experimentally, to say nothing of practical deployment. If she was caught by surprise, even Maya Yotsuba could be fatally wounded by a single shot.

Tatsuya had hurried to the scene of the bombing fully prepared to use Regeneration in front of other people if he had to, but now he'd confirmed Maya's immediate safety. They wouldn't be able to talk for a little while—not that he had anything particular to say—so Tatsuya was considering simply returning to school. However, he just caught sight of a certain familiar red uniform.

"Ichijou," Tatsuya called, though he wasn't trying very hard to be heard over the din of the frantic triage.

Masaki nonetheless responded firmly to the hailing: "Shiba."

He must have come here looking for his father, Gouki. Masaki's stride was quick as he cast his gaze all around him. Tatsuya approached him.

"I see you've come, too, Miss Shiba." Masaki looked beside Tatsuya to his sister, his expression a complicated mix of pleasure, disappointment, resignation, and yearning.

Miyuki was *not* holding Tatsuya's arm.

She wasn't clinging to him at all.

If anything, the space between them had widened. And yet, to Masaki, this seemed like evidence that they had gone from siblings to lovers.

"Yes, it's awful." It wasn't hard for Miyuki to read Masaki's thoughts as he looked at her. Even setting aside the impassioned engagement proposal that came immediately after the announcement of her and Tatsuya's betrothal, Masaki's expression, though complicated, was incredibly easy to understand.

In point of fact, Miyuki was more than a little bit annoyed with Masaki. While the Ichijou family's interference had not weakened her position as Tatsuya's fiancée, she was still unamused by complications suddenly cropping up immediately after the revelation that her fondest wish would very likely come true.

That being said, Miyuki was not so childish as to confront Masaki himself with that annoyance. Even if she found his actions displeasing, she personally bore Masaki no ill will at all. It was a simple enough matter for her to summon a pleasant smile, even at a time like this.

Still, since colder treatment would have helped him give up more quickly, that might have been the better tack for her to take—for both her sake and Masaki's.

Because, even in a moment like this, Masaki couldn't help but feel his mood lift after receiving a smile from the girl he had a crush on. "Yes, it really is," he said, the affection evident in his voice. "Are the family heads over there?"

"Yes. It seems they're being interviewed by the police."

"Wait, what?!" Masaki was not so bewitched that he'd lost track of his priorities. "I'm sorry—you'll have to excuse me," he said with a bow before heading toward his father, alarmed at the prospect of the family heads being questioned as a group.

As if trading places, Katsuto emerged from behind the wall of uniformed officers interviewing the leaders of the Ten. If he alone was being released, it had to be out of consideration for his status as a minor. (In the past, the age of majority had been lowered to eighteen, but it was raised back to twenty in 2070. This was a reaction to the lowering of the age of majority during the Twenty Years' Global War Outbreak in order to increase the share of the population who could be mobilized, and it had been a global trend. In extreme cases after the war, ages of majority as young as sixteen were suddenly raised as high as twenty-five.)

Once he emerged, Katsuto headed straight for Tatsuya and the other students. Evidently, he'd kept track of them after Izumi had been dragged away.

"Shiba—" he began. The reason Katsuto spoke that name and nothing more was because he didn't really know which sibling he should speak with or exactly how to address them. Or at least, that was Tatsuya's guess.

"It's good to see a First High alum here, Juumonji. Have the police finished any of their questioning yet?" Tatsuya directed Katsuto's attention toward himself and established that his position here relative to Katsuto was not as a member of one of the Master Clan families but rather as an underclassman from the same school.

Katsuto seemed to accept this, and his general demeanor relaxed quite a bit. "No, I just thought I should come over and explain the situation to you guys."

He looked over at Tatsuya's other companions. He knew Kasumi and Izumi. He'd never met Minami or Takuma before, or at least he didn't consciously remember ever conversing with them.

"Are you by any chance Mr. Shippou's...?" Katsuto offered to Takuma.

"Yes, I'm Takuma Shippou." In contrast to Tatsuya, Takuma addressed his elder as a fellow member of one of the Ten Master Clans. While there was still the difference between a patriarch and the son of the patriarch, they were still on somewhat equal footing, given that both of their families were a part of the Master Clans.

"I'm Katsuto Juumonji. Nice to meet you."

"I'm pleased to make your acquaintance as well."

Equal footing notwithstanding, the upperclassman-underclassman hierarchy still existed, so they naturally fell into that pattern. Takuma didn't have enough nerve to instantly act chummy with Katsuto, whom he'd only just met.

"This is Minami Sakurai, and she's a freshman our family's looking after," Tatsuya said, carefully timing his interjection to introduce her. Minami faced Katsuto and bowed politely. Katsuto was able to surmise from her general attitude that to some extent, Minami was a servant of the Yotsuba family. He acknowledged her with a nod, then returned to the subject at hand.

"You all came here because you got a disaster notification, right? As you can see, Ms. Yotsuba, Mr. Saegusa, and Mr. Shippou are all safe. They're not even slightly wounded."

Disaster notification messages were a network service accessed by personal terminals to inform family and friends that the user had been involved in an incident, using short-range wireless communication to gather relevant fire or earthquake reports and send them to preregistered recipients. The messages included whatever information about the incident the local authorities had gathered, along with a three-tiered urgency level based on the user's lifelog as recorded by the terminal: "Safe," "In Danger," and "Deceased."

However, this information was only a snapshot of the situation at the time the initial alert was sent, and so long as the user hadn't opted into continuous transmission, there was no way of knowing from one message how the incident was developing. That was why everyone had hurried to the scene with such urgency.

"Yes, it seems not. But incidentally, would you mind telling us what happened here?" Takuma asked.

"Sure. But I have other people I need to explain things to, so I'm going to have to keep it simple."

At Katsuto's words, Tatsuya scanned the area. He saw some Yotsuba-affiliated people unobtrusively lingering around—specifically some of the butler Hanabishi's staff, who handled situations requiring the use of force, along with a few others, who were probably relatives of other families. Unfortunately, he could make out no sign of any of the terrorists responsible for the bombing.

"If you would, please," said Tatsuya with a polite bow meant to convey that even a simple explanation would do. Katsuto nodded understandingly.

"Honestly, most of the details are uncertain," he began, before explaining that the meeting had been interrupted by suicide bombers, that the family heads had escaped via the roof, and that the bombers were reanimated corpses. "We don't even know for sure that we were the real target. We're quite certain that they were targeting the Master Clans Council, but the police haven't drawn any firm conclusions, either."

"Excuse me, Katsuto—er, I mean, Mr. Juumonji," Kasumi interrupted, hastily correcting herself. The sisters had known Katsuto since before entering First High, so in their minds he was more of a friend than an alum. The fact that Mayumi called him Juumonji while Kasumi used Katsuto was a point that Kasumi and Izumi preferred not to over-scrutinize.

"What is it, Kasumi?" He seemed to feel the same way.

"What are the police asking Father—no, all the family heads?"

"They're being asked what happened. We were on the scene and saw it with our own eyes."

"So Father and the others aren't being interrogated as suspects, then?" Izumi interjected from beside Kasumi. It was a rather natural thing to do, but Tatsuya and Miyuki were both slightly surprised by Izumi's sincere concern for her father.

There flickered a hint of hesitation in Katsuto's eyes as he considered the other Saegusa sister. Nonetheless, he didn't attempt any temporary obfuscation of the truth. "They're not suspected of collaboration. But the police are concerned that it was a conflict among magicians that invited the terrorist attack."

"No, that's not…" Izumi murmured, stunned, clenching her little hand into a fist.

…*fair*, she was surely thinking.

The anger wasn't limited to Izumi. Takuma had carefully played the role of the listener, but his frustration was obvious as he clenched his jaw.

Tatsuya noted the effort his underclassmen were putting into containing their feelings and grumbled for them, "That sounds like the same logic the anti-magician organizations often use."

The Saegusa sisters, Takuma, and Minami all stiffened at the suggestion.

"Brother, surely there aren't any humanists in the police…?" Miyuki asked.

"I doubt it," he agreed, eliciting a wave of relieved sighs around him. "If that were the case, the interrogation would undoubtedly be a lot more severe."

Tatsuya thought back to after he'd fought the ancient magicians manipulated by Gongjin Zhou's Taoists at Arashiyama in Kyoto and the relentless questioning he'd received from a detective who was none too fond of the Ten Master Clans.

His statement seemed to calm Miyuki and the freshmen, but Katsuto's raised eyebrows and widened eyes suggested that some doubts lingered with him. "Shiba, I thought you two were cousins now, not siblings."

Before Miyuki's dismay could become obvious, Tatsuya smiled and replied, "Oh, you mean Miyuki addressing me as 'brother'? Well, until a few days ago, we thought we *were* siblings, and old habits die hard."

"Ah, I see. That makes sense." Katsuto's doubts immediately evaporated. It wasn't that he was especially gullible, but rather it was that Tatsuya's response was so smooth and natural. He was like a born liar, showing no visible trace of either guilt or pleasure at speaking falsehoods.

"Wait, is that *my* brother?" With convenient timing, Kasumi's voice rang out, diverting Katsuto's attention away.

"Oh, it's Tomokazu," Katsuto noted of the young man who was waving at them. "Shiba, did you have anything else you wanted to ask me?"

"No, nothing else."

"What about you, Shippou?" Katsuto turned to Takuma.

"I don't have anything, either."

Katsuto nodded. "In that case, I'll be going." With that, he headed toward Tomokazu.

Just then, Izumi spoke up to Tatsuya and Miyuki. "Miyuki, Shiba—my brother looks rather lost, so we'll get going as well. I figure we'll head home with him, so please don't worry about us."

"Shiba, Miss President, we'll be going as well. See you later, too, Sakurai!" Kasumi added, bowing to the siblings and waving to Minami. The twin sisters then followed behind Katsuto toward their brother.

"Tatsuya, is that person really Izumi and Kasumi's…?" Miyuki wondered as she watched them go.

"Yes. Tomokazu Saegusa, the eldest son of the Saegusa family. He's Izumi and Kasumi's half brother by a different mother."

"I see…" Miyuki's voice contained a note of understanding in it; she had noticed the somehow distant tone in Kasumi and Izumi's use of the word *brother*. "Oh, by the way, Tatsuya, about what you were saying before—"

"Ah, right, the possibility that the police have been infiltrated by elements that discriminate against magicians. Well, like I said, I don't think we have to worry about that," Tatsuya said, anticipating the question. "In fact, it might be simpler if that *were* the case," he finished with a sigh.

"…I should think it would be a major problem if the police have been corrupted by any sort of ideology, whether or not it's militant humanism, wouldn't it?" She looked up at him with the question mark practically visible over her head.

"If a branch of the police has been tainted by prejudice against magicians, we'll simply have to *deal* with them," Tatsuya replied grimly, his thoughts clear on his face. "In any case, there's no need for us to get involved. We can just pass the information along and let the police deal with the matter internally."

"I can't imagine this would happen, but…what if police who are hostile toward magicians became the majority? What would we do then?"

"There'd be nothing *to* do," Tatsuya explained, shaking his head with a bitter expression. "So long as there's no technology that can stand up to magic, the police will still need its own magicians in order to oppose the magicians that continue to exist, whether they like it or not. The government would act before things got to that point, I think…"

"Is there some possibility it wouldn't play out that way?" Miyuki pressed the point anxiously.

"Even without any ideological shift in the police force to worry about, the more urgent matter right now is that the Ten Master Clans may be held partially responsible for this terrorist attack. If the ideologically neutral police start thinking that way, then there's a good chance the apolitical masses will do the same thing."

Tatsuya turned his gaze to Maya. The clan heads were still surrounded by a throng of officers.

"Public opinion could change a lot depending on how the media covers this attack. And unfortunately, I think there are a lot of people who will interpret what happened here as 'ordinary folk suffered because of magicians.'"

Tatsuya turned from the crowd of officers to the line of ambulances. It looked like the most seriously injured victims had already been transported, but there were still over a dozen wounded lingering. Given these numbers, it seemed unlikely that the final body count would come in under ten.

"The ones responsible for terrorism are terrorists. But even if people feel the same way I do, once the media repeats their 'the magicians who endangered innocent bystanders share the responsibility' story enough times, more than a few are going to start believing what they hear."

"But we're Japanese citizens, the same as them," Miyuki mourned, looking down. She didn't stay that way long, though, proving that she was not the frail little girl she might appear to be. "Still—not all media are biased against magicians. Last April, some of the coverage acknowledged the rights and viewpoints of magicians, even if it was in the minority."

Just as Miyuki said, when news stories maligning magicians had shot up the previous April, in the latter part of the month some of the coverage had pushed back against the wave of scorn.

But this time there were casualties—a lot of them. The circumstances were considerably worse this time around.

"That's true. And the Master Clans Council isn't going to just sit by and do nothing."

The truth was, Tatsuya didn't want to say anything to make her worry more. Whether he saw the future pessimistically or optimistically, things would happen as they happened. There was nothing either of them could do about the future in this moment, so there was consequently no point in worrying about the possibility of conditions worsening.

"Anyway, we've made sure that Mother's all right, so we may as well head back to school."

Having talked to Katsuto, Tatsuya had a general grasp of the situation, and it didn't seem likely that they'd be able to accomplish anything else no matter how much longer they hung around. Here, at least, there was nothing to be gained by any further meddling, so it was best to leave the rest to the professionals.

With an "Okay, Tatsuya" and a nod, Miyuki agreed with her brother's assessment, and Minami indicated her willingness to follow orders with a crisp bow.

"What're you going to do, Shippou?"

"I'm…going to stay here a bit longer," replied Takuma to Tatsuya's question.

"Okay." Tatsuya neither supported nor opposed Takuma's decision. He had no obligation to look out for Takuma, and it would actually be inappropriate of him. Tatsuya gestured to Miyuki and Minami, and they started to leave.

"Um, Shiba—" came Takuma's hesitant voice from behind them.

"What is it?"

"About what we were talking about earlier," Takuma started, only to suddenly say, "no, never mind."

It was obvious that he was feeling tentative about something, but Tatsuya merely offered, "Okay," again and kept going.

A burned-down hotel with a large group of casualties and fatalities.

The mastermind of this gruesome act of terrorism watched the results of his work from an isolated house in Odawara, approximately nine kilometers from the scene.

Gu Jie's suicide-bombing plan had succeeded with the smallest amount of losses he'd projected.

The explosives hidden all over the town hadn't been caught by the bomb detectors. Even if they were obsolete, the USNA's military produced quality munitions indeed. From far enough away, their shielding was effective against even modern-day explosive-detection sensors.

The flesh puppets he'd controlled with Reanimation, his corpse-controlling magic, hadn't been caught by the sensors, either. Or even anyone in the hotel.

He didn't mock their naive security measures. By Gu Jie's estimation, the city's security level was no worse than the USNA's, where he'd lived until the previous month. But his skill had proven to be superior this time. He nodded to himself, satisfied.

Although he'd failed to so much as scratch any of the heads of the Ten Master Clans, that, too, was all according to his plan. He felt no regret, since he'd assumed from the start that explosives from mere hand-held missile launchers wouldn't be enough to touch them.

As planned, the Ten Master Clans had protected themselves. They'd protected *only* themselves and left the others at the scene to die. Gu Jie, a master of magic who manipulated death itself, put the number of dead at over twenty. Add the wounded and the number of casualties couldn't be fewer than fifty.

The suffering of some fifty people lay at the feet of the Ten Master Clans' selfishness.

That was what Gu Jie wanted to show the people of Japan: that the Ten Master Clans would leave you to die if it meant preserving their own lives.

It was their fault that their fellow countrymen were dead.

The Ten Master Clans, the Yotsuba family—they would be hated by Japan's people and would lose their place in this nation.

Just as he no longer had a place where he belonged in his homeland of Dahan.

A dark joy rose within Gu Jie, and he smiled, standing to leave. At his feet were the scattered bodies of the family who'd originally lived in the house he had taken for himself.

In a room at the USNA embassy, the number two in command of the Stars, Major Benjamin Canopus, watched a live feed of the scene at the Hakone terrorist attack.

His refined, masculine features were darkened by a frown. He couldn't help but feel outrage and distress at the sight of noncombatants paying the price for terrorist acts, even when they didn't hail from his country.

Canopus felt that every proper soldier had to be dedicated to protecting the distinction between combatants and civilians as defined in classical rules of engagement, so his duties with the Stars—which were frequently covert operations that involved concealing his military identity—were often opposed to his personal beliefs. He constantly felt conflicted. This made him all the more determined to take any and all measures necessary to avoid civilian casualties of any kind.

If he'd been allowed to, Canopus would have wanted to stop Hague's (Gu Jie's) plan. Even if it meant revealing the shameful fact that his nation had allowed obsolete weapons under their supervision to be stolen, he dearly wished he could've cooperated with the Japanese authorities to prevent the deaths of innocent civilians.

But he had not been allowed to. He had been forbidden from revealing the fact of the weapon theft to the Japanese. And to keep that truth hidden, cooperation with Japanese military and law enforcement was also not authorized.

The mission given to Canopus was the assassination of Hague. The mission came with a condition—not to give the Japanese authorities any reason to accuse the USNA of a violation of their sovereignty. It was made clear that the optimal outcome would be to lure Hague out into international waters and dispose of him there.

For someone who was a soldier through and through, Canopus had good political instincts. But he understood that being a soldier meant following orders and that the moment he disobeyed them, he ceased being a soldier and became an outlaw doling out violence based on nothing more than his personal preference.

So Canopus decided, for now, to remain a soldier and perform his duty.

After the questioning was finally over and they were released by the police, the leaders of the Ten Master Clans took the helicopter that Masaki had arrived in to the Kanto branch office of the Magic

Association. Of course, Katsuto was with them and Masaki, too, as were Kasumi, Izumi, their older brother Tomokazu, and finally Takuma.

After reaching the Magic Association building, the family heads all assembled in a meeting room, leaving Masaki, Kasumi, Izumi, Tomokazu, and Takuma to wait in a separate room. Despite the urgent circumstances, once all ten of the family heads were seated around the meeting room's roundtable, their eyes naturally turned to Mai Futatsugi, who was the eldest.

"Given the circumstances, let's not waste time with pointless formalities. I'd like to hear from all of you how we should deal with this emergency." As she sat at the focal point of nine separate gazes, Mai looked at each individual sitting at the table.

After her gaze had traveled all the way around the table, it settled on the person directly across from her—Kouichi.

"It will be difficult to keep the media in check," Kouichi noted pessimistically. Among the Ten Master Clans, he was the most skilled at media manipulation. "Currently, there are sixteen fatalities. Given the people they've yet to find in the rubble, the final figure will probably be above twenty—that's more than enough victims for the discourse to turn toward hysteria."

"That doesn't mean we can sit idly by and simply watch it unfold," objected Isami, whose seat was separated from Kouichi's by one place, which explained the lack of force in his voice.

"I can't help but wonder if a wait-and-see approach isn't called for at the moment," Gen Mitsuya interjected, articulating a more conservative path. "If we act rashly and openly, the public will see right through it, which will only worsen the backlash."

"I agree. We're victims, too, and we're not obligated to explain anything. There's nothing to be gained by being hasty and inviting more suspicion," Raizou Yatsushiro stated.

"But if we just stay silent, we'll only be demonized. The blame will fall entirely on us. Magicians everywhere will end up under increased scrutiny," Ichijou added.

"I agree with Mr. Ichijou. Of course, we can't be overzealous and risk a backlash, but I don't think silence is the right path, either. If we don't push back now, our enemies will only tighten the noose around our necks."

Both Gouki and Atsuko Mutsuzuka argued for a proactive response. The meeting had only barely gotten started, but already the mood was tense, and a clash seemed imminent. Mai furrowed her brow at this and tried to draw out other viewpoints from council members who had not yet spoken.

"Mr. Juumonji, what do you think? Please don't hold back. Feel free to speak your mind."

Katsuto inclined his head slightly at the others sitting around the table. "I believe media manipulation will be a waste of effort. On that point, I'm in agreement with Mr. Saegusa," he said, surprisingly articulate and direct.

"So you believe we should do nothing?" asked Raizou, his expression one of surprise and amusement.

"No," Katsuto replied, shaking his head as he fixed the man with his gaze. "I think we should assert our position without any manipulation or tricks. Specifically, I believe the Magic Association should issue a statement condemning all terrorism."

"I see," Raizou said, nodding at the unexpected response. It felt as though everyone had been so fixated on subtle, behind-the-scenes maneuvers that they'd lost sight of the obvious course of action.

"I believe we need to seriously consider the efficacy of Mr. Juumonji's proposal," Takumi Shippou said.

"I feel inclined to agree that issuing such a statement through the Magic Association is an excellent idea," Raizou agreed, lightly raising his hand.

"Oh, I thought you felt there was no need for any excuses or apologies, Mr. Yatsushiro," Atsuko remarked with a small degree of derision.

Gouki scowled at the rather impertinent comment, but Raizou merely laughed and let it go.

"What are your thoughts, Ms. Yotsuba?" Not even Atsuko seemed perturbed by Raizou's lack of conviction. She briskly turned to Maya for her opinion.

Before parting her crimson lips to speak, Maya looked not to Atsuko but to Kouichi, who sat next to her. "It doesn't seem to me that we need to limit ourselves to one response."

"That is true," said Kouichi, nodding evenly at what could have been seen as a provocation from Maya. "We should release a statement through the Magic Association. In it, we should not only condemn the terrorism but also pledge our full support and cooperation in apprehending those responsible." Kouichi glanced around the roundtable to confirm that no one was in opposition to his proposal, before continuing. "Of course, I also think we should proceed with the aforementioned media manipulation."

"But it won't be easy to control the media here. You yourself said as much, Mr. Saegusa."

Kouichi nodded with an empty smile at Gen's point. "Indeed. I doubt we'll be able to avoid the rise of voices claiming that magicians bear some of the responsibility. But I don't think it would be in our best interests to do nothing, either. Even if magicians are partially responsible, I believe we must still act to encourage the message, in the media's coverage, that terrorists are the real villains."

Gen was not satisfied with this answer. "I wonder if it will be so simple. Once an anti-magician narrative is established, it won't be easy to dislodge it."

"Addressing the trend of hostility toward magicians will be a long-term project. But if we can harness the public's greater hatred for terrorism, the unease they feel toward magicians could be eased. If we can catch the terrorists and show that we have in fact *taken* responsibility, that animosity would smoothly shift—"

Gouki interrupted Kouichi and Gen's argument. "Catch the terrorists ourselves? That would involve considerable risk."

"For the leaders of the Ten Master Clans to openly act, we would need the approval of the Joint Chiefs of Staff. Even with approval per the unofficial rules that fall outside of national law, considering our relationship with the government, we still can't ignore protocol."

"Mr. Ichijou," Kouichi asked, "how likely is it that we'll be able to get their approval?"

Gouki shook his head. "That's not even the only problem. If, in our attempt to capture the mastermind, we allow a second or third attack to occur, the Clans' influence will crater. And it won't just be us. Magicians everywhere will face more hardship and persecution."

"But we can hardly afford to leave *this* attack unaddressed."

Maya's statement caused the council to murmur. Gouki, whose view she'd directly contradicted, wore obvious wide-eyed surprise on his face.

"In order to prevent both subsequent terrorist attacks and copycat incidents, we of the Ten Master Clans must stake our reputation on either capturing or eliminating the criminals behind this."

To see Maya supporting Kouichi like this was completely unexpected by everyone except Maya herself.

"However, I also understand Mr. Ichijou's caution."

"…What do you mean by that?" Gouki wasn't the only one looking at Maya dubiously. From behind the tinted lenses of his glasses, Kouichi was also watching her carefully.

"I mean that I don't think it would be in our best interests to be seen directly engaging in a search for the fugitives. In addition to the consideration for how our reputation will suffer if we fail to catch him, we need to also stay vigilant to stop further outbreaks of aggression."

"You're saying we should prioritize counterterrorism readiness?" asked Mai.

"Exactly." Maya nodded.

"So who will we delegate the search for the actual culprits to?" Atsuko asked. Her question was not directed just to Maya but rather to the entire council.

Maya answered with her family's position: "The Yotsuba family is prepared to offer Tatsuya's services."

Immediately after, Gouki spat confrontationally, "We will give the task to Masaki."

But just before each family head could begin nominating their relatives for the task, Mai stymied them. "Ms. Yotsuba, Mr. Ichijou, wait please. Tatsuya and Masaki are both still high school students, are they not? It often takes considerable time to flush out a criminal who's gone into hiding. I'm not sure how I feel about asking high school students to forgo their studies for an assignment that has the potential to last so long."

Gouki was at a loss for how to reply to this very reasonable point.

But Maya was unfazed and smiled warmly at Mai. "I appreciate your concern, Ms. Futatsugi. But there's no need to worry," she said. "It's quite true that finding an enemy who's gone into hiding is far more time consuming than striking an enemy standing right in front of you. But even taking that into consideration, with Tatsuya on the job, backed by the Yotsuba family, it won't take more than a month to track the terrorist down. That shouldn't seriously impact his academic progress."

Mai found herself overpowered by Maya, who sounded not so much confident as precognizant, utterly certain of the outcome. "Still…" Mai started. But she, like Maya, was the head of one of the Ten Master Clans, and she wasn't speechless for long. "…the fact remains that Tatsuya is a high school student. No matter how capable he may be, I can't help but wonder about the optics of tasking someone so young with a counterterrorism operation."

Maya met Mai's objection with a faint smile, which seemed to say, *Now this is a problem?*

The details of the April 2095 terrorist attack on First High School had been kept secret for well over a year, but by this point, the broad strokes of the incident were well-known among the Ten Master Clans.

The particulars of the magic Tatsuya had used had been kept under wraps. However, after Tatsuya's connection to the Yotsuba family was made public, the fact that he and Katsuto had been at the center of the terrorists' defeat had spread out from the Juumonji family—in other words, from Katsuto—to the other members of the council.

Likewise, the assassination of No-Head Dragon's leadership was being kept secret, but the events that occurred at the international conference hall during the Yokohama Incident were widely known from the outset. As far as the parasite incident went, the specifics were classified, but Tatsuya's involvement there was also known. Maya herself had recently revealed that he'd been responsible for ending Gongjin Zhou the previous autumn. It was, as Maya pointed out, a bit late to claim that such situations were too dangerous for a mere high school student.

"Might we consider Tomokazu to lead the hunt?" Kouichi asked, nudging the deadlocked mood along. "My oldest son has finished his studies, and his job can make his time available. He's also close to the scene in Hakone, where we may find clues as to where the terrorists are hiding. The Kanto-Izu region is the responsibility of my family and the Juumonji family."

Kouichi watched the reactions this elicited from the other members around the table.

"If the fact that I had secret communication with Gongjin Zhou makes me untrustworthy, then I'm quite willing to cede command on the ground to Mr. Juumonji and have Tomokazu report to him."

Gouki looked to Mai, Isami to Atsuko, and Takumi to Raizou. Kouichi's true intentions were opaque to them.

"Do you really think that will make up for your misconduct?" Gen demanded, not bothering to make eye contact with either Mai or Maya.

Kouichi acknowledged the question with a calm, serious expression. "I don't expect this to be enough to regain your trust, but I hope this can become the first step in clearing the black mark from my name."

"I don't see a problem with this," said Maya crisply, supporting Kouichi's proposal without even glancing in his direction. "Kanto does fall under the jurisdiction of the Saegusa and Juumonji families, after all. If Mr. Saegusa is giving us his assurance, then I think we can entrust him with this," she continued, offering Mai a calm smile.

It was not Mai who replied, though, but rather Katsuto. "As I'm sure you're all aware, I would also like to undertake this duty. If it is necessary, I will ask Tatsuya to assist as well, so please feel free to speak."

"That's very gracious of you. I believe Mr. Ichijou will also be willing to assist us."

"Of course, we will offer our full support. Please use Masaki in whatever way you deem necessary." Katsuto bowed briefly to Maya and Gouki, then turned his attention to Kouichi. "Mr. Saegusa, while I'll be nominally in charge of this effort, Tomokazu will be the one giving actual direction."

"Thank you very much." Kouichi acknowledged Katsuto—who was young enough to be his son—with a bow.

But Katsuto was not finished. "However, Tatsuya of the Yotsuba family and Masaki of the Ichijou family will report directly to me."

For just a moment, Kouichi's eyes narrowed suspiciously. The tinted glasses he wore even indoors, however, kept anyone else from noticing the fleeting expression. "I will admit I don't see the point of that, but I don't mind," he said, giving Katsuto an indulgent nod.

This time it was Katsuto who met Kouichi's statement with a serene bow.

"Very well. We'll issue a statement through the Magic Association condemning the terrorist attack, and Mr. Juumonji will be responsible for the apprehension of the ringleader, with Mr. Saegusa directing the main effort. Are we all agreed on this course of action?" Mai asked, seeking consensus.

Raizou raised a casual hand. "I have no objection to the proposal itself, but how can we be sure the terrorist leader is even in Japan?" he asked, pointing out that the corpses could have been controlled from abroad.

"We are certain he is," said Gouki decisively. "The magic used to manipulate the bodies was not the type that uses preprogrammed actions. The activation timing, at the very least, would have relied on remote control. Sending a command to so many people would have required him to be hiding fairly close by."

"How close is 'fairly?'" Isami pressed.

Gouki thought about the question for a moment before answering. "That depends on the power of the caster but a ten-kilometer radius at most," he said, then added, "assuming he wasn't using a technique that we don't know about."

"Well, that's not something we can take into account," said Katsuto. "If the target can use magic beyond our knowledge, then capturing him won't be possible, regardless of whether he's in the country or not."

"That's a good point. I think our current plan is a good one," Raizou encouraged, giving his support to the consensus Mai had presented to the council.

As if that were their signal, one by one the rest of the members voiced their assent.

With consensus reached, the impromptu Master Clans Council came to a close.

The family heads all promptly made haste for their respective home bases to quickly increase precautions meant to prevent a second terrorist attack from happening in the regions that fell under their supervision.

That said, there was no way the Ichijou family, for example, could keep the entire Hokuriku-Sanin region under continuous observation, nor could the Mutsuzuka family prevent any illegal use of magic in the entire Tohoku area. The regional responsibilities of the Ten pertained to the discovery of and response to events after the fact.

Prevention of terrorism was the job of law enforcement. All the Ten Master Clans could do was provide assistance. But in order to ensure the smooth deployment of that assistance, the family heads could not afford to be away from their bases. Or—as in the case of the Yotsuba family—the heads needed to be present at home in order to ensure that the assistance (or maybe interference, as it were) was given discreetly so their involvement would remain invisible.

In either case, the circumstances meant that the family heads needed to hurry home.

Gouki Ichijou, along with Masaki, was returning to Kanazawa by helicopter.

Just as the helicopter rose from the helipad at the Magic Association's Kanto branch office, Gouki addressed his son. "Masaki."

"Yes?" he replied in a formal tone, inferring the nature of the conversation from his father's voice.

"I'm going to explain the Master Clans Council's plan for addressing this terrorist attack."

"Yes, sir."

"The Ten Master Clans will release a statement through the Magic Association denouncing the attack, simultaneously beginning a search for the mastermind with the ultimate aim of bringing whoever's responsible into our custody. Mr. Juumonji will be responsible for the search, with Mr. Saegusa's eldest son, Tomokazu, assisting him."

"What role will the Ichijou family play?"

"Aside from Mr. Juumonji, the family heads of the Ten will be focusing on preventing a second attack. You, Masaki, will pursue the terrorist leader at the direction of Mr. Juumonji."

"Yes, sir," Masaki replied, straightening his posture. His face was colored not with apprehension but excitement. He considered the role of tracking and apprehending the terrorist leader to be a prestigious one.

"You'll probably have to take some time off school. I'll make arrangements with the principal to have it treated as a sort of holiday."

"I understand."

Masaki loved his school life. In his heart of hearts, he wasn't eager to leave it. But still more important to him was his duty to the Ten Master Clans. His expression was already tight, but his face turned even more serious at what his father and family leader said next:

"Tatsuya Shiba from the Yotsuba family will also participate in the search under Mr. Juumonji's supervision. Show him what you're made of, Masaki."

"Yes, sir!" Masaki replied with a fierce nod.

The eventful day of February 5, 2097 was finally coming to an end.

Having rushed to the scene of the terrorist attack in Hakone earlier, Tatsuya and Miyuki (and Minami) were enjoying a moment of peace in their home.

Tatsuya had felt briefly reassured after confirming Maya's safety, but he now had the premonition that beginning tomorrow, magicians would face a rising tide of public animosity. Even though he had to admit it all came with the vague sense that this shouldn't be his problem.

As far as the terrorism itself went, he felt an *ordinary* amount of outrage at it.

He felt an *ordinary* amount of sympathy for the victims and their families.

But it was also plain fact that he was relieved that Miyuki had not been targeted.

He was not approaching the incident with an eye toward resolving it. As always, the most important thing to him was his sister. Even his concern for Maya was simply because in this moment, compared to her absence, Maya's presence was more convenient—and safer—*for Miyuki*.

While it was a lower priority than Miyuki, if First High was attacked, Tatsuya would have been unable to ignore it.

But outside of that—for example, if the council was targeted—Tatsuya would not have felt any particular motivation to act.

Unless he was ordered to.

Tatsuya had banished all thoughts about the terrorist incident from his mind and was in Miyuki's room helping her with her practical magical studies homework, until the phone suddenly started ringing. Before Miyuki could press the ANSWER CALL button, the receiver display switched to indicate a call in progress. Perhaps Minami had picked it up? The call had come not to Miyuki's private number but to the house's.

Just as Tatsuya shifted his broken concentration back to the homework, the phone beeped again. It was the notification of a call being transferred.

"Hello?" Miyuki asked, pressing the ANSWER CALL button and speaking into the mic.

*"Miyuki, there's a call from the family head for Tatsuya,"* came Minami's voice from the speaker.

"Understood. I'll take it in the living room," Tatsuya said as he stood. Not even pausing to wonder what the call could be about, he headed for the first floor.

Miyuki, of course, followed him.

"Sorry to keep you waiting, Aunt Maya." Tatsuya greeted her with a bow when he came into the visiphone's field of view, where Minami had remained rather than putting Maya on hold. When other people were around, Tatsuya made it a point to call Maya "Mother," but around close relatives, he still used "Aunt." Of course, Minami hadn't been informed of the truth that Maya and Tatsuya weren't really mother and son, still just aunt and nephew, but their trust that she wouldn't go blabbing about such things to outsiders meant that she was treated as a relative.

*"And I'm sorry to be calling at such a late hour,"* Maya replied smoothly.

"No, we were still up studying." It was the truth, but even so, it elicited a smile from Maya.

*"So even you study, eh?"* she asked, genuinely amused.

"Well, I *am* a high school student, after all, so I can't exactly neglect my schoolwork," he replied and then waited for her to get to the point.

*"Well, I suppose it's true that a student's job is studying. It's too bad I can't let you give it your undivided attention."* Maya's honest amusement gave way to her usual artificially pleasant face as she regarded Tatsuya from the other side of the display.

Tatsuya naturally straightened and prepared to receive his orders.

"Tatsuya, I am tasking you with apprehending the mastermind of today's terrorist attack."

"Apprehending? Not assassinating?"

"Ah, I suppose I misspoke. Find him and neutralize him. Dead or alive, it matters little."

"Affirmative, Aunt Maya." Tatsuya brought his heels together and bowed crisply. The only reason he didn't reflexively salute was because he'd been conscious ahead of time of the need to perform a civilian bow. The fact that he'd still said, "Affirmative," rather than a simple "Understood," was thanks to the not-inconsiderable influence of the Independent Magic Battalion.

Of course, even if he had given a military salute, Maya probably wouldn't have found it particularly notable or cared.

"The search is being carried out on the orders of the Master Clans Council. Mr. Juumonji is overseeing with the Saegusa family providing the bulk of the forces."

"So does that mean I'll also be operating under the direction of the Saegusa family?"

"No. Per Mr. Juumonji's request, you'll report directly to him," Maya said before dropping a bomb. "And by 'Mr. Juumonji,' I mean Katsuto. At the recent Master Clans Council, he succeeded his father as head."

But the bomb may as well have been a dud.

"I see," Tatsuya stated dryly.

"So you're not surprised?"

"In the Independent Magic Battalion even two years ago, I was hearing that Katsuto was already the de facto authority figure of his family, so no."

"My goodness…you can never let your guard down around the military. Or maybe it was the doing of that young lady."

By "that young lady," Maya was referring to Kyouko Fujibayashi. She was well aware of Kyouko's other name—the Electron Sorceress.

Then, with no particular preamble, Maya lobbed a second

bombshell. *"Masaki Ichijou will also be participating in the search and also reporting directly to Mr. Juumonji."*

"Ichijou?!" As far as Tatsuya was concerned, this bomb also fizzled, but it had an immediate effect on Miyuki, who was standing meekly beside him. "Er, I'm sorry," Miyuki quickly added, blushing red.

*"I don't mind one bit. Your surprise is quite understandable,"* Maya offered generously through the screen.

Miyuki wasn't exactly emboldened by this, but she regained enough composure to pose the question that came to mind. "I don't mean to bring up an earlier topic, but what about our studies? Taking orders from Mr. Juumonji means the search will take place in the Kanto region, correct? I can't imagine we'd only be there for a week."

On the other side of the screen, Maya smiled brightly at Miyuki. *"I have no intention of letting this become some time-consuming affair. We already know the name and particulars of the target you'll be neutralizing."*

At this, Tatsuya was finally surprised. But not at the fact that Maya already knew who the terrorist mastermind was. Rather, he was stunned that despite being a known entity, the terrorist still managed to make a clean getaway.

*"The man's name is Gu Jie. His English name is Gide Hague. Publicly, he's a stateless refugee from Dahan associated with the Kunlun Institute. Apparently, he escaped before its destruction. He appears to be a man in his fifties with dark skin and white hair. Although by this point, he could have changed much of that."*

The individual Maya described matched the information Lina had given them. Tatsuya surmised that their sources were the same.

"Do you have an image of his face?"

*"Unfortunately, no. Only a description."*

This was hardly different from having no leads at all, Tatsuya thought. Maya had given him a name and a description, but names could be changed. It seemed very optimistic to imagine that the search would be concluded quickly.

Tatsuya didn't let his pessimism reach his face, but Miyuki looked obviously concerned.

"You needn't worry too much about this, Miyuki. We'll use some divination on our end to narrow down his possible hiding places."

Evidently, some of the Yotsuba family's magicians had sensory magic available to them that even Tatsuya was unfamiliar with—perhaps upstream time traversal like postcognition or psychometric detection of residual thoughts. He inferred as much from Maya's use of the word *divination*. He could also imagine that the Kuroba's specialty of espionage was supported by the existence of such magic. Tatsuya realized all over again that there was a lot he and Miyuki didn't yet know about the Yotsuba family.

But this was not the time for such musings.

"Your part will come after that, Tatsuya. Once we've managed to identify him, he won't escape, will he?"

Tatsuya recognized the question Maya put to him as an order and bowed crisply. "Gongjin Zhou very nearly did escape, but…I will do everything in my power, yes."

Once her call to Tatsuya was concluded, Maya's pleasant demeanor immediately shifted.

Behind her, as ever, Hayama stood at the ready.

Maya looked back at her trusted butler with an intensity on her face that she rarely showed. "Hayama, have you found any leads yet?"

"I'm afraid not, madam."

"I see," Maya said, irritation dripping from her voice. She hadn't let Tatsuya see this mood nor had she let it slip in front of the other family heads.

Hayama did not tell his mistress to be patient. She knew just as well as he did that the memories of the dead victims wouldn't disappear in only three or four days.

Rather than counseling patience, Hayama decided to ask after the source of her frustration. "Are you regretting not being able to put the intelligence from Colonel Balance to use, madam?"

Maya reflexively began to refute this, but she stopped herself with a deep sigh. "...I suppose I should know better than to try to put on a brave face in front of you, Hayama." Her irritation gave way to an exhausted half smile. "Yes, I'm regretting the fact that despite getting advance warning, the enemy still managed to get the drop on us."

It was no wonder she was exhausted. She'd escaped from a terrorist bombing on the second day of the already demanding Master Clans Council. She'd been interviewed by law enforcement, then pressed on to a second meeting to discuss how to respond.

Maya was an outstanding magician, but physically she was no different from an average person. Her youthful appearance was not merely external; she was just as healthy as she appeared to be. Nonetheless, she possessed only the fitness of a woman around thirty and nothing extraordinary.

"Madam, I understand how you feel, but there is no use in agonizing over things that have already happened. Even the Yotsuba family is not omnipotent."

When physical exhaustion affected mental energy, it was a message from the body that it needed rest. If Maya wasn't accepting that herself, then she needed someone who would help her do so.

Fortunately, Maya's psychological condition had not deteriorated so much that she had become unable to recognize her body's needs. "...You're right. I don't intend to spend more time than necessary on this, but it's not going to be wrapped up by tomorrow or the day after, no matter what I do. I'll get some rest. If anything happens, please tell me in the morning."

"You may rest assured I will do so, madam."

As Maya left her study, Hayama saw her off with a respectful bow.

# [ 7 ]

February 6, the morning after the terrorist attack.

A fine mist of rain had been falling since before dawn and looked unlikely to abate, but Tatsuya left for Kyuuchouji temple as usual.

He received the usual rough welcome from the disciples.

But once he was face-to-face with Yakumo, Tatsuya took an action that was not at all usual.

"So you want me to teach you how to counter Qimen Dunjia, eh…?"

Tatsuya trained with Yakumo, but he wasn't, strictly speaking, among his disciples.

Nor did Yakumo owe Tatsuya a favor.

Yakumo was merely acting as Tatsuya's training dummy. Previously, this job had fallen to Kazama, but recently Tatsuya's skill had become comparable with his, and sparring with Tatsuya was now good practice even for Yakumo.

He'd helped the young man develop the psionic bullet technique during the parasite incident because it wasn't something he could ignore, and he'd helped during the Parasidoll incident for the same reason—their interests aligned.

Yakumo occasionally lent a hand during investigations. It was something like a hobby to him, and he enjoyed it.

The reason he lent out the underground installation beneath the temple, however, was simply because he had no use for it himself.

"Tatsuya. I've given you a variety of instruction over the years, but I've never taught you specific techniques. I thought you understood the reason for that."

"I do understand. It's because I'm not a disciple of *Kyuuchouji temple*," Tatsuya replied, returning Yakumo's cool gaze with an even, unconcerned one of his own. He had a thorough understanding of the nature of their relationship. He didn't have to be told that he had no right to ask this of him. And yet, here he was because of an urgent need.

Tatsuya wouldn't let a target escape once he'd found it. Maya had said as much, but Tatsuya knew perfectly well that she was overestimating him. In reality, his power alone hadn't been enough to neutralize Gongjin Zhou. If it hadn't been for Saburou Nakura's seal, drawn with his own blood at the cost of his life, Tatsuya wouldn't have been able to counter Zhou's Qimen Dunjia, and Zhou would have escaped.

Neither Lina nor Maya had said it out loud, but it wasn't hard to reach the conclusion that Gu Jie was the one behind Zhou. Raymond S. Clark had told Tatsuya directly—or, well, via a video recording—that Gu Jie was pulling the strings for Blanche and No-Head Dragon. So clearly Gongjin Zhou, who'd been closely connected to both Blanche and No-Head Dragon, was also Gu Jie's subordinate.

The master was not always more powerful than the disciple. It was hardly rare for a disciple's ability to outstrip their master's. But to assume that Gu Jie couldn't do something that Gongjin Zhou had done wasn't just optimistic; it was downright naive. Tatsuya felt that at the very least, he needed to take some precautions.

Whether or not Yakumo understood Tatsuya's position, his tone was not friendly. "Indeed. You're neither an itinerant monk nor a *shinobi*. As a *shinobi myself*, you are ultimately an outsider. And I cannot teach secret techniques to an outsider."

"If the technique weren't magic, would it still be subject to nondisclosure?"

Yakumo smirked at the very modern phrase *nondisclosure*. But his expression soon regained its seriousness. "If it's not a secret technique, then it's exempt from that prohibition, yes, but...Tatsuya—are you suggesting that you want to learn a way to counter Qimen Dunjia that isn't reliant on magic?"

Tatsuya met Yakumo's piercing gaze without so much as a flinch. "As you know, master, my ability with magic is extremely uneven. Even if you were to teach me a high-level magic technique, I would unfortunately be unable to use it."

"I doubt that very much. If we're talking about techniques that adhere to the principles of modern magic, it's true that you're at a disadvantage. But in terms of your ability to control spirit, you're at the level of a master, despite your age. If anything, I'd guess you'd have more aptitude for the ancient secret techniques rather than less."

"I thought that the operating principles of modern and ancient magic were the same."

"Ancient and modern magic techniques that rewrite phenomena are essentially similar. But from our perspective, there is more to technique than rewriting phenomena. Many of the esoteric methods hidden within our martial art do not involve rewriting phenomena but using spirit to create waves and flows—and control them, and interrupt them, even destroy them."

"Master, this 'spirit' you're talking about—are you referring to psions? 'Waves' could be psionic waves, and 'flow'... Is that psionic conduction?"

"Turns out you *have* been studying. That's basically correct," said Yakumo, a strange light glittering in his narrowly opened eyes.

That moment, Tatsuya felt the strange sensation of being thrown into a formless space with no up or down—but which was nonetheless unlike a zero-gravity environment.

"For us, the technique of manipulating spirit is among our esoteric arts. And countering Qimen Dunjia is indeed something that can be done through manipulating spirit."

Yakumo's voice seemed to assault Tatsuya's body from all directions. There was nothing to stand on and no way to attack or escape.

With no idea where his opponent was, evasion and defense were also impossible.

He could see Yakumo's form. But without the ability to trust his senses, meaningful resistance was impossible.

His trust in Yakumo was irrelevant. The man across from him held absolute power over him, and Tatsuya had to force down the sense of doom welling up from inside him. He turned his attention inward, to his own body, to his own internality.

His blood continued to pump normally. It was very different compared to the feeling of free fall that came with flight magic. In opposition to gravity, his head was on top, and his feet were at the bottom. Using not nerve impulses but psionic signals, Tatsuya regained control and broke through the illusion of being trapped in directionless space.

The feeling of gravity's effect on his limbs returned.

His feet were firmly planted on the ground, and he was looking up at the sky.

"Master, just now…"

"I didn't teach you a thing. And I certainly didn't expect you to break through that illusion entirely under your own power." Yakumo's face was the picture of innocence. He was practically whistling. "Even Kazama couldn't break free on his first try."

"Was that Qimen Dunjia?"

Yakumo seemed as though he wanted to divert the conversation into idle chitchat, but he answered Tatsuya's bluntly posed question with a quick "It was not. Qimen Dunjia affects a group, an area. What you just saw was an illusion directed at just one person." Yakumo's smile turned mischievous. "Of course, casting an illusion on you was hard even for me, so I'm a little spent."

Yakumo didn't explain what he meant by "spent." Tatsuya was about to ask, but his attention was pulled away from that by what the man said next.

"In a way, you could call that the rudimentary technique that comes before Qimen Dunjia."

He said it as though it were an incidental detail, but Tatsuya realized that this was Yakumo's answer to his request to be taught how to counter Qimen Dunjia.

He wasn't sure exactly how the illusion had been put on him, but if it was the rudimentary version of Qimen Dunjia, then the countermeasure had to be something in the direction of what he'd just done. Now all he had to do was practice it.

"—Master, thank you very much."

"Like I said, I didn't teach you a thing. Now then, shall we start our training?" Yakumo insisted, moving on to their usual *physical* martial arts practice.

"Yes, I'm ready." Bowing, Tatsuya assumed his usual ready stance.

Despite its somewhat unusual start, Tatsuya finished his daily training session with Yakumo and returned home.

After that, he went to school as usual. Yes, he had been assigned by Maya to track down the terrorist mastermind, but at the moment, he was still waiting for more information.

But his usual routine only lasted until lunch.

With the conclusion of Miyuki and Honoka's cold war, Tatsuya and his friends had resumed gathering in the dining hall to have lunch together. Miyuki, Honoka, and Shizuku has staked out a table, and the rest of the group was assembling there.

Then, just as they were all starting to eat lunch, the dining hall's large display switched to a broadcast of breaking news.

"'Terrorists claim responsibility'?" Mikihiko murmured, his brow furrowing. As he did, the newscaster began to read the statement.

The gist of the pompous, overwrought prose was as follows:

—*We are responsible for the recent attack on a Hakone hotel.*

—*This is our holy war, which we undertake in order to extinguish the evil power known as magic from the Earth.*

—*The target of this attack was the Ten Master Clans, who hold this nation's magicians in their thrall.*

—*However, these contemptible individuals used innocent civilians as shields to make their escape.*

—*We will continue to fight to free humanity from these mutants who call themselves magicians.*

—*So long as the people of Japan refuse to purge these magicians from their midst, the number of casualties will rise.*

The newscaster then moved on to detailing the damage and casualties that resulted from the attack.

Of eighty-nine guests using the hotel, there had been twenty-two fatalities, and another thirty-four had suffered light to heavy injuries.

Of the thirty-three uninjured guests, twenty-seven had been magicians.

The newscaster added that none of the casualties had been magicians—and suggested that if instead of escaping they'd prioritized saving lives, there might have been fewer victims.

"Why do we have to put other people's lives before our own, huh?" spat Erika as she watched the screen, where a politician was now offering some comments to the newscaster. There wasn't any point in complaining to the television, but apparently she wasn't in any kind of mood to care.

"Sometimes, people have to put others' lives first, because of their occupation or social standing. But yeah, it's pretty annoying to see someone talking about that like it should be obviously unconditional," Mikihiko agreed in an uncharacteristically strong voice, his obvious loathing also motivated by the nature of the commentary.

"Weren't there almost fifty suicide bombers? How do they think we could've stopped that many? Do they think the Ten Master Clans are made up of invincible supermen?" Leo complained.

"It's important to provide mutual aid during a disaster like that, but demanding that we put other people's lives first is nothing more than forcibly imposing their conveniently heartwarming values on us. It doesn't sound like magicians' lives are included among the lives that should've been prioritized," Tatsuya added sharply, unable to remain simply sarcastic this time.

Nobody seemed to have anything to add to that. They turned their attention back to the broadcast.

The politician was just condemning the terrorists. If he'd said anything openly critical about the Ten Master Clans, it would have been construed as supporting the terrorists.

But as the newscaster's initial comments had suggested, the mood of misplaced self-righteousness would only increase. And magician-hating politicians would gleefully pounce on the opportunity. Tatsuya wasn't the only one gloomily contemplating the prospect of something similar to the previous April happening again.

That evening, Tatsuya was invited to the Juumonji family's estate.

*Estate* wasn't quite the right word—it was more like a modern-style home that was slightly on the larger side. It was bigger than Tatsuya's home but nothing compared with where Shizuku lived. The only thing really notable about it was its garden, which was so large it was hard to believe it was in Tokyo.

Tatsuya pushed the doorbell button at the front gate, and Katsuto came out personally to greet him. "Good of you to come. Let's head inside," he said.

Tatsuya had heard from Maya that Katsuto had already taken over leadership of the family. He couldn't decide whether being received personally by the master of the house meant that he was being treated as an important guest or simply that their household was thinly staffed. He quickly decided the question was of no importance and set it aside.

"Thank you for having me over."

Aside from its roominess, the entryway was not notably luxurious. And even its size was only roughly double that of the entryway in an average single-family home. There were no notably fancy furnishings, either. The only thing that caught Tatsuya's eye was a pair of neatly aligned, youthfully styled ladies' pumps.

If the publicly available data was to be trusted, the Juumonji family's youngest generation consisted of Katsuto, a brother in his second year of middle school, another brother in his first year of middle school, and a sister in her fifth year of elementary school. Tatsuya wondered if there was another guest here. He had the feeling that he knew who it was, but he didn't confront Katsuto with that deduction.

Tatsuya followed behind Katsuto, and eventually they came to a sitting room, where the exact woman Tatsuya had expected was sitting.

"Good evening, Tatsuya. You're right on time," said Mayumi, looking over her shoulder from the sofa in front of him.

"It's been a while, Mayumi. Since December, I believe."

"Yes, that's what—three months? Feels like a long time and yet hardly any time at all."

"You're going to make me nervous if you just keep standing there. Have a seat, Shiba," Katsuto instructed.

Tatsuya sat as directed on the sofa next to Mayumi. It was, incidentally, a three-person sofa, and there was an empty seat between the two of them.

Katsuto sat opposite Tatsuya rather than his other guest.

Once the three were seated, they all glanced at one another as if to determine who would speak first, but just then there was a knock at the door of the sitting room.

A woman of about sixty emerged from the doorway. "Your tea," she said, setting down a saucer in front of Tatsuya, then placing a teacup on it with a neat, practiced motion. She then refilled Mayumi and Katsuto's teacups, bowed, and left the room.

"She's very elegant," Tatsuya noted, impressed. His sister's bearing was just as beautiful, but the elegance gained from so many years of humble service was something that even Miyuki could not simply imitate.

"Shiba, Saegusa, I'm sorry to make you come all the way here today," said Katsuto, not acknowledging Tatsuya's murmured compliment. On a second glance, he seemed to be a bit embarrassed.

Tatsuya suddenly got the sense that Mayumi was about to burst out laughing beside him.

"Not at all. It's not as though it was particularly far."

The truth was that point to point, some thirty kilometers lay between Tatsuya's residence and Katsuto's home, but if they provoked Mayumi any further, the resulting awkwardness would fall entirely on them. Tatsuya did his level best to perform a serious mood.

Thanks to his efforts, Mayumi was able to regain her composure. "Well, now that Tatsuya's here, Juumonji, are you going to tell us what this is about?"

At this, Katsuto's mood also shifted. Tatsuya had never seen him look quite so tense.

"I need your help with a matter related to the recent terrorist attack."

Katsuto's request was what Tatsuya expected. But at the same time, it was surprising.

"The Yotsuba family head has also ordered me to assist, and I will be happy to cooperate," Tatsuya stated, glancing aside at Mayumi.

Her face was solemn and unreadable as she gazed steadily back at Katsuto.

"But why are you asking Saegusa as well? I was told that the Saegusa family's eldest son was tasked with joining the hunt for the terrorists."

"Unfortunately, I can't answer that question, Shiba," Katsuto stated before turning to Mayumi. "Saegusa, what I'm asking of you is not a request from the Juumonji family to the Saegusa family. It's a favor from one friend to another. You don't need to concern yourself with our family circumstances. If you don't want to, you can just refuse. I won't be offended."

Mayumi left a soft breath escape. The small sound had a note of frustration in it. "You've got it backward, Juumonji. Telling me it's a favor from one friend to another makes it *harder* for me to refuse."

"Oh, I see. Sorry."

"You don't look very sorry."

"No, that really wasn't what I meant…" Katsuto shrank under her dubious gaze. Tatsuya hadn't had a chance to see the two act so familiar around each other before, and there was something refreshing about watching them behave like this.

Katsuto and Mayumi noticed Tatsuya watching them and simultaneously coughed to compose themselves.

"Anyway, what is it you want me to do, Juumonji? Saying 'I need your help' doesn't help me decide anything. I can't agree to do something that's impossible for me."

"I see your point," Katsuto said, reaching for his tea and taking a sip in order to buy time to consider how to *officially* explain what he needed. "The search for the terrorist leader is being conducted in a somewhat unconventional fashion."

"I know that. You are in command, but my older brother is the one directly managing the bulk of the resources, right? Not very efficient. This doesn't feel like the right time for our families to be thinking about appearances."

Evidently, Mayumi had interpreted the strange organization of the terrorist search to be a product of the Saegusa and Juumonji families playing politics with their shared responsibility for the Kanto region.

The real reason was something else entirely, but that wasn't something that Katsuto could tell Mayumi. He couldn't very well say, *This is part of your father's amends for his disloyalty.*

"It's true. If Tomokazu and I don't coordinate closely, we won't be able to avoid wasted effort. That's why I want you, Saegusa, to act as a liaison between us," Katsuto decided upon at last. "I have no intention of hiding the details of my investigation from Tomokazu, and I expect he doesn't, either. But during its course, we'll assuredly have to use secret techniques and classified information networks. I can't risk passing along information obtained like that via outsiders. The nature of the information could very well lead someone to deduce how it was gathered."

"I see. So you want me to be the go-between? That's what you're saying? Because you'll be relaying things that can't be revealed to a mere messenger."

"Exactly. I don't even mind if you exercise your discretion and censor information that would reveal Saegusa family secrets to me. All I want is for you to pass along anything necessary for the investigation."

"Wow, you sound so official..." Mayumi was wearing a skeptical smile, but there was worry in her tone, too. Katsuto had said she could use her own judgment to filter out the information, but that meant there was a nonzero chance that she could filter out something important that ended up allowing their target to escape. It wasn't something she could agree to lightly.

"...All right. I'll do it. I have to admit I'm probably the best person for the job."

"I appreciate it."

"Don't worry about it. I mean, it's a problem for my family, too."

The truth was that the request for Mayumi to perform this duty had come from Kouichi. Kouichi hadn't explained his reasoning, but Katsuto had the faint sense it was because doing so would increase the opportunities Mayumi and Tatsuya would have to interact.

It was true that there was a need for someone to coordinate communication. But cooperating with Kouichi's somewhat underhanded plan pricked at Katsuto's conscience. That was why he was being more circumspect than was necessary, but Mayumi gave no sign of having noticed any ulterior motives.

"So practically speaking, what should I do? Maybe I need to take some time off from school."

"I was thinking I'd work that out with you after this," said Katsuto, then turned to Tatsuya, who by this point was something of a third wheel. "I don't mind you moving freely until we've found a useful lead, but I'd like to stay in close contact. As much as they can be, our meetings should be in person. When would be convenient for you? If possible, I'd like to meet daily to at least catch up on any progress that might've been made."

This insistence on in-person meetings, like Mayumi's appointment as communication coordinator, had come at Kouichi's strong request. However, it was a perfectly reasonable precaution in and of itself.

Perhaps because of that, Tatsuya gave no indication of having noticed this little intrigue playing out. "Anytime is fine with me," he said without any hesitation.

"All right," said Katsuto, and returned his attention to Mayumi. "What about you, Saegusa?"

"I can't promise that I'll be available every single day, but generally I think that will be fine."

"That's more than enough. Where shall we meet?"

"If it were just me and Juumonji, I'd say somewhere close to the Magic University, but..." Mayumi looked over at Tatsuya to check his reaction.

"That's no problem," said Tatsuya, again without any hesitation. This wasn't out of any deference to his seniors, but rather because the Magic University was also very convenient for him.

"But is there a suitable location near the university?"

It was easy enough to meet in person instead of communicating electronically, but they would still be wise to take precautions against eavesdropping. A civilian residence wouldn't be secure enough.

"I'll make those preparations. I'd like to start our intelligence briefings the day after tomorrow," said Katsuto.

"Gotcha," said Mayumi.

"Understood. Where should we assemble and when?" asked Tatsuya.

After a moment's thought, Katsuto answered Tatsuya's question with a time and place. "…All right, the day after tomorrow at 6:00 PM, in front of the main university gate."

Tatsuya did a quick mental calculation. If he skipped his student council duties, Tatsuya could be home in time to head back out and make it there by 6:00 PM. He nodded. "Understood."

Around the same time that Tatsuya, Mayumi, and Katsuto were meeting in the Juumonji home to decide on their plan, Gouki Ichijou was visiting a well-known and exclusive Japanese fine-dining restaurant near his home. In addition to the cuisine being excellent, the staff was exceedingly well trained, and the establishment was often used by politicians in the area for discreet meetings.

Gouki himself had used it to entertain politicians four or five times himself. Such activities weren't his forte, but as the patriarch of one of the Ten Master Clans, they were an unavoidable part of his duties.

However, the individual he was entertaining this evening was no politician.

Sitting across from Gouki was the principal of Third High School, Chizuru Maeda.

"Ms. Maeda, thank you for making time in your busy schedule to—"

"Oh, come on—let's just skip the formalities, please. It's just you and me here."

…Hearing her talk this way made it sound like she couldn't

possibly be a teacher, much less a principal, but this woman was unmistakably the principal of the National Magic University Third Affiliated High School where Masaki attended classes.

"...It's hard to imagine they let you be a principal, Chizuru. Magic High School is a national-level organization, you know," Gouki teased.

"Don't be stupid, Gouki. Most of the time I hide this side of me, obviously," Principal Maeda said, shamelessly unfazed by the teasing. "And Magic High School is an upper secondary school. Even if it's national level, it's not like an arm of the military," she continued with a fierce grin.

Gouki hadn't meant to imply that Magic High School and the Academy of Defense were the same thing, but he decided not to quibble. He was perfectly aware of Maeda's complicated feelings about the military.

Principal Maeda had served in the Maritime Defense Force until her late twenties. Her final rank was first lieutenant. She'd had some sort of trouble with a superior (Gouki had been told it was coordinated sexual harassment) and had ended up retiring young. Afterward, she changed professions to become an educator and, at the age of forty, was selected as the principal for Third High—an unusual and singular career path.

She had also been one year ahead of Gouki while they'd *attended* Third High. During school, she'd been a holy terror, her talent allowing her to defeat a string of campus hotshots and shine as the most skilled student they had; Gouki himself had the dubious honor of having his nose broken by her once. She would always be something of a domineering upperclassman.

"Okay, Gouki, let's hear what you have to say. You don't invite me out like this often, so it's gotta be important."

"It's a personal matter," replied Gouki to Maeda's opening jab. His tone was dignified and even a little bit defiant.

"Oh-ho...don't tell me you want me to bump your kid's grades up or something."

"It may amount to something like that," said Gouki.

Maeda's eyes shone with a keen light as she nodded for Gouki to continue.

"I assume you heard about the terrorist attack in Hakone the other day."

"I heard. Awful."

"So you also know about the statement issued through the Magic Association?"

"Of course. But it's not going to have much of an effect, right? Condemning the terrorists is such an obvious thing to do, and to anyone who already has an unfavorable view of magicians, it's going to seem like we're merely trying to shift the blame," Maeda said, then added, "I mean, the actual blame shifting happened when they started faulting the magicians who were the target, but still."

"We are under no illusions that condemning the terrorism will be enough to defuse the situation."

"Now that you mention it, the statement did say something about cooperating to the fullest possible extent in capturing those responsible. So that wasn't just lip service?"

Gouki nodded. "The Ichijou family has sent Masaki to aid in the search."

Maeda didn't suggest that was excessive. Instead, she simply said, "And?" in a manner that implied she knew where this was headed.

"With Mr. Juumonji coordinating the search and beginning from the scene of the attack in Hakone, it's projected to take anywhere from a few weeks to over a month. I expect to have Masaki stay at a separate residence in Tokyo for the duration. He'll have to be excused from a significant amount of school."

"And you're asking me to treat this not as an absence but as a scheduled holiday?"

"Yes. The work of the Ten Master Clans is not public service. It is, if anything, a personal matter, and I recognize that it's a lot to ask.

But in order for my son to be able to devote himself to this without worrying about his future, I am making this unreasonable request."

"It *is* a big ask," Maeda said coolly to Gouki's bowed head. "Just because he's from an important family doesn't mean I can grant him favors like that. If anything, my job is to stamp out instances of special treatment whenever I find them."

"...I understand." Gouki did not press further. Maeda was not an inflexible person; in fact, Gouki knew her to be exceedingly empathetic. But he also knew that once she'd settled on something, she never went back on her word. "It was a foolish request. Please forget it."

"No, I can appreciate your position. And I do see the necessity of sending your son to Tokyo. So while I can't excuse his absence, I can make a request with Mr. Momoyama."

Not understanding why Momoyama's name had come up, Gouki's expression was muddled. "Huh? Mr. Momoyama as in Principal Momoyama, the principal of First High?"

"That's right."

"What sort of request?"

"To have your son admitted there."

Maeda didn't deliberately cut her explanation short. Rather, the pace of Gouki's follow-up questions was so rapid that she didn't have time to elaborate.

"Now, hold on," she said, raising a hand to forestall any further time-wasting interrogation from him. "I'm not saying I'll have him transferred. All I mean is that I'll make it possible for him to keep up with his theoretical studies at First High. Personalized instruction via terminal is standard these days and not just in magic high schools. Schools using the same magic curriculum can exchange academic records via the Magic University system, so I expect he'll be able to continue his classes at Third High using First High's facilities. His practicum and physical education classes won't be possible, of course, but I don't think a month of absences in those areas will hurt him too much."

"So you're saying you'll let my son attend First High for the duration of his duties? As something like an auditor?"

"It's not like he's going to be investigating full-time like some kind of detective, right?" Gouki nodded, and Maeda continued, "It would probably be less trouble for him if we could get permission to let him study at home, but we're not allowed to transmit academic data from the magic high school system outside of the university network. I know the environment and social situation might be rough for him, but with the general education and theoretical magic curriculum available at First High, the absence on his record shouldn't have any adverse effects."

Gouki's expression finally started to show acceptance.

"You've already worked out where he's going to live, right? I'll make arrangements for him to start at First High next Monday, and he can finish out this week at his current school. Time wise, how does a month sound? Running through March 9. And of course, if the case is solved before then, I'll make sure he can come back whenever he needs to."

"Thank you so much, Chizuru. I truly appreciate it."

From a parent's perspective, this was even better than having Masaki excused from class. Gouki had absolutely no complaints, and his bow to Maeda was a deep one.

Maeda proceeded to keep Gouki out until the wee hours, where she drank him under the table.

The denouncement of Hague, as many magicians had suspected, only stirred up public opinion. The media was flooded with castigation for magicians. It was admittedly worse because of the recency of the event, but the recipients of the torrent of public anger had little cause for optimism, knowing that the media was much quicker to take up the banner of outrage than it was to call for calm.

The students at First High were also obviously agitated. Despite knowing there was nothing they could do, students filled the halls, checking the news between classes. In whispers and grumbles, they complained to one another about the biased media coverage.

Reactions to the news among the students of First High were broadly divided into three groups. The largest group was outraged that magicians, and not the terrorists, were being cast as the villains of the incident. Many of these students were boys. Another group, mostly girls, was more worried about the rising tide of hostility toward magicians. And the final group was frustrated with people who had numbers in their family names.

Even once classes ended, the news coverage continued broadcasting in the student council room. Normally, they didn't even so much as play quiet music there, in order to avoid interfering with their work—and also because their music tastes differed—but today everyone was unavoidably concerned about what was going on. Predictably, productivity had plummeted.

Tatsuya would be taking a break from the student council beginning the next day, and his successor didn't need any extra work. Tatsuya was therefore silently grinding away at the mountain of in-progress tasks. Without this, the student council's duties would probably back up with an entire day's worth of work.

What stopped him was overhearing a conversation he couldn't ignore. The speaker who caught his attention was not the former student council treasurer, Kei Isori, who'd been invited to attend a meeting on next month's graduation party, but rather Kanon Chiyoda, who'd tagged along.

"Wait, Chiyoda, are you saying we're in the wrong?"

Tatsuya looked up to see Izumi, the vice president—who along with Miyuki, the president, was participating in the council meeting—

protesting whatever it was Kanon had said. Izumi's question was as restrained and polite as ever, but she couldn't hide her displeasure.

Tatsuya's only relation to Izumi was as her senior, being a year ahead of her in school, and even though they both served on the student council, they weren't particularly close. He didn't feel as though he was in any position to chide her, but even if Miyuki had said the same thing, Tatsuya probably wouldn't have spoken up. What Kanon had said was more than enough to incur Izumi's wrath.

Kanon had said, *"What a pain... Thanks to the Ten Master Clans screwing up, we're all paying the price."*

It was a thoughtless remark tossed out during the post-meeting chatter, in response to the exceptionally harsh anti-magician tone of the current news broadcast. But she wasn't the only magician who felt that way. It was a complaint often raised against the most powerful Numbered families.

"I mean, obviously the terrorists are the bad guys here, but it's just a fact that the Ten haven't handled things well, either."

Kanon wasn't the only one complaining. Tatsuya could hear similar statements coming from some of her nearby classmates. The fact that she wasn't alone in her sentiment was emboldening her. On top of that, she knew she was going against the grain, which only made her dig her heels in deeper.

Izumi wasn't losing her cool, just as she hadn't while confronting the police detectives at the scene of the attack. "So what are you saying they did wrong?" she asked with a polite tone and a composed, chilly expression.

On the other hand, Kanon was getting worked up. She correctly interpreted Izumi's attitude as contempt. "Of all the other people who happened to be in the same place as them, they didn't bother to save even one civilian! Is anyone really surprised they're getting blamed?"

Kanon hadn't started ranting. At most, she'd only raised her voice a bit. But letting herself be more strident might have been a better way to handle this argument. In retrospect, if she'd used her position as a more senior student as a shield, she might have avoided the argument that ensued.

"'Civilian'? What do you mean by 'civilian'?" Izumi asked.

Kanon wasn't immediately able to answer. "What does that have to do with…?"

"Do you mean a citizen? Or do you mean someone who's not a public servant? Because in that case, the heads of the Ten Master Clans aren't military or government employees, which makes them civilians as well, doesn't it?"

"What are you trying to say?"

"I'm just wondering why some 'civilians' are responsible for putting the safety of other 'civilians' above their own, that's all…"

Izumi casually covered her mouth with her left hand.

Kanon felt her ridicule. "Why you…!" She pushed back away from the desk, the legs of her chair screeching against the floor as she stood.

"Kanon, calm down!" Isori hissed, standing and putting his hand on her shoulder.

Opposite the two, Miyuki had been silently listening to their exchange, and she finally spoke up. "Hey, Izumi, I'm sorry but could you go buy everybody something hot to drink? Here's some money." She held out the student council's money card.

The student council room had a pantry equipped with a hot water dispenser, a pot, and a coffee maker. There were also tea leaves and coffee beans in the room. Generally speaking, there was no need to leave the room to get something to drink.

In other words, Miyuki was encouraging Izumi to go cool off.

"All right…" Izumi stood with a glum expression. Being scolded by her beloved Miyuki had instantly doused her anger.

"I'll help," said Minami, standing.

"Yes, please do," Miyuki instructed.

Minami bowed to Miyuki, then walked over to Izumi and took her hand.

Izumi and Minami disappeared out of the door and down the hall.

After confirming they were gone, Isori turned to face Kanon. "...Okay, that was your fault, Kanon. Even if the Ten's family heads had the opportunity to save the people who ended up as casualties, they weren't obligated to. It's wrong to demand virtue be mandatory."

"But..." Kanon started grudgingly, but one look from Isori cut her off.

"I mean, if somebody's fallen right in front of you, I think it's morally questionable to just walk past them. But if you're in a life-threatening situation and you have to escape, I can't say I think you should have to go around looking for other people to help when you don't even know where they are. Being in the Ten Master Clans doesn't make you immortal."

"I...I guess so."

"We don't even expect firefighters to plunge headfirst into a deadly fire with no regard for their own lives. Going into a situation like that without a thought for their own safety in order to save someone is admirable and courageous, but forcing them to do it and saying 'It's your duty to risk your life and go in there,' is nasty and ridiculous, in my opinion. I feel like that's something only their chief, who's responsible for their lives and is sharing that risk, can order them to do."

Kanon looked away from Isori and down at the floor.

"And I think it's inexcusable to condemn people after the fact for failing to meet an obligation they never had in the first place. I don't want you to do things like that, Kanon. If someone attacked your father like that, you'd be just as angry, wouldn't you?"

"...Yeah." Kanon nodded, wilting under Isori's gentle questioning.

"I'm glad you understand. Now, you'll have to apologize to Saegusa once she gets back."

Kanon nodded again.

◇ ◇ ◇

Kanon apologized to Izumi when she returned to the student council room, and Izumi in turn apologized to Kanon for her chilly attitude. Things had been successfully patched up between them, but this was because they were already on speaking terms, and Isori had been present as a reasonable moderator.

Most non-magicians had very little personal interaction with magicians. Out in the world, there was no one to act as a mediator between magicians and the rest of the population. The fact was that the casualties of the attack had been entirely non-magicians, and there was nothing for that resentment to do except build.

There were some who defended magicians. But their voices were too quiet. No matter how reasonable their arguments, if they did not reach the intended ears, they accomplished nothing.

Given the circumstances, it seemed that magicians could do little but endure the injustice. This realization was difficult for the hot-blooded younger generation to accept.

Among these youths was Takuma Shippou, head of the Shippou, who had recently been added to the Ten Master Clans.

He was only sixteen—just the age when no matter what the nature of young people's frustration or anger with society was, lacking any means to put up a fight, many would throw their pent-up energy into an activity like sports, music, or writing. Of them, a few would explode into misguided violence.

However, Takuma had an idea of where to find someone who could, in fact, provide him with a means to resist. Unfortunately, from his perspective, this was a relationship that was very much in the past tense. Still, he had no choice but to rely on her.

Until the previous spring, it should have been an equitable relationship. Although he had in fact been quite one-sidedly on the receiving end of all the help, his pride had managed to soldier on uninjured.

But now his pride was the last thing on his mind. The position among the Ten Master Clans he'd so dearly hoped to gain now existed only to protect the rights of magicians. Takuma felt this very strongly.

If it was in service of actions he felt were worthy of the Ten Master Clans, Takuma would prostrate himself at the woman's feet. With his mind made up, he paid a visit to the apartment where the actress Maki Sawamura lived.

He'd been prepared to be turned away at the door, but contrary to his expectations, Maki smoothly invited him in.

"Good evening. It's been quite a while, Takuma."

"Uh, hi, Maki. Yeah, it has."

It was only 9:00 PM, but Maki was already dressed for a late evening's relaxation. Specifically, she wore a calf-length bathrobe, under which he glimpsed the lace-trimmed hem of a negligee.

"Sorry, were you about to go to bed? I can come back another time," Takuma said, preparing to leave without so much as sitting down.

"Wait, Takuma. I don't mind, so come have a seat, won't you?" said Maki from her sofa.

Thus invited, Takuma sat across the table from Maki.

The distance between the two of them was farther than it had been when Takuma had visited this apartment the previous spring.

"What would you like to drink?"

"Ah, don't trouble yourself, please." All too conscious of having arrived unannounced, Takuma demurred, trying to spare her the trouble of serving him anything.

Hearing his answer, Maki's eyes widened. "...So is coffee okay?"

"Sure, thanks. Sorry."

Maya pushed an unobtrusive button on the armrest of her sofa. "Coffee, please," she said. Sitting directly across from her, Takuma couldn't be sure, but apparently there was a microphone hidden somewhere.

"I'm surprised you knew I was off work today, Takuma."

"Uh, no, I had no idea. If you weren't here, I was going to leave a message on the intercom and try again later."

"*Really?*" Maya asked skeptically. As ever, there wasn't the slightest hint of artifice in the movements of her face or the sound of her voice, and Takuma had no idea whether she was being sincere or wearing a mask. "If you were going to go to all that trouble, you could have just called ahead."

Takuma flashed a somewhat hapless smile. "It was just…hard to call somehow. If I'm being honest, I turned around quite a few times before I finally made it here."

She didn't ask why it was hard to call. Technically, they'd had an amicable breakup. She'd played her part in it beautifully. But Takuma had his pride, and even Maki could understand why he wouldn't want to call the girl who had dumped him. "And it still didn't occur to you that it might be a waste of your time?" she asked instead.

"Since I'm asking a favor of you, I was prepared to walk as many times as it took," he stated seriously.

Just then, the living room door opened.

A woman slightly older than Maki, carrying a tray, approached Takuma from his side. With a practiced, elegant motion, she set a saucer down on the table in front of him, then placed a cup of coffee on the saucer.

"Thanks," said Maki.

The woman bowed wordlessly and left the room.

"…She wasn't a 3H, was she?" asked Takuma.

"Nope," Maki said, letting a smile slip. "She's my new housekeeper. You know perfectly well I hate 3Hs."

"Oh, I remember. That's why I was surprised." It was just a bit of incidental small talk, but it brought to Takuma's mind a vivid memory of Maki saying, *Having a 3H look at me is like having a surveillance camera stuck in my face. It makes my skin crawl.*

There was a time when Takuma wouldn't have paid attention to such incidental details. His memory had always been good, so he'd been able to keep track of things like this all along, but so long as it didn't affect him, he hadn't concerned himself with the likes and dislikes of others.

Now it was Maki's turn to look seriously at Takuma.

Takuma suddenly felt uneasy under her gaze and averted his eyes.

This meant that when Maki spoke, he didn't catch the expression on her face.

"Takuma…you really have changed."

There was a note of praise in Maki's voice that made him flush bashfully. "Y-yeah, I guess, maybe a little," Takuma murmured, still looking away and reminding himself that she was an actress, and she could sound however she wanted to.

"No, more than a little."

But even as he kept looking away, Maki's voice had a strange way of penetrating his consciousness.

"Boys grow up so quickly at your age… You're not quite an adult yet, but that's part of the appeal…"

Maki hadn't moved from her place on the sofa opposite him, but the sweet scent of her skin seemed to be wafting toward him.

"Whatever shall I do? I've been told not to lay a hand on you, but…just once couldn't hurt…"

Her amorous sigh seemed to be right at his ear, despite the distance between them.

"Maki, I have a favor to ask!" said Takuma with sudden vigor, as though trying to dispel the illusion.

"A favor…?"

With his field of view taken up entirely by the floor, Takuma couldn't see it, but Maki's expression was one of total astonishment. No trace of her enticing demeanor remained.

Previously, their relationship had been one in which Maki had granted a variety of requests from Takuma, so it wasn't terribly strange for Takuma to be asking something of her. It was Takuma's deeply bowed head that Maki found so surprising.

Takuma had interpreted this not as receiving a handout from her but as her investing in him. Whatever her true thoughts on the matter, she had said as much to him.

Perhaps that was why whenever Takuma had previously asked something of her, he'd done so with only the minimum of humility. It was the logic of youth to want to avoid showing weakness precisely because the relationship was so one-sided.

And yet now he had no qualms about bowing so deeply his upper body was parallel with the floor. It was so different from the Takuma who Maki had known that for a moment she wondered if he was doing some sort of stretch.

"First, you can sit up, Takuma."

Maki had not forgotten Tatsuya's threat. She'd welcomed Takuma into her home, but she'd planned only to toy with him a bit and send him home feeling good. She had no interest in inviting a scandal, but she had reckoned that neither Tatsuya Shiba nor those backing him would bother coming after her for a little bit of mischief.

But seeing Takuma's bearing, she had changed her mind. "What do you want me to do?"

Men didn't have a monopoly on disregarding risk and making decisions based on gut feelings. Maki wanted to help Takuma, who seemed like a different person compared to the boy he'd been only a little more than six months earlier. A warm desire to embrace him welled up in her, as though she were an older sister regarding her rascally younger brother who was desperately trying to grow up.

Maki's kind smile was a far more favorable reaction than Takuma had anticipated, and he was completely taken off guard. He composed himself and spoke, his enthusiasm coloring his voice with grim determination.

"I assume you've heard about the terrorist attack the day before yesterday."

"The one in Hakone? It sounded like they were hit pretty hard."

"Yeah. Despite magicians being the ones targeted, it's turning the tide of public opinion against us."

"But there was a reason they were targeted, right? Innocent bystanders got caught up in the violence, so you can't blame people for being upset."

Maki did not discriminate against magicians. On the contrary, she actively made efforts to get along *very* well with magicians. The point she was making was, if anything, what she imagined ordinary people in the world to be thinking.

Takuma either understood that or simply endured it, but in any case, he showed no anger at Maki's comment. "What you're saying is *probably* right. That's just the nature of human emotion. But we can't afford to let our kind be cast as the villains. If we don't stop this soon, it won't be long before we lose the ability to uphold the human rights of magicians at all. Eventually, we might even see witch hunts and have people call it justice."

Maki didn't suggest he was overthinking things. In fact, she thought it was a reasonable prediction. "Okay. Am I right in thinking that you're asking more for my father's help than mine?"

Takuma flinched; she'd had hit the bull's-eye. Maki's father was the president of a holding company that owned several large media companies, including a television network.

But his hesitation did not last more than a second. "I know it's presumptuous. Even I think so. There's no upside for your father in allying himself to magicians. Given the current environment, it's decidedly unwise. Even so…please!"

If he had been in a Japanese-style room, he'd have had his forehead pressed down against the tatami mat.

"You're the only person I could think of to ask for help, Maki…"

It struck Maki as convenient that neither of them could see the other's face in that moment.

She found her chest swelling with affection for this boy almost ten years younger than her.

But she was an A-list actress. She didn't need to cover up her emotions with anything as blatant as a cough or a throat clearing. "All right, Takuma. I'll do it."

"Maki…!" Takuma looked up, his face overjoyed.

"But eventually, you'll have to pay me back."

"Of course, I'll do anything I can!"

In the near future—three years to be precise, in 2100, the final year of the twenty-first century—Takuma would come to deeply regret those words, but he would not break his promise. This is the secret story behind the dashing silver screen debut of a certain Magic University student-turned-actor.

Late that night, two individuals went to the police morgue where the bodies of the people who'd actually carried out the terrorist attack were being stored.

One visitor was a middle-aged man wearing a trench coat along with a fedora pulled low over his face, who—if one was inclined to be generous—looked something like a detective. The other wore a newsboy cap and large sunglasses with a muffler covering the lower half of their face, keeping their features totally obscured. They were tall for a woman but short for a man. Their body was completely hidden in an overbroad wool coat, hiding their build. It was impossible to tell just by looking that she was a young woman of twenty.

The lone coroner remaining in the facility at that late hour let them in. He traded places with them, leaving the morgue. He wasn't being controlled, nor was he being threatened. The coroner had been bribed by the man in the fedora—Mitsugu Kuroba.

Mitsugu looked at the body bag in one corner of the room, then at the corpses laid out on the beds. This was where all the attackers had been brought—every body that was determined to have been one of the suicide bombers. Owing to the nature of suicide bombing, there weren't many intact corpses, but a few of them had suffered relatively little damage. These were the ones on the beds before him.

For Mitsugu and his companion's purposes, all they needed was the cranium. A cleanly severed head was just fine, and even if it was missing a brain, there wouldn't be a problem. As long as there was something recognizable as a head, it would be a worthwhile clue.

"Yoshimi," Mitsugu whispered to the woman with him.

Underneath her cap, sunglasses, and muffler, Yoshimi nodded and touched the forehead of one corpse with a leather-gloved hand.

A faint psionic glow appeared around the point of contact between hand and forehead. It was similar to the light emitted from a CAD when a program activated. The core principle of what was actually happening was the same—the injection of homogenous psionic waves with neither meaning nor distortion, then the reading of the psionic signals that bounced back. In some respects, the corpse was acting as a CAD, and the psionic information bodies that remained within it were like an activation program.

The woman called Yoshimi was practicing psychometry. She was a psychometrist by trade, skilled in reading the traces of psionic information that could linger in the human body.

In modern magic theory, psions were the particles that gave ideas and will form, and pushions could be conceptualized as the particles that formed the emotions that in turn gave rise to thoughts and intent.

Of course, that was only a hypothesis.

Very little about the nature of pushions was understood with complete certainty.

That said, there were observations of the human mind affecting psions.

Magic programs were also psionic information bodies. So even if someone's physical body were subjected to external magical interference, that person's active and passive psychoactivity would immediately distort and disperse the now-useless program.

But corpses felt nothing and thought nothing. Which meant that any psionic information bodies that remained within them—and any magic programs that had been written into them—would linger for much longer than they would in a living body, preserved with a low amount of degradation.

The Yotsuba family had developed a technique to read the

psionic information bodies contained within a dead body—a corpse's memories—and the Kuroba family used this in its espionage activities.

"Yoshimi."

"It's still good," she said, her voice muffled by the fabric wrapped around her face. She moved on to the next corpse.

"Don't go in too deep. You won't be able to find your way back out."

Seemingly unconcerned, Yoshimi proceeded from one corpse to the next, retrieving more information.

Then, just as she stood back from the sixth dead body, she exhaled a sigh. "I found it."

"Good. Now let's get out of here."

Mitsugu pulled Yoshimi's gloves off her hands. She then reached into her coat pocket and produced a new pair of gloves, which she put on.

With his companion in tow, Mitsugu left the morgue. Somewhere along the way, Yoshimi's gloves disappeared from his hands.

It went without saying that the Ten Master Clans weren't the only ones looking for the terrorists. A large-scale attack taking place within a stone's throw of the capital was a terrible blow to the pride of law enforcement and more than enough impetus to drive the top brass insane with rage.

The case fell not to the Kanagawa regional police department (known as the Kanagawa Prefectural Police—not the regional police or former prefectural police) but instead to the Ministry of Police's Wide-Area Special Investigation Team (nicknamed the "Japanese FBI"). Normally, the case would've gone to the regional law enforcement, but the national-level search team had summoned investigators to the southern Kanto region and poured all their manpower into getting the investigation rolling.

Inspector Toshikazu Chiba just happened to be standing by at headquarters, so without waiting for the mid-transfer detectives to assemble, he immediately commenced his investigation. He had felt as much outrage at the attack as anyone, and in a rare occurrence, his urgency showed as he made his rounds.

And yet the investigation ran into snags immediately.

"What do you mean, every single one of the attackers is dead?" Toshikazu grumbled, sitting in an unmarked patrol car.

"Well, things like that happen when you're dealing with suicide bombers," said Toshikazu's driver, Assistant Inspector Inagaki, in an attempt to mollify him. But the truth was that Inagaki also found it strange, so his voice didn't have much conviction in it.

"The ones who actually blew themselves up being dead, I can understand. But don't you think it strange that even the bombers with no evidence of being near any explosions all wound up in the morgue? Some bodies have barely a scratch on them."

"And the autopsy results put the time of death as at least a day before the actual attack. Adding in the possibility of refrigerated preservation of the corpses, they could've been dead for up to ten days prior to the attack… Do you think the bodies walked in carrying the explosives themselves?"

"I wish I could laugh that off as something out of a schlocky horror movie…" Toshikazu muttered with a beleaguered smirk.

"You're thinking there was some kind of corpse-reanimation magic used, aren't you, Inspector?" Inagaki asked.

Toshikazu nodded reluctantly, then realized Inagaki, who was driving, wouldn't be able to see the gesture and added, "Yeah, I am. I hate to say it, but…given the circumstances, it's the most logical guess."

The luxury of relegating magic to the realm of fiction when pursuing investigations had died the previous century. Magic was now a factor that law enforcement investigators couldn't ignore, and Toshikazu himself was in fact a magician. Denying magic would entail denying his own existence.

That said, as a user of modern magic, he couldn't help but find the prospect of corpse-manipulation techniques very fishy.

"Do you think we're gonna need to talk to a specialist?"

"Oh, you have a necromancy guy on speed dial?" Toshikazu scowled at Inagaki's suggestion. Even if there was a magician somewhere with expertise in corpse manipulation, there would be unavoidable ethical issues involved. They wouldn't exactly be able to just hang a sign up advertising their services. "But yeah, we're way out of our depth here. It'd sure help to have somebody to walk us through the possibilities."

"Searching the Ministry of Police's database for necromancy only turned up hits for postmortem divination, too." Despite being the one to make the suggestion, Inagaki seemed aware that finding someone with expertise in this area wouldn't be easy.

As his subordinate sighed, Toshikazu dropped his objections. "Yeah… But it's not like we have any hot leads. So we might as well try. Take us to Roter Wald, Inagaki."

"The information broker, huh? Copy that," Inagaki sighed defeatedly, heading the car to Yokohama.

Roter Wald was a café with a forest cottage design nestled in a residential Yokohama neighborhood. Upon entering the tranquil little establishment, Toshikazu automatically scanned the interior, looking for someone.

*Who am I looking for?* he immediately thought. He remembered the time just before the Yokohama Incident that had shaken all of Japan—and eventually the entire world. Then, as now, he'd come to this café looking for leads on illegal immigration, and he remembered the woman he'd met: Kyouko Fujibayashi.

He hadn't seen her since they'd parted ways in front of Sakuragi Station during the Yokohama Incident. They hadn't been romantically involved; they were merely cooperating in the course of their respective duties. But Toshikazu's feelings did not end there.

Afterward, Toshikazu had been relegated to the cleanup investigations into any lingering illegal immigrants and had no time to contact Fujibayashi. Just when he thought the fallout might have been tapering off, the vampire incident happened, and his hands were immediately full with the resulting investigation. He'd been mostly away from the Kanto region since the previous spring, and it had given him little opportunity to think about her.

Coming again to this café—the place where they'd first met—was what brought her to mind again. What was he, some kind of sentimental romantic? Or was he just wondering what might have been? Toshikazu shook his head ruefully as he took a seat at the counter. Such musings were unusual for him.

As Inagaki came into the edge of his field of view and sat down beside him, Toshikazu ordered. "Two coffees."

It would've been a mistake to try to lean on the proprietor.

As he waited for his coffee, Toshikazu idly looked around the inside of the café. As always, it was busy with patrons but not completely full.

Toshikazu turned back to the counter before his gaze attracted any suspicion.

When he looked over his shoulder at the sound of the cowbell attached to the café's front door, it wasn't out of vigilance or suspicion. It was merely the physical reflex of someone who had nothing better to do.

He immediately stood—which was also a largely unconscious act. Toshikazu was no longer off guard.

"Hello there, Inspector," said a beautiful woman approximately his age as she took in his face, her eyes wide.

"Ms. Fujibayashi…"

The one who'd come through the café's door was none other than the woman in his memory, Kyouko Fujibayashi.

"It's been a while, Inspector Chiba. Is this seat taken?" asked Fujibayashi, looking just as he remembered her. Her makeup was deliberately understated, but closer attention revealed a face that was nonetheless carefully composed.

"Ah, please sit!" Toshikazu nodded, completely failing to notice Inagaki's scowl.

Fujibayashi smiled and sat down.

Toshikazu realized he was suddenly feeling unaccountably nervous. It didn't occur to him, though, that his nerves were not really "unaccountable" at all.

"A coffee for me, please," Fujibayashi told the proprietor, placing the same order as Toshikazu had and laying her coat on the empty seat next to her. "You haven't changed a bit, Inspector."

"I'm just stubborn, that's all." Toshikazu felt his voice about to crack.

"How modest of you," she quipped, with a meticulously constructed smile.

Toshikazu felt his smile tense slightly. "So, Ms. Fujibayashi, are you off work today?"

Just because she was dressed casually didn't mean she was off duty, given her line of work. Toshikazu knew as much, but he didn't want to directly ask her if she was on a mission here in public, where he didn't know who might overhear.

"I am. But the coffee here is so delicious—so." She shrugged. The proprietor happened to be looking her way at that moment and gave her a slight bow, acknowledging the compliment.

If Toshikazu had said the same thing, the proprietor probably wouldn't have given him any reaction at all. Evidently, despite living nowhere near the shop, Fujibayashi was a regular.

"And you, Inspector? Are you off duty?"

"Well, you know... That actually reminds me, Ms. Fujibayashi, you know quite a bit about ancient magic, right?" Toshikazu was more than a little flustered, but he hadn't forgotten about the investigation, and it was the detective part of his brain that recalled this particular aspect of the woman in front of him.

"I suppose I know a thing or two about it, yes," she said, peering at him curiously.

"If you have time, there's something I'd like to know a little more about."

Just then, the proprietor's voice cut in. "Here you are," he said, placing coffee cups in front of Toshikazu and Inagaki.

"I don't mind. But first, Inspector, don't you have something to discuss with the proprietor?"

Toshikazu suddenly remembered the reason why he'd come to this café in the first place.

Unfortunately, it seemed he wouldn't be able to claim he hadn't neglected his job.

Toshikazu had written his request—"I need to find someone with expertise in corpse-manipulation magic"—on a slip of paper and passed it to the proprietor, who had returned the slip with his answer written on it. After thoroughly memorizing it, he returned the slip to the proprietor. Judging by the proprietor's slight smile, Toshikazu inferred that this had been the right thing to do.

It seemed that Fujibayashi really had come just for the coffee, and she exchanged some small talk with the proprietor.

"Here's for the bill. I'm also taking care of these two. I don't need any change." Before Fujibayashi could object, Toshikazu slipped the proprietor a high-denomination money card. Inagaki stood a beat late, and his eyebrows lifted in surprise when he saw the amount. It was well above the going rate for such information.

"I believe I may have a bit too much here," the proprietor said with a mild frown.

"Keep it on my tab for next time, then," Toshikazu replied.

The proprietor didn't attempt to force the issue. "I look forward to your next visit," he said with a slight bow.

After exiting Roter Wald, at Fujibayashi's invitation, Toshikazu joined her in her car. Inagaki followed them in the unmarked patrol car.

"So, Inspector, is what you want to talk about something related to the Hakone terrorist attack?" Fujibayashi asked as soon as they were underway, immediately cutting to the point.

"...Indeed," he said, setting aside all his conversational preparations, silently grateful that he wasn't going to have to go through the effort. "There are some very odd details surrounding it."

"Odd?"

Although Fujibayashi kept her hand on the gearshift, the car was currently driving autonomously. There was nothing dangerous about her looking over to Toshikazu in the passenger's seat. Nonetheless, Toshikazu's deeply internalized police training made him feel a certain chill at the gesture, despite knowing there was no danger.

It might have shown on his face. Fujibayashi immediately turned back to the road.

"Yes. None of the actual attackers are alive."

"...Are you sure they didn't escape?" she suggested quite reasonably.

"No, that much is certain," he stated firmly. "They were concentrated only at the hotel that was the target, and the traffic cameras all around the area continued to function perfectly after the attack."

"So you're saying none of the traffic cameras recorded any attackers escaping the site of the bombing after it was over?"

"Correct. All the attackers were caught on camera as they infiltrated the hotel. And they've all been identified. There's one body that wasn't found, but we can say with absolute certainty that none of the terrorists fled the scene."

"The perpetrators were caught on camera, but you still weren't able to prevent the attack?"

Toshikazu was stuck for an answer, but undaunted, he quickly offered a rebuttal. "The explosives they used didn't trip our sensors. They looked like ordinary people going about their day, and there was no reason to stop them from entering a hotel that was open for business."

"...So you're saying that if the Ten Master Clans had used the Magic Association's meeting facilities or booked the entire hotel, this attack wouldn't have happened?"

"Well, putting aside whether it was preventable or not, the number of casualties probably could have been lowered."

Fujibayashi was connected to the Kudou family, which up until the day of the Master Clans Council had been one of the Ten Master Clans. Toshikazu's point might have been correct, but it made the atmosphere unavoidably awkward.

Toshikazu moved on to the matter at hand in an attempt to clear the air. "Actually, there's another mysterious point... To make a long story short, the evidence suggests the attackers were already dead at the time of the incident."

"I see... So *that's* why you're going to talk to the Dollmakers."

"Dollmakers?"

Toshikazu thought he was heading to the home of a magic researcher who specialized in necromancy. He had no thought of calling on a dollmaker or puppeteer.

"The individual you're trying to contact is not simply a magic researcher but a practitioner of an ancient magical technique called a 'Dollmaker.' He's rumored to use forbidden magic to turn dead bodies into puppets, and the Magic Association has marked him as a person of interest."

"That's..."

"If you want someone to tell you about techniques to control a corpse, he'll certainly be able to. Publicly he *is* a researcher, after all." Fujibayashi turned to regard Toshikazu again. "However, Inspector, please be cautious. I have been told that Kazukiyo Oumi the Dollmaker has not inconsiderable ties to the magicians from Dahan."

Toshikazu nodded in reply to the warning, his face tense.

◇ ◇ ◇

Friday, February 8, 5:57 PM. As instructed by Katsuto, Tatsuya arrived at the front gate of Magic University.

After returning home briefly, Tatsuya made his way to the university's public transit stop, dressed in a comfortable half coat over a tailored jacket. It was widely accepted that students at Magic University tended to look a bit more mature than the people who attended other colleges, but dressed like this, he didn't stand out, since he often seemed older than he was, too.

"Hi, Tatsuya."

It was a little less than five minutes past the meeting time when Mayumi emerged from the campus gate and greeted Tatsuya. She was casually dressed, wearing a duffle coat and knee-length skirt, paired with thick tights and high boots. Between her style and the thin tote bag hanging from her shoulder, she practically radiated college-girl energy.

She undoubtedly would've been annoyed to hear it, but next to Tatsuya's buttoned-up appearance, he looked like the elder of the two.

"Sorry, have you been waiting long?" she asked with a breathless smile.

"You're within the margin of error. Don't worry about it," answered Tatsuya honestly.

Her smile instantly fell into a pout. "C'mon…you're supposed to say, 'No, I just got here myself.'"

Evidently, she'd expected the standard response from him. Tatsuya didn't understand the purpose of her request, but he was certainly willing to accommodate it in the spirit of service.

"I just got here myself," he said.

This didn't seem to improve her mood at all, and she glared at him glumly.

Unflustered and unconcerned, Tatsuya continued the conversation as though nothing had happened. "Incidentally, is Juumonji not with you?"

Mayumi huffed a performative sigh. "…He's gone ahead to a place where we can talk. He told me where to go, so just come with me."

Then, either satisfied or resigned, she started walking, gesturing for him to come along with her.

Tatsuya briskly drew along her right side.

Mayumi switched the tote bag from her right shoulder to her left.

She started to reach out with her hand several times, but in the end, she continued walking without taking Tatsuya's arm.

After just over ten minutes of walking, their destination turned out to be a modestly fashionable-looking single-family residence. Its most prominent detail was a single round table surrounded by four chairs on a roofed terrace.

However, upon entering, it turned out the first floor was a small restaurant. The reason it didn't have a sign was either because Katsuto had rented out the entire establishment or perhaps because the owners preferred to only serve regulars and people their regulars vouched for.

Just as Tatsuya was considering the matter, Mayumi cleared things up with the actual answer. "This is an invite-only establishment. Plus, apparently Juumonji reserved the whole place, so we won't have to worry about the eyes and ears of other customers."

Apparently, he'd been right with both guesses.

The exterior notwithstanding, their shoes remained on since it was a restaurant. Mayumi's booted heels made a pleasant click with each step she took.

"Sorry to make you wait, Juumonji," she said.

"It's fine. I just got here."

Tatsuya didn't show it on his face, but he was impressed with Katsuto's reply. He'd said just what Mayumi wanted to hear. How had he gotten it right? Perhaps because he'd known her for so long.

"Have a seat," Katsuto said.

Tatsuya did so, betraying no hint of his thoughts as he sat across from the man.

Mayumi sat next to Tatsuya on the same side of the table. Presumably, this was simply because they'd walked up to the table side by side, rather than any kind of message about them being together.

Tatsuya's conversation with Mari was still fresh in his memory, so he couldn't honestly claim to be completely unaware of Mayumi. But as to the question of whether he could see Mayumi in *that* way, well—no, he could not.

Tatsuya had accepted Miyuki's feelings and become her fiancé. But that did not mean he returned those feelings.

To him, Miyuki was still his sister.

He could not conceive how their relationship could be a romantic one.

Even if he'd decided how to answer her feelings, his heart had yet to reach that point.

Tatsuya's capacity for considering romance at all was already completely maxed out with just Miyuki. If he tried to make room for Mayumi, too, it would start affecting his work. So he had already decided not to count her as an option in that regard.

He was honestly very grateful that so far Mayumi had continued to treat him as she always had.

From the way Mari had talked to him earlier, she must have already egged Mayumi on quite a bit. Even if Mayumi hadn't thought much about Tatsuya before that, her friend's urging could certainly have had an effect. Someone's intense encouragement would be all the more convincing when they were close to you. Tatsuya understood such things not as a matter of passion but in the context of coercion and conciliation. However, the psychological principles involved were the same.

So Tatsuya was on guard, but fortunately Mayumi hadn't shown any outward indication of having been obviously influenced. He didn't know what she was thinking, but neither did she. They were on even footing.

"So just to get things started, have either of you learned anything?" Katsuto started abruptly.

Tatsuya and Mayumi exchanged a glance. Mayumi decided to

speak first. "Unfortunately, at the moment I don't have any promising leads. The terrorist came to Japan from America on a freighter and made landfall at Yokosuka Port, but beyond that we don't know anything. And even that much is mere deduction."

"I obtained some information from the USNA," Tatsuya stated simply.

Mayumi looked shocked, and even Katsuto seemed surprised.

"From America? And exactly what sort of connection gave you that info?"

The international movements of high-level magicians were very strictly regulated. As a result, if they weren't attached to a governmental agency, it was near impossible for a magician to build up a good information network that reached overseas. Within the Ten Master Clans, the Mitsuya family was known to have unusually good information thanks to their arms-trading partners, but neither Katsuto nor Mayumi had ever heard anything about the Yotsuba family having an overseas information source.

"Well, you know. This and that," Tatsuya said evasively.

"...I shouldn't have asked. Sorry," Mayumi replied with an embarrassed little bow. Even when you were talking to a fellow member of the Ten Master Clans, it wasn't exactly admirable to demand they reveal something they were obviously keeping a secret.

Tatsuya acknowledged this with a short "It's fine" and then went on. "According to what I've learned, the terrorist ringleader is a former Dahanese magician named Gu Jie. His English name is Gide Hague. He appears to be a man in his fifties, with dark skin and white hair. Unfortunately, the reliability of this is unknown."

Maya had already been informed that Tatsuya was sharing the information about Gu Jie with Katsuto and Mayumi. Tatsuya hadn't asked permission; it had been Maya who instructed him to share it with the Saegusa family to aid in the search.

"Even if it's not conclusive, given our lack of any other leads, it's excellent information. Saegusa—"

"Right." Mayumi nodded as Katsuto's gaze met hers. "We can use this description to run a search for any foreigners who've entered the country within the last two weeks matching it."

"It seems pretty likely he smuggled himself in, though."

"That's probably true," Mayumi agreed. "But when people move, they always leave tracks. If we shake out the area between Yokosuka and Hakone, we should be able to find some leads. We'll get the police to help us."

The magician family with the greatest amount of influence over the police was the Chiba family, nearly half of whom were said to serve on the force (mostly in the anti-riot squads) as magician inspectors, but in the Kanto region's investigations division, it was the Saegusa family who predominated.

And even if they hadn't, this had been a huge incident. The police wouldn't need outside encouragement to be pursuing the criminals to the absolute extent of their ability. They would be hungry for any leads, no matter how minor.

Katsuto didn't need to have something so obvious explained to him. "Okay. Saegusa, you head up that end. Shiba, you keep tracking down leads."

"Sure thing," she replied.

"Understood," Tatsuya agreed.

The three met one another's eyes and nodded.

"Do either of you have any suggestions? Or anything you want to ask me?"

Tatsuya and Minami both answered in the negative.

Katsuto nodded. "What are you two doing for dinner?" he went on. "If you want to eat, I'll have something prepared right away."

"I'm sorry—I have plans at home," Tatsuya said first, turning the offer down.

"…I'll pass today, too," Mayumi added with a brief glance at Tatsuya. "Might take you up on that tomorrow, though," she finished apologetically.

"All right. So does this time tomorrow work?"

"Fine by me," said Mayumi.

"For me as well," said Tatsuya. "If anything changes, I'll contact you."

The "anything" Tatsuya was envisioning was the possibility that his search might run late into the night.

Katsuto either understood that or was hesitant to butt into Tatsuya's personal life, but in either case, he didn't push for details. "Sure. I have another meeting after this, so Shiba—would you escort Saegusa home?" he said—not necessarily as a quid pro quo, but still.

"Huh?! No, no, you don't have to!" she protested, flustered. They were currently opposite the train station as seen from the university. If any of her acquaintances saw her walking alone with Tatsuya at this hour, it would be perfect fodder for rumors.

"It's already dark outside. I'm not doubting your ability to handle yourself, Saegusa, but we have no idea where our terrorists are hiding right now. I can't let a woman walk around alone when there's every reason to think we might be targeted."

It was hard to refute the point that individuals might be targets for the terrorists. And besides, pushing back too stubbornly seemed to make her that much more conscious of Tatsuya, which only exacerbated her embarrassment.

"I'll escort you home, Saegusa."

Backed into a corner, Mayumi finally relented to Tatsuya's offer. "...All right, thanks. We'll see you tomorrow, Juumonji."

"Right. Take care."

Mayumi and Tatsuya left the restaurant together.

It was about a ten-minute walk from the restaurant to the university and another ten minutes from the university to the cabinet station. Night had fallen, and there was neither moon nor starlight, but thanks to the streetlights, they could still see where they were going. Nonetheless, visibility was still poorer than it was during the day, and as a result, Mayumi's walking pace was a little bit slower.

The darkness was no impediment for Tatsuya, but he didn't go striding ahead through the gloom or try to drag Mayumi along by the hand. He simply matched her pace and continued to walk alongside her.

No words were exchanged. The silence was clearly awkward for Mayumi, but Tatsuya didn't have anything to talk about, either.

"Oh—" Just as they were passing by the entrance to the university, Mayumi suddenly spoke. "It's snowing."

Mayumi stopped and looked up at the sky. As if her voice had been their cue, snowflakes started to flutter down from the clouds overhead, which were faintly glowing from the city's illumination.

Tatsuya produced separately an umbrella and then its handle from within a dedicated pocket inside his coat. Thanks to improvements in materials, it was slim and light enough not to be burdensome while stored, but if the grip was as thin as the shaft, it would be difficult to hold, and so the handle had to be stored separately and attached when the umbrella was opened. (With most umbrellas, the switch to open it was actually on the grip itself.)

Tatsuya opened the umbrella and looked over to Mayumi, who was still gazing up into the sky as snow continued to fall.

"I would recommend using an umbrella, Saegusa," Tatsuya said.

Mayumi looked over her shoulder at him with an awkward smile. "...I don't have one on me." Her smile remained as her eyes glanced this way and that.

Tatsuya had to consciously suppress a sigh. He couldn't believe there were still people who failed to be prepared for the weather, despite the accuracy of modern weather forecasting. "What, you didn't look at the forecast before leaving your house...?"

"I was really rushing, so..." Mayumi answered, her expression so sheepish it looked like she was about to face-palm.

Tatsuya held out his umbrella. "You can use mine."

"Huh? Oh no, I couldn't," Mayumi said. "It's just snow not rain, and it's not even coming down that hard…"

"Exactly. It's just a little bit of snow, so I'll be fine without my umbrella. You should use it."

"But—"

"If you happen to catch a cold, Juumonji will definitely punch me."

Mayumi couldn't help but giggle at Tatsuya's overserious face as he held the umbrella out. "I don't think that would be enough to make Juumonji resort to violence," she said, and instead of taking the umbrella, she drew closer to Tatsuya and curled her left arm around his right, bringing their shoulders close enough to touch.

"Shall we both use it, then?"

An oncoming car passed by on Tatsuya's left. The car's headlights momentarily illuminated Mayumi's happy face.

Her smile was as innocent as a child's.

"…All right," Tatsuya said.

Still smiling, Mayumi let go of Tatsuya's arm.

Tatsuya tilted the umbrella over to the right, in her direction.

Tatsuya saw Mayumi off at the cabinet station. He had planned to accompany her all the way to her door, but upon hearing Mayumi's threat/warning—"Oh, you want to come to my home? You're going to get quite a welcome, then,"—he had no choice but to back down.

When he got back home, Miyuki was there to greet him in the entryway as always. As she helped him out of his half coat, she furrowed her brow at the slight whiff of Mayumi's perfume that she caught on it, but she said nothing, not even making a joke of pouting about it.

Despite her intentions, Miyuki was finding herself unable to simply act as she always had, back when she had only been his younger sister.

When she had only been his sister, all she'd cared about was that Tatsuya didn't resent her.

But now Miyuki realized she'd never really felt a true sense of crisis about the issue back then.

*What if he hates me?* The mere thought made her chest hurt. She had a vision of lashing out at him in a fit of jealousy, angering him, ruining her affection for him—and that made her blood run cold.

As his sister, even if he disliked her, they weren't strangers. They still had the bond of brother and sister.

But an engagement could be severed by exasperation or disgust.

Finally having gotten Tatsuya only to lose her position as his fiancée—the possibility was an unbearable nightmare. It wasn't just difficult to bear; she knew she would be unable to stand it. When the anxious thought that she might not get him occurred to her, it made it that much more difficult to let go of him. If he were ever to cast her aside, Miyuki was quite sincerely certain that she would be unable to go on living.

Tatsuya had turned to let her remove his coat, and once it was done, he turned back around to face her. "Anything happen while I was out?" he asked.

"There was a message from Mr. Hayama," Miyuki replied. "I'd like to talk about it over dinner. Will that be all right?"

She flashed him a smile that gave no hint of the anxiety boiling in her heart.

Minami joined them at the dinner table, while Miyuki explained the content of Hayama's message.

"Kamakura, huh?"

"Yes. Apparently, there's a safe house Gongjin Zhou purchased under an assumed name in the western hills of Kamakura, and that's where Gu Jie is hiding out."

"And they're that certain..." Tatsuya wondered how they'd managed to zero in on the location. But more than that, he wondered why they hadn't moved to capture him if they were so certain about the location.

"Is there something bothering you about it, Tatsuya?" asked Miyuki, noticing the concerned expression on his face.

Tatsuya didn't mention the questions that had come to mind. If he had, Miyuki would undoubtedly hear it as a criticism—*Why didn't you ask about those details?*—even though it wasn't one.

"No, I was just thinking about what kinds of preparations we'll need to make," he said instead.

Tatsuya was incredibly attuned to the changes in his sister's expression, and so he noticed. What was it that she was so afraid of? But there was nothing he could do about it in that moment, because he was still unable to whisper in her ear the words he knew she truly wanted to hear.

"I'll ask Hayama later how we'll need to prepare," Tatsuya decided, setting aside the topic.

Just then, Gu Jie was leaving the safe house in Kamakura.

About an hour earlier, he'd picked up via Hlidskjalf a transmission that the individual responsible for planning the terrorist attack in Hakone was hiding in Kamakura. The precise address was off, but it was close. If he lingered, the noose would close around him, and he'd be unable to escape. Gu Jie knew he didn't have much time left, but he had no intention of carrying out a suicide bombing personally.

Not even Hlidskjalf could tell him how his pursuers had managed to close in on his location so quickly. That part hadn't been included in the intercepted data, which caused him considerable concern. If he didn't know what was in his opponent's hand, he couldn't prepare a counter.

If he spent some time sifting through Mitsugu Kuroba's communication history, maybe there would be a reference to the answer hidden somewhere in the past. But if he narrowed the search terms down too much, he would likely give away the fact that he himself was a Hlidskjalf operator.

*No,* Gu Jie thought. Even if the other Hlidskjalf operators knew that he was one of them, it wouldn't cause him much real trouble. He wasn't going to be around much longer. But if intelligence officials were tipped off about him by another operator, Gu Jie realized that the Yotsubas themselves might be considerably damaged in the process.

But there was no time to lose. His top priority was getting away from the current location without being noticed. When he'd first searched the safe house, he'd done everything he could to cover his tracks. After taking some measures to make tracing him that much more difficult, he set out on the snow-dusted road carrying the absolute minimum of supplies with him. Using every one of his five senses and more, he took in the area around him but detected no observers.

"I'll leave the hospitality for the next guests to you," Gu Jie said to the puppet he'd just made and headed for the next safe house.

The West Coast of America, February 8, 7:00 AM local time. After a modest breakfast, Raymond S. Clark turned on his Hlidskjalf terminal and began to investigate the Hakone terrorist attack.

He wasn't "investigating" in the sense of searching for the truth behind what had occurred. He'd known that since the attack—and even before, from his observation of the preparations for it. What Raymond wanted to know was what the hero who would bring the incident to its resolution was doing.

Without an incident, there could be no hero.

This was why he never provided the relevant authorities with any information that could prevent things from coming to a head. It wasn't any fun to *watch* the villain escape and the case get wrapped up, unsolved.

So whenever the investigation was bogged down, he provided some leads or manipulated information in order to help the hero. Somehow, giving the hero the hint needed to catch the villain just when he was on the verge of escaping made Raymond feel important. It was his favorite game.

In Hlidskjalf, Raymond checked the events of the previous day and furrowed his brow.

Events were not playing out the way he would've liked them to. As far as Raymond was concerned, the villain's use of Hlidskjalf to obtain information that let him elude the hero's pursuit was against the rules.

Of course, all he knew was that Gide Hague had used Hlidskjalf and discovered that the Yotsubas had found his location. He didn't yet know if that had resulted in his fleeing the safe house. But the fact that Hague had used the information network to get intel that he would otherwise never have had was itself difficult for Raymond to forgive.

Raymond thought of Hlidskjalf as a tool for a scriptwriter or director. It was meant to be used by people working behind the scenes in order to set the stage. A character *in* the play using it introduced a tremendous information imbalance into the mix, which could ruin the entire drama. To the audience and the backstage staff alike, it was an unforgivable breach of conduct.

While Hague himself had been a backstage figure, there had been no problem with his use of the program, of course. But now that he was personally standing on the stage, he could no longer be allowed access to this tool that could upset the plot so easily.

As Raymond's introduction of himself as the Seven Sages implied, Hlidskjalf had seven operators. But Raymond was the only one among them who used the name Seven Sages. And as the only Seven Sages, he decided to send a request to Hlidskjalf's administrator, who only he knew, for the deletion of Hague's account.

Saturday, February 9, before dawn.

With at least two hours to go before the sun rose, Tatsuya set off for Kamakura on his electric motorcycle.

His trusty bike got him to the western hills of Kamakura before 5:00 AM, and he soon arrived at the vacation house where Gu Jie was supposedly hiding.

Standing there, wearing large sunglasses despite the predawn gloom with a muffler covering the lower half of their face, was an indistinct figure, tall for a woman but short for a man.

Their thick coat made it impossible to glean any clues about their gender. Of course, Tatsuya couldn't have cared less what *her* gender was.

Tatsuya took the glove off his right hand and thrust it into his jacket pocket; then with his left hand, he took out his portable terminal and turned its screen toward her. She likewise bared her right hand to the cold air and held up her own terminal.

At the same time, each touched the screen of the other's terminal with their index finger.

The scanners behind the displays engaged, reading their fingerprints.

Roughly simultaneously, they each nodded and returned their terminals to their pockets, then re-gloved their hands.

"Show me, please," Tatsuya commanded.

"This way," Yoshimi said with a nod, leading the way. Tatsuya left his bike and followed.

Yoshimi stopped in front of a vacation house. There didn't seem to be anybody around, but Tatsuya knew that the area was surrounded by Yotsuba family forces. The way they'd hidden themselves wasn't like the Kuroba household troops, though. Tatsuya wasn't sure which branch family they were from. He didn't sense Yuuka Tsukuba or Katsushige Shibata, so perhaps it was the Mashiba, Shiiba, Mugura, or Shizuka families.

Not that it mattered at the moment. And his questions from last night were answered, in any case.

It had been the Kuroba family that found the safe house, but for whatever reason, another family had ended up with the job of actually taking control of the attack site. It would have taken time to make that switch, Tatsuya deduced.

Gu Jie was supposedly able to magically control corpses—and not by manipulating the spiritual being within it but rather by direct control of the body after death.

Illusions created via mental interference wouldn't work on such corpses, nor would their insensate, pain-immune bodies be affected by the Poison Wasp technique that Mitsugu Kuroba and his subordinates specialized in. Moving away from the Kuroba family when it came to executing the combat operation was a sensible management choice.

One Kuroba agent remained—Yoshimi, presumably in case of Gu Jie's escape, as her presence would let them quickly recover any leads.

"Here? I seem to remember a different address," Tatsuya noted.

"Wrong address," came Yoshimi's muffled voice. Her terseness was deliberate. Tatsuya had heard she always took care to leave as little trace of her own presence as possible. Whether that was a standard attitude for an espionage agent or a taboo passed down among those who specialized in her type of magic, he wasn't sure. Still, she wasn't someone he'd be working closely with, so he decided to put it out of his mind.

Tatsuya drew his Trident and peered into the safe house using Elemental Sight.

He could make out three humanoid shapes.

They weren't corpses. They were living humans.

However, they weren't ordinary humans—

"All units, heat-resistant anti-magic shields!" Tatsuya shouted as he pulled the trigger on his gun-shaped CAD, Trident.

The magic program targeting him and Yoshimi dispersed.

The safe house went up in flames the same moment.

Tatsuya activated Leap and jumped back and away from the conflagration. Yoshimi had jumped even farther back, and without looking behind him, Tatsuya spoke to her in a loud, clear tone.

"Gu Jie's not here. There are three Generators in the house."

An ambush had been laid—three strengthened magicians, Generators. Which meant that details about their raid had been leaked.

But neither Tatsuya nor Yoshimi wasted time with questions about how that had happened or whether there was a mole.

The only thing Yoshimi said was, "Leave all three bodies intact, please." If Tatsuya used Mist Dispersion on them, there'd be no leads left to investigate.

But this also meant there was no particular need to keep them alive, which considerably simplified the difficulty of the combat. Tatsuya, never particularly inclined to grant killers many exceptions, was grateful for this latitude.

"Stay back. I'll handle this alone," he said.

Yoshimi nodded and leaped backward again. At the same time, the branch family forces slowly closing in around the perimeter halted their advance.

From within the burning safe house came a magical attack— Blaze. There was no expansion of the activation sequence.

*These Generators must be specialized to a near-psychic level*, Tatsuya surmised as he dismantled the Blaze program that had been aimed at his allies, who were hiding in the bushes and buildings surrounding them.

Regardless of the predawn hour, the fire department would undoubtedly come to respond to an inferno of this size. Since they were mostly vacation homes, a majority of them were fortunately unoccupied, but there was no doubt that residents in the neighborhood would soon start to notice the disturbance.

There wasn't much time to lose.

After all, Tatsuya's Dismantle couldn't extinguish natural flame.

Plus, dismantling the building's material would simply expose all the flammable material at once, resulting in an explosion of flame. It was possible the sudden combustion would exhaust all the available oxygen in the area, extinguishing the fire, but the resulting shock wave might cause serious damage to the surrounding buildings. And Tatsuya himself wasn't exactly immune to a sudden absence of oxygen.

So what he targeted was not the entire building. He aimed Dismantle at the house's support pillars.

The burning safe house collapsed in on itself as though crushed from above.

The flames rising from the ruined roof immediately ceased.

This was nothing to be surprised at—a magician who specialized in creating fire would also be proficient in extinguishing it. Whoever had been casting magic from within the house had probably been wearing flame-retardant clothing, but evidently it wasn't so effective as to withstand lengthy direct exposure to an intense blaze, to say nothing of radiant or convective heat.

Three human figures pushed their way out of the rubble and stood.

The Generators, all wearing flame-retardant clothing, cast Blaze at Tatsuya simultaneously.

Magic programs surrounded him, their light reflecting in his eyes.

Tatsuya instantly projected psions out from his body.

Even uncompressed, the activated psions easily blew away the programs, operating on the same principle as Program Demolition. It was an ad hoc technique that only someone with a psion count as high as Tatsuya could execute.

Without missing a beat, Tatsuya fired three dismantling spells with his CAD in rapid succession.

The event influence radius that the Generators had been expanding collapsed.

The information reinforcement armor that had been protecting the Generators themselves was blown off—

—and fist-sized holes opened up in their chests.

Blood, however, didn't seep from the wounds.

Tatsuya pulled the trigger two more times.

The three Generators fell backward, their hearts gone.

His CAD still held at the ready, Tatsuya approached the rubble, stopping just a step short of it.

As he looked down at the corpses, Yoshimi came up from behind him. Despite the bulky silhouette of her oversized coat, her movements were surprisingly agile.

It wasn't just her, either. The previously hidden members of the branch family also began to emerge from their hiding places.

The siren of an approaching fire truck was audible in the distance. The fire had been reduced to ashes, but that wasn't going to make the firefighters pull a U-turn. They would need to vacate the scene quickly.

Yoshimi moved ahead of Tatsuya, stepping over the rubble—which was not only no longer on fire but also not even warm—and approached the bodies. The combat unit, after posting lookouts, also surrounded the corpses.

From within, the bodies of the felled Generators emanated a faint psionic light. It was the initiation of a delayed-activation program. Probably a technique that used the death of its target as an activation key.

Tatsuya brought his right hand up, holding his CAD ready.

The literally heartless Generators leaped to their feet, launching themselves at the nearest person. Their sole target was Yoshimi.

—A magic technique that turned a corpse into a puppet: Necromancy.

Yoshimi reflexively recoiled, stumbling over the rubble.

Her evasion magic wouldn't activate in time.

Tatsuya leveled his CAD at the corpses closing in on her and pulled the trigger.

—A magic technique that dismantled information bodies: Program Dispersion.

The psionic light emanating from the Generators faded.

The three Generators, their hands still outstretched in aggression, collapsed into the rubble.

The puppets were once again corpses.

"Th-thank you." As she looked over her shoulder, Yoshimi's face was still obscured by her muffler and glasses, but her voice betrayed a mixture of relief and gratitude.

"It should be all right now," said Tatsuya.

Yoshimi nodded. "Carry them out," she ordered the combat unit.

Leaving Yoshimi and the unit to finish their work, Tatsuya headed for his bike.

◇ ◇ ◇

Although Gu Jie had completely eluded the initial pursuit, Tatsuya was still ahead of anybody else in chasing down the terrorist mastermind.

Inspector Toshikazu Chiba, likewise engaged in the hunt for the terrorists, was still running around looking for a lead and had yet to find so much as a trace of the man responsible.

Proceeding from the principle that an investigation began at the scene of the crime, Toshikazu had headed to Hakone, where he received a phone call that made his eyes go wide even as he held the speaker to his ear.

*"Hello, is this Inspector Chiba? This is Fujibayashi."*

Her voice was unmistakable.

It was more or less unthinkable that someone had hijacked the communications infrastructure to impersonate her, but the fact of her calling was so unexpected that the thought occurred to him, nonetheless.

*"I'm sorry to call you during work."*

"It's fine. I'm always happy to get a call from you, Ms. Fujibayashi. What can I do for you?" said Toshikazu, moving away from the group of investigators. When Inagaki approached out of curiosity, Toshikazu shooed him away with a gesture.

*"Oh, I wouldn't say I need you to 'do' anything... I'm just worried about yesterday."*

"And that's why you went to the trouble of calling?" Despite the overall unfavorable circumstances, Toshikazu could feel his heart leap.

*"Yes. After your meeting with the Dollmaker, did anything...odd happen?"*

"Anything odd...? Well, I ended up pretty exhausted after hearing a bunch of geeky trivia about necromancy that didn't help my investigation at all."

*"No, not like that, I mean... Did your head hurt, or did you feel sleepy, or look pale—anything like that?"*

"No, nothing like that," said Toshikazu in his usual easygoing voice, inwardly scolding himself for feeling like a schoolboy talking to his crush.

"*I see...*" Her relief was palpable on the other end of the call.

Toshikazu was unaware of the smile on his own face. He also didn't hear Inagaki's murmur of "What's going on with him? Creepy."

"Were you worried about me?" asked Toshikazu.

"*...I was worried. But it looks like I didn't need to be.*"

Fujibayashi's voice sounded a little bashful, which made Toshikazu's smile even more pronounced.

"*Well then, Inspector, I'll be praying for your quick success in your efforts to apprehend the mastermind of this terrorist attack.*"

"Thank you very much. Good luck to you as well, Second Lieutenant Fujibayashi."

The call ended, and Toshikazu rejoined the other investigators, at which point Inagaki met him with an exhausted expression.

"Inagaki, what's wrong? You don't look well."

"I just had to exert considerable effort. Don't worry about it," he replied, rubbing his temples as though his head ached.

"Well, don't push yourself," Toshikazu said breezily, walking off with a chuckle and thinking nothing at all of his partner's gesture.

Her call with Toshikazu concluded, Fujibayashi looked to the female noncommissioned officer who sat in front of her, watching a monitor.

"There's no sign of interference with his consciousness," said the officer to Kazama, looking up and announcing the results of her analysis.

She was a specialist in psychological analysis and an expert in detecting and removing brainwashing from enlisted men and officers. To answer the question put to her, she could use vocal pitch and inflection, talking speed, breath interval, ocular movements, pulse and body temperature fluctuations, all to determine the presence or absence of subconscious suggestion. Even in situations like this one, where she had access to only the vocal transmission data, military-grade acoustic analysis equipment could derive a pulse rate from that. For a specialist, that was enough to ascertain the absence of being under the influence of mental suggestion.

"Kazukiyo Oumi is clear?" Kazama asked before nodding to the specialist. "Good work. You're dismissed."

The specialist stood, saluted, then pushed the cart carrying her equipment out of the room.

"I'm sorry you have to do such dirty work, Fujibayashi."

"It's fine… But, Commander, wasn't it dangerous? Even if the Chiba family is an authority in modern magic, their techniques do lean in the direction of physical control. Their resistance to mental interference is an unknown quantity."

The truth was that Toshikazu had been sent to the Dollmaker at Major General Saeki's direction. But it wasn't because she was targeting him. Rather, since the inspector was searching for anyone with a background in corpse-manipulation magic in the course of the Hakone terrorist investigation, in order to guide that search toward magicians suspected of being escaped remnants from the Kunlun Institute, Kazama's people had seeded lists of such suspects with information brokers to camouflage their source and nature.

Roter Wald was one example. The proprietor wasn't cooperating with Kazama in any real sense. The broker Toshikazu had been introduced to was completely random. Fujibayashi had been patronizing Roter Wald for a few days in order to follow through on the ruse, but it had been completely by chance that the proprietor had made the introduction to Kazukiyo Oumi.

So it wasn't as simple as Fujibayashi having used Toshikazu as a stooge, but nonetheless her conscience nagged at her.

"If we're going to go to such roundabout extremes to smoke out collaborators, perhaps we should also be participating in the terrorist attack investigation."

"Lieutenant. This unit—no, this entire brigade—is not participating in the Hakone investigation. This comes directly from General Saeki."

"Yes, sir…"

"It is absolutely imperative that the 101st Brigade avoid any appearance of supporting the Ten Master Clans."

"Yes, sir. Understood, sir."

The National Defense Force's 101st Brigade that General Saeki instituted had been founded to oppose the military potential that magicians—led by the Ten Master Clans—represented. Saeki was viewed as the political rival of the grand old dean of the Ten Master Clans, the retired General Kudou, and even if he himself didn't particularly consider himself such, it was simply reality that a considerable portion of Saeki's base of support within the military was composed of anti–Ten Master Clans, anti–Retsu Kudou elements.

However, behind the scenes, the 101st Brigade had a cooperative relationship with the Yotsuba family, which had assumed a leadership role among the Clans. If that relationship were to come to light—well, there would be room for spin, but it would preclude the possibility of further discreet cooperation with the Ten Master Clans.

"Good work, Lieutenant."

"Yes, sir." Fujibayashi saluted Kazama and left the room.

Fujibayashi returned to the cramped office that was given her as part of her duties as battalion adjutant. It was her private room, situated next to the battalion commander Kazama's office.

She sat down at her desk and considered the phone call she'd just had. The battalion hadn't specified the intelligence that had been provided to the information broker, and a broker at the level of Roten Wald's proprietor could easily bypass any pressure projected by the National Defense Force. Even without her intervention, Toshikazu would have found his way to the Dollmaker. And yet Fujibayashi could not clear her conscience so easily.

Upon rationally considering all the details, one could just as easily say that Fujibayashi had actually been providing Toshikazu support, given the real concern of brainwashing. But it was also true that the battalion had intercepted his phone calls and used him to their own end. Her guilt lingered.

As she thought back on the phone conversation, Fujibayashi couldn't help but let a giggle slip.

Toshikazu had called her Second Lieutenant Fujibayashi. He obviously didn't know about her promotion.

Although the military and the police were different organizations, they were alike in that promotions were announced in their official updates. If Toshikazu had been interested, he certainly could have found out. All he'd have to do was register his interest with a search agent.

*Last autumn, I got the feeling that he was coming on to me pretty strong, but...I guess he wasn't that serious.*

*But I was being pretty suggestive with him, too, so...maybe that goes both ways.*

Fujibayashi considered this and decided to laugh the matter off.

She decided that the flicker of genuine loneliness she felt was simply her imagination.

# [ 8 ]

Sunday, February 10, shortly before 3:00 PM.

With Miyuki in tow, Tatsuya visited the Kitayama family estate.

Though, in the interest of accuracy, perhaps it was better to say that Miyuki had her brother in tow.

The siblings were visiting the Kitayama family because yesterday in their classroom, Shizuku had invited Miyuki over. At first, Miyuki had misunderstood the invitation for tea as a formal, traditional tea ceremony and had been wondering if she ought to wear a proper kimono for the occasion, but upon being told by Shizuku that they'd be serving black tea, she had been rather embarrassed by her misunderstanding.

Their shoes still on due to the nature of the house, they were shown into an elegant Western-style room. Looking at the paintings hanging on the walls and the vases standing next to them, Tatsuya wondered how much this all must have cost, but he soon stopped thinking about it. Miyuki wasn't some unruly child who without supervision might break a valuable object, but pointing out how expensive everything must have been would surely make her feel awkward.

Shizuku was already sitting in the room when they entered it. She was wearing a collared, knee-length dress and high heels. It wasn't quite so neatly ceremonious as to be a formal afternoon dress, but it unmistakably brought that sensibility to mind.

Miyuki, in fact, was dressed similarly. Tatsuya had consulted with her as to whether casual or formal dress was more appropriate, and he inwardly breathed a sigh of relief that she hadn't misread the situation.

Tatsuya, per Miyuki's advice, had worn an unremarkable dark suit. He'd considered coming in his school uniform, but he'd gone with the suit in order to better match Miyuki's outfit.

Shizuku stood upon seeing Tatsuya and Miyuki. "Welcome to my home," she said, bowing with her hands politely clasped.

"Thank you so much for inviting us," Tatsuya said, returning her bow. Though his reply may have lacked a certain elegance, it was certainly polite enough. A half step behind her brother, Miyuki also bowed, and hers was faultlessly graceful.

"Please," Shizuku insisted formally, gesturing to the seats that had been prepared for Tatsuya and Miyuki. She was being as reserved with her conversation as ever, but her manners were twice as polite as they even normally were. Whatever the reason, she was fully in "elegant young lady" mode today.

Shizuku looked to a maid who was standing off to one side. The woman looked to be in her thirties. She was well put together, but both Miyuki and Tatsuya could immediately tell that she had been chosen not for her appearance but for her skill.

She placed a stylish kettle on top an induction heater, then pressed a switch. The sound of boiling water soon emanated from the kettle. She had probably heated the water in advance before bringing it to a boil.

The maid took a teapot out of the warmer, placing a generous amount of black tea leaves inside the thoroughly warmed pot.

As soon as the water in the kettle reached a boil, she turned off the induction burner, and briskly poured its water into the pot. She quickly placed the teapot's lid on top, then took a step back, her eyes lowered.

"Tatsuya, if you'd prefer coffee, I can have some made right away," she whispered. Her way of talking was as usual, but the atmosphere was different. Shizuku seemed faintly nervous.

"No, that's fine. I enjoy black tea, too." Tatsuya decided to at least speak to her normally, like they were classmates. He didn't pry into what was making her nervous. They would probably find out soon enough, so he felt no need to hurry things.

"By the way, Shizuku," Miyuki said, following Tatsuya's lead and using a more informal register. "Will Honoka be here, too?"

"Ah, no. That is, well…"

Shizuku was prevaricating—practically begging them not to ask the reason for Honoka's absence.

Her words stumbled to a halt. Not even Miyuki, the most socially adept of the three, attempted to pick up the conversation where it had left off.

"Miss," said the maid from next to Shizuku, breaking the silence suddenly.

"Ah, er, thank you!"

It was the maid warning Shizuku not to oversteep the tea. Shizuku removed the lid from the pot, stirred it gently with a spoon, then replaced the lid.

Then, picking up a ceramic tea strainer in one hand and the teapot in the other, she poured the tea evenly into three teacups. She served the one into which the last drops fell to Tatsuya and the one next to it to Miyuki.

"Please," she said.

"Thank you," Tatsuya said, with Miyuki wordlessly bowing before picking up her cup.

"It's delicious," Miyuki said after a sip. Next to her, Tatsuya nodded emphatically. "You're just as good at making black tea as you are at matcha, aren't you?" she finished.

"Oh, it's nothing special…" Shizuku said, looking away bashfully.

"You've had Shizuku's matcha, Miyuki?" Tatsuya asked.

"Yes. It's really quite delicious, you know. I'd certainly want my brother to be able to taste it."

"…You were better at it, Miyuki," Shizuku said abruptly—clearly to cover up her own embarrassment—fixing her once-averted gaze back on Miyuki. "And, your 'brother,' Miyuki?"

"Hmm? Oh…" For a moment, Miyuki didn't grasp what Shizuku was getting at, but she soon understood the question: *Why are you still calling him your brother when he's your cousin?*

But this was an odd time to be asking such a question. Shizuku must have seen and heard Miyuki referring to Tatsuya as her brother dozens of times at school.

Still, Miyuki kept her answer polite. "I've been calling him that since middle school… I guess old habits are hard to break." In addition to looking somewhat abashed, she even added some unnecessary explanation.

"Since *middle* school?"

"Yes, um, it's sort of…"

Miyuki trailed off vaguely. She had started calling Tatsuya her brother in their first year of middle school, during the incident that summer in Okinawa. Before that, her mother had strictly forbidden them from treating each other like siblings.

Even though she'd been only a child and hadn't known the reasoning behind anything, Miyuki still hated the memories she had of all the days when she'd been rude and dismissive toward the brother she would later come to love so much. That she'd ever done so was a secret she couldn't bear to tell anyone.

Another awkward silence fell over the table.

But this time, a distraction arrived with perfect timing: There was a knock at the door.

A different maid than the one who had helped prepare the tea went to the door and opened it.

"Miss, the master of the house has arrived."

"See him in," answered Shizuku, without asking Tatsuya or Miyuki their inclinations.

Tatsuya soon realized that today's invitation must have come from not Shizuku but rather her father.

"My apologies for interrupting your conversation," said Shizuku's father, Ushio Kitayama, coming to stand alongside his daughter as he greeted the already-standing Tatsuya and Miyuki. Ushio wore a button-down shirt and a double-breasted knit jacket over it, giving him a casual, rougher style—although he didn't look even slightly sloppy.

"I'm sorry for the intrusion," Tatsuya said. If Ushio really was the person responsible for their invitation, it would've been appropriate to thank him, but for now, Tatsuya decided to continue with the assumption that they were here at Shizuku's behest. It made things easier for both sides.

But why would a major player in finance be so roundabout? Tatsuya felt more caution than curiosity at the question. He surely didn't think of them as ordinary high school students. Someone with the Yotsuba name would be a desirable ally for just about everyone operating at the top levels of the finance world, and there was value even in being recognized as their rival.

Previously, Tatsuya had been told to stay away from Shizuku by her mother, but that had only been an emotional reaction—a parent's desire to protect her daughter from someone she didn't comprehend. But it didn't make sense that a similar reason could possibly have motivated Ushio's invitation.

"No, no, I'm the one brazenly intruding upon you young people here. You'll have to excuse me, really."

"There's nothing brazen about it. By rights, as guests in your home we ought to have greeted you properly. Please pardon our impropriety."

"Well, Shizuku is the one who invited you, so I hardly think that's necessary. But apropos of my brazenness, would you mind if I stayed to chat a bit?"

"If you don't mind our company, certainly not."

"Oh, lovely. Let's sit and talk, then," Ushio said, taking a seat across from Tatsuya. A beat later, Tatsuya, Miyuki, and Shizuko all followed suit.

"Now then, there's hardly anything to talk about except this anti-magician negativity campaign."

The topic was within Tatsuya's range of supposition, but he was surprised to see Ushio plunging into it so directly.

"Both my wife and daughter are magicians, after all, so I can't help but be concerned about the recent developments. I wonder how the Ten Master Clans intend to deal with this wave spreading across the nation that's trying to make magicians out to be the enemy."

"I can't speak in specifics, but I was acknowledged as a member of the Yotsuba family just this past New Year's. Miyuki was also raised separately from the main family. At the moment, neither of us are in a position to know very much about what the Ten Master Clans are planning."

Ushio nodded magnanimously, betraying no doubt about Tatsuya's answer. "That makes sense. Well, my wife tells me that as the leaders of Japan's magical community, the Ten have a variety of unusual customs."

Tatsuya nodded lightly, but only to indicate that he'd understood. Obviously, Ushio was going somewhere with this statement.

"But surely, you haven't heard nothing, right? Are you simply not permitted to tell me anything at all?"

All Tatsuya had heard was what was necessary to carry out his own particular mission. And he hadn't been told *not* to discuss that mission's details.

"I imagine you know this, since it's already been publicly announced, but the Ten recently began a search for the person behind the terrorist attack. The police will ultimately be responsible for apprehending him, but I'm also participating in the search."

"I see. So this is following through on the statement issued through the Magic Association of Japan. I wonder if the media will play a countermove of some kind."

"I haven't heard anything about that," Tatsuya admitted.

"Indeed…" Ushio sighed, as from beside him the maid placed

a teacup in front of him. He acknowledged her with a glance, then took a sip from the freshly poured tea. "Well, as I said, I can't pretend as though this anti-magician talk has nothing to do with me. If the Ten Master Clans wanted my cooperation, I might be able to speak to some people in the media."

It was true that Ushio Kitayama's financial resources gave him a certain amount of influence in the mass media. Even if he couldn't single-handedly turn the rising tide of anti-magician sentiment, he could certainly dampen its energy.

It ought to have been an offer Tatsuya was pleased to hear. He wasn't ignorant about the power of public discourse. Even the Yotsuba family couldn't stand fully apart from the rest of Japanese society. Magicians were not in any position to declare their independence and form a self-governing territory—not *yet* anyway.

But Tatsuya's answer was a negative one. "Unfortunately, I can't act as a representative of the Ten Master Clans. Neither Miyuki nor myself can even represent the Yotsuba family to the Master Clans Council. Also, given the circumstances, I don't think that taking the magicians' side and intervening with the media would lead to a desirable outcome for Shizuku."

Ushio's eyes glittered. He'd worn the face of an affable father thus far, but now he was nothing short of a captain of industry who represented all of Japan. "And why is that?"

"The anti-magician activities are only one aspect of a general anti-social movement. Magicians are simply a convenient outlet for a more fundamental frustration plaguing society. If anything, your position as a wealthy man would make you a convenient focal point for that frustration, and I don't think you should give these agitators another tool to use in their instigation. These people will not draw fine distinctions—there's a real danger that their malice would extend not just to your wife and Shizuku but even to Wataru."

Ushio brought his teacup to his lips, taking a moment to consider Tatsuya's statement.

"…While I think it's dangerous to categorize all anti-magician criticism as anarchism, I can tell that you're genuinely concerned about my son and my daughter. But do you really think I should do nothing?"

"If a magician—no, if a student of First High—becomes a victim of a crime, then I expect we'll ask for your assistance then."

"…And you don't intend to prevent that harm before it happens?"

"It's impossible to protect the entire student body every moment they're away from school. We'll encourage caution, but anything beyond that is difficult, I think."

"You make a good point." Ushio gave Tatsuya an appraising glance, but it was quickly replaced with a self-possessed smile. "I understand your position. I'll stay quiet for the moment. But if the situation deteriorates, do please come and check with me. I don't mean to be a broken record about this, but I truly do consider this my problem as well."

"Understood. I'll be counting on you when the time comes," Tatsuya said with a bow.

Ushio stood. "Well, I've imposed enough. Please enjoy your afternoon," he said, bowing to Tatsuya and Miyuki before leaving the room.

Tatsuya had turned down Ushio Kitayama's offer because media manipulation simply wasn't his job.

But the Ten Master Clans hadn't yet decided if media intervention was unnecessary. The evening of the day the Shiba siblings visited the Kitayama residence, Kouichi Saegusa invited a Diet member named Kouzuke to an expensive restaurant.

Representative Kouzuke was a young politician in the ruling party whose constituency was in Tokyo and who was known to have a favorable view of magicians. Many considered him to be all but guaranteed for a cabinet position in the next term, but the recent rise in anti-magician sentiment had put him in a less certain position. That didn't mean he was suddenly going to flip to the anti-magician camp, but he'd been forced into silence for the past few days.

When the after-dinner coffee was brought in, Kouichi told the garçon that they were not to be disturbed for a while and had the doors to their private dining room closed. He then directed his attention back to Kouzuke.

"I trust you enjoyed the dinner?"

"Yes, it was spectacular."

"I'm glad to hear that. I'll make sure to pass your compliments on to the chef."

"Oh, please, let me do it myself. There are so many prying eyes and ears around Akasaka and Shinbashi that I haven't been able to properly relax in some time. An establishment like this is a treasure."

Kouichi and Kouzuke were roughly the same age, and their conversation flowed with ease and familiarity.

"Now then, Mr. Saegusa. I'd love to hear whatever it is you have to say to me." Cutting away the pleasantries, Kouzuke pushed toward the evening's real topic. "From what I can guess, you want to deal with the media?"

"You're as perceptive as ever, Mr. Kouzuke. Just as you say," Kouichi said, casually flattering the man. But Kouzuke only smirked bitterly. Given the circumstances, there was no other reason for Kouichi to come calling. He wasn't annoyed about it, but given the obvious motivation, Kouzuke felt no pleasure at the flattery.

"A request from none other than Mr. Saegusa. Well, I'm prepared for a certain amount of risk. Shall we put pressure on the media? Or would you rather push the narrative that the real villains here are the terrorists, while magicians are simply victims, just like the bystanders?" Kouzuke grinned. He was still a young politician, but he already had the confidence and bearing of an official backed by the ruling party who'd triumphed through hellish power struggles to achieve his current position.

"No, I wouldn't ask for anything so forceful," Kouichi said, undaunted by Kouzuke's brashness. If he'd taken the offer at face value, he'd be considerably indebted to Kouzuke, which would put the Saegusa family at Kouzuke's beck and call for any number of requests.

Kouichi was a veteran of more negotiations than any other family head in the Ten Master Clans. Kouzuke didn't have the skill it would take to steal the initiative from him.

"What I need from you, Mr. Kouzuke, is when magicians are harmed by anti-magician groups, to keep an eye out and make sure that those stories don't get smothered in the national discourse."

Kouichi's request was considerably more conservative than what Kouzuke had proposed.

"Obviously, we won't permit criminal activity, but…are you sure that's sufficient?" Kouzuke asked dubiously.

Kouichi laughed, shaking his head. "It's the wish of every virtuous citizen for obvious things to be treated as obviously important, Mr. Kouzuke! For example, if a student from First High is assaulted by an anti-magician demonstrator, the attacker could claim that it was in self-defense simply because the victim was a magician."

"No, surely not."

"You don't think so?"

Kouzuke got the strange sense that behind Kouichi's sunglasses, his artificial eye glittered with a suspicious light. Kouzuke was now the more intimidated one of the two.

"*They resorted to violence because of the latent danger that magic might be used against them. It was justifiable self-defense.* Can you really say that the media and certain members of the opposition party wouldn't say such a thing?"

Faced with Kouichi's quiet smile, Kouzuke's breath caught in his throat.

"Despite employing intimidation and harassment themselves, they use convenient logic to justify resorting to violence at the first sign of resistance. And politicians and the media defend them and embolden them. Do you really think this is impossible?"

"Well…"

"When their misinformation or unlawfulness is threatened with exposure, it's not at all rare for these groups to resort to agitation, threats, and outright violence in order to suppress their opponent's grievances. But for the adversely affected party, this isn't admissible. Even when magicians are victims, their complaints go unheard. Such is the deplorable state toward which I fear this nation is headed."

"Mr. Saegusa, surely you're not…" Kouzuke's voice wavered, but not out of fear of the scenario Kouichi had laid out. "Surely you're not considering using First High students or Magic University students as sacrifices to alter public opinion…?"

The faint smile on Kouichi's lips vanished, and he looked into Kouzuke's face. "My dearest hope is that nothing at all happens. But it's not possible *for us* to prevent every incident of unjust violence against a magician."

Gazing steadily at Kouzuke, Kouichi's smile returned, this time with a sly significance.

"Even if the police are out on patrol in full force, they can't do anything *until an incident actually happens*. So I'm asking that if such an incident does come to pass, that it be handled *correctly*. I look forward to your cooperation, Mr. Kouzuke."

"…I…I understand," Kouzuke stammered his acceptance, which Kouichi received with that same mysteriously glittering smile.

Monday, February 11. Tatsuya walked to school with Miyuki and Minami as he usually did, but on his way to his classroom, he noticed a strange commotion around the campus.

The morning after Gu Jie's declaration of responsibility, the school mood had also been unsettled, this was different somehow. There was anxiety, yes, but a sense of curiosity seemed to predominate. In that way, it reminded Tatsuya of the day Lina had come to the school for her study abroad.

The mood in Class 2-E was no different.

"Good morning," Mizuki said.

"Morning," Tatsuya replied. "Hey, Mizuki. Seems like everybody's restless this morning. Did something happen?"

"I'm not totally sure myself, but…apparently Ichijou from Third High is here for some reason."

"Ichijou?" Tatsuya couldn't disguise his surprise.

Masaki simply visiting Tokyo wasn't itself cause for attention. Maya had told Tatsuya that Masaki had been put on the hunt for the terrorists under Katsuto. It was also within the realm of possibility that he would miss a considerable number of school days and live in Tokyo for a while.

But even if so, there wasn't any need for him to attend First High. Hachiouji, where First High was located, was part of old central Tokyo, but it was quite far away from the Juumonji family's estate. Magic University, where Katsuto was enrolled, was in Nerima, which also wasn't close. It was very difficult to imagine Masaki visiting First High because he just happened to be in the neighborhood.

Surely he wasn't…*transferring*…?

"Who did you hear that from, Mizuki?"

"Me," came the answer from behind Tatsuya. Instead of leaning in through the window, Erika had entered the classroom and come up behind him.

"Morning, Erika. So where did you spot Ichijou?" Tatsuya asked over his shoulder.

"I didn't directly *spot* him, per se," she replied, not even bothering with a disappointed expression as she gave up on startling Tatsuya. "Some girl saw the vice principal escorting him into the principal's office. I asked around, and it seems like a bunch of people are saying the same thing, so I'm pretty sure it's accurate."

Erika had a much larger circle of acquaintances than Tatsuya. His face was more well-known around the school, but Erika knew far more students than he did. If this information was what Erika had concluded after running around asking her contacts about it, then Tatsuya was inclined to believe that Masaki was indeed here at First High—and that he'd been escorted to see the principal by the vice principal.

"The principal's office, huh…"

Tatsuya was starting to think the unlikely scenario he'd just imagined might actually be true.

Like Tatsuya, Miyuki wasn't in a position to appreciate the rumor.

"As I'm sure you all know, Ichijou is a student at Third High, but because of some family circumstances, he will be living in Tokyo for about a month." It was vice principal Yaosaka, not the guidance counselor, who stood in front of Class 2-A with Masaki beside him.

It was surprising enough that Masaki was here at all, but the fact that the vice principal was introducing him personally was so shocking that none of actual content of the introduction was entering the students' heads.

None of the students would dare try to whisper to one another in front of the vice principal, but the classroom practically hummed with excitement, which only increased at Yaosaka's mention of "family circumstances." There wasn't a single student in Class 2-A who didn't know what that meant. Family circumstances—in other words, Ichijou family circumstances. Every boy and girl in the class knew it had to have something to do with the terrorist attack a few days earlier.

But there was a difference of temperature between the gazes of the boys and those of the girls in the class.

One of the girls raised her hand. "Vice Principal, do you mean that Ichijou is transferring from Third High into *this* class?" she asked with a hopeful note in her voice.

This had already been explained, but Yaosaka patiently repeated himself. "He is not transferring. As you can see from his uniform, Ichijou will continue to be enrolled in Third High School. However, since it's not practical for him to commute to Third High in Kanazawa from where he is currently staying in Tokyo, he will be allowed to use a terminal in this classroom to access the Magic University and magic high school network to continue his curriculum at Third High."

Class 2-A had unfortunately lost a student the previous month. The unoccupied desk had remained open since then.

"He won't be able to transfer credits from practicums or laboratories, but he'll still be studying alongside all of you. I think this will be a good opportunity to learn and grow for both Ichijou and this class. I hope you'll all get along in the spirit of friendly competition. Now then, Ichijou."

At Yaosaka's prompt, Masaki took a half step forward.

"I'm Masaki Ichijou from Third High School. I appreciate the kindness you're all showing me by allowing me to study with you. It may not be a very long time, but I look forward to the coming month."

A warm round of applause greeted Masaki as he bowed. Class 2-A had the experience of Lina joining them during her exchange, so they were more used to bombshells like this than the rest of First High—which was part of why Principal Momoyama had placed Masaki with them.

It certainly wasn't the result of the proposal the Ichijou family had recently made to the Yotsuba family.

—And yet, Miyuki couldn't help but be suspicious. Even as she clapped along with the rest of the class, she sighed in her heart.

During lunch, Masaki didn't sit at the same table as Miyuki. He seemingly prioritized improving his relationship with the boys in the class and mingled with Morisaki's group of friends.

"That's unexpected," murmured Erika as she looked on from a slight distance away. "I was so sure he'd stick to Miyuki like glue."

"If he did that, both the guys *and* girls in the class would immediately hate him," commented Mikihiko with a smirk.

"Lina was a girl, so it seemed totally natural that she would hang out with Miyuki, but Ichijou's a guy, so it's different," agreed Honoka with a smile.

"Yeah, good point. If he went around chasing girls' tails on his first day, it'd wreck his Prince Charming image, I guess."

"Chasing tails? Erika, way to be blunt…" Mizuki chided.

"Did I say something wrong?"

"Yeah, 'tails'…"

"That's no good? Butts, then."

"Erika…"

"What kind of girl was Lina?" Shizuku asked Honoka, leaving Erika to her one-sided teasing of Mizuki.

"Oh, that's right—you didn't get a chance to talk to Lina much, did you, Shizuku?"

Lina had come to First High on the pretense of being an exchange student. The other half of the exchange had been Shizuku. Shizuku left the country just as Lina was arriving, so she hadn't gotten to know the American girl at all.

"I heard she was blonde and superhot."

"She totally was. Blonde hair and these vivid blue eyes. She was really pretty."

"Prettier than Miyuki?"

"Huh? Of course not…" Honoka sputtered, glancing at Miyuki with a nervous smile. "But…they were different types, you know? Like Miyuki's the 'elegant beauty' type."

Shizuku looked briefly at the increasingly awkward Miyuki before nodding at Honoka to continue. As close friends, Shizuku and Honoka had similar behavioral patterns.

"But Lina was more like the 'cute' type, I think. She had a face like a porcelain doll, but her vibe was more casual…like, easy to approach, energetic, lively, and cheerful."

"I think those last two are basically the same thing."

"Ngh…! W-well, anyway, she was really American seeming."

"Sounds like you're prejudiced toward Americans…"

Honoka tried to bulldoze her way past Shizuku's teasing. "And she was a really strong magician, too. She was even a good match against Miyuki!" she concluded.

"She was as good-looking as Miyuki? Whoa." This seemed to catch Shizuku's interest, and she abandoned her teasing.

"Well, she did some here as a representative of the USNA, in a way," Tatsuya said, eliciting grins from Erika and Leo—although both of them were well aware that Lina's true identity was a secret. They wouldn't blab about it here where there was no telling who might overhear.

Shizuku, the only one who *didn't* know Lina's true identity, cocked her head in confusion at Erika's meaningful smile.

"Her magic abilities aside, she was a fun girl. I'm sure you'd like her, too, Shizuku—she was plenty easy to tease."

"It's not like I'm the king of teasing or anything."

"Tatsuya…I think you're being a little rude to both Shizuku and Lina, honestly," Miyuki rebuked.

In response to successive objections from Shizuku and Miyuki, Tatsuya smiled and apologized. "Sorry."

"Anyway, I never dreamed that Ichijou would start studying at First High. Was there any explanation at all as to why he transferred here?" Mikihiko interjected, leaving the subject of Lina aside for the moment and posing the question the three students from Class 2-A had been wondering about all morning. He phrased the question politely since Miyuki was there.

"They said it wasn't a transfer."

"He's going to be staying in Tokyo for a while, so they're going to let him use a terminal at our school to continue his academic classes at Third High online. That's why he's still wearing his Third High uniform instead of a First High one."

"Family circumstances? Like, the Ichijou family?" Mikihiko asked, after hearing Honoka's explanation, furrowing his brow. "I figure these days they've got their hands full with the terrorist attack stuff, but…Tatsuya, do you know anything about this?"

Tatsuya neither lied nor exercised his right to remain silent. "You know the statement that was issued through the Magic Association, right?"

"Uh, the one that said they were gonna track down the terrorist mastermind? That one?"

"Ichijou is in Tokyo on that mission. Incidentally, Mayumi Saegusa and Katsuto Juumonji are also participating in the search. And so am I."

On reason for the mission was to demonstrate to the world that the Ten Master Clans were not simply standing idly by. The media-directed statement through the Magic Association had been another part of that calculated response. Tatsuya understood this, so there was no reason for him not to explain the situation.

"Huh… Hey, Tatsuya."

"What?"

"Uh…should I help, too?"

Mikihiko's reaction came as a surprise to Tatsuya.

The Ten Master Clans were not searching for the terrorist Gu Jie to retaliate for the attack. It was the job of the police to track down a criminal responsible for abetting murder, injury, and use of explosives in the destruction of property—it would be a misplaced overstep of their authority for the civilian Ten Master Clans to undertake the search themselves.

The Ten Master Clans were *aiding* in the search as part of a campaign to sway public opinion. There would be little point in someone not from one of those families joining the effort.

"I think you'd be better off keeping an eye out for anti-magician groups," said Tatsuya, trying to direct Mikihiko's concern in a different direction. But it wasn't a diversion—the matter in question was also of critical importance.

"Anti-magician groups?"

"You're the one who told me about people who were verbally harassing and photographing students from this school, Mikihiko."

"Oh, right—that." It had been the substance of a report from the disciplinary committee the second Monday of the new semester. "I'm surprised you'd remember such a minor detail."

"I was just thinking how surprised I was that you'd forgotten about it."

Mikihiko blinked rapidly at the unexpected scolding from Tatsuya.

"It started happening even before the terrorist attack. Public opinion is turning against magicians, and we can no longer ignore the possibility that groups who don't look favorably on magicians—like the humanists—will be increasingly aggressive or even violent toward students."

Tatsuya's decisive words spurred Mikihiko to action. For a moment, it seemed like he was just staring at his feet, but then he pulled out his portable terminal and seemed to check some data. "There still aren't any reports of physical violence...but the number of harassment incidents occurring off campus has clearly been increasing."

Mikihiko was looking at data the disciplinary committee had assembled from student reports.

"I'm sorry, Tatsuya. It looks like I really dropped the ball here. Until you pointed it out just now, I'd been totally focused on on-campus matters," Mikihiko muttered, but there was reason to sympathize with his inattention. Ever since Gu Jie's declaration the previous Wednesday, the student body had been anxious and irritable. The slightest nudge would cause quarrels, and there had even been a few scuffles that turned physical. It was an unstable situation, and Mikihiko, as the president of the disciplinary committee, had to prioritize school matters first and foremost.

"Would you pass that data along to the student council? The reports through last week are finished, so I'll incorporate them and make a report," said Tatsuya.

That said, given the anxieties the students were voicing, the faculty office would have to be informed. What Tatsuya meant by his statement was that, separately from the disciplinary committee, the student council would prepare its own report based on student consultations.

"Understood. I'll do my best to make sure all the information makes its way to you." Mikihiko nodded firmly.

"We'll be counting on you, disciplinary committee president!" yelled Erika. She was half teasing, but Mikihiko could tell she was also genuinely trying to encourage him.

After the day's classes ended, Tatsuya visited Class 2-A's room.

Miyuki's keen senses picked up on his approach, and she came out into the hall to meet him. "Tatsuya, did you come to pick me up?" she asked. It was relatively rare for Tatsuya to meet up with Miyuki on the way to the student council room rather than the other way around.

"Yes. I also had something I wanted to talk to Ichijou about."

Miyuki looked slightly crestfallen. "Oh, Ichijou? I see. I'll get him."

She didn't dwell on her disappointment, though, and turned around with a smile, heading back into her classroom.

That smile gave Tatsuya a sense of unease. It was new as of this year, and he'd seen it several times already. He first started noticing it ever since they'd returned from the New Year's celebration.

There was an undesirable shift happening within Miyuki. Tatsuya's gut told him that if he neglected the situation, there would be unpleasant consequences.

But at the moment, he didn't have the luxury of digging into the matter.

Here and now, dealing with Masaki took priority.

"Thank you," Masaki said politely to Miyuki before addressing Tatsuya. "What is it, Shiba?"

"Ichijou, do you hear about the meetings Juumonji is holding?" Tatsuya didn't need to re-explain their mission; as fellow members of Ten Master Clans families, they were both perfectly aware of their orders to find the terrorist mastermind.

But having just arrived in Tokyo, Masaki hadn't learned any more than that. "No, I hadn't..." he said.

"It's not really a formal meeting so much as it is Saegusa, Juumonji, and me all taking the opportunity to mutually share relevant information. Do you want to come?"

"Hmm." Masaki stopped to consider Tatsuya's invitation but not for more than about ten seconds. "As long as I wouldn't be in the way, I think will, yes."

Masaki was well aware of the need to exchange field intelligence and build consensus during the search. What he'd been worried about briefly was whether the presence of a Third High student would disrupt the mood in meeting made up of one First High student and two First High alumni. But he soon decided this was no time to be worrying about such minor details.

"All right. Today's meeting is at 6:00 PM. Get out your terminal, and I'll forward you the location."

"Uh, okay," Masaki said, slightly surprised, as he produced a portable terminal from his pocket. In a conversation like this, a Third High student would've just said, *Okay, we'll go together.* He hadn't felt particularly inclined to walk somewhere side by side with his romantic rival, but upon learning that they really would be traveling separately, he felt rather deflated.

He suddenly felt very keenly that this wasn't Third High, and it sparked a bout of loneliness.

Tatsuya's eye hadn't missed the change in the other boy's expression, but he had no interest in Masaki's thoughts or feelings at the moment. "Did you get the data?" he asked in a businesslike tone.

"...There it is."

"All right, I'll see you at that location. Six PM." Masaki nodded, and Tatsuya took his leave. "Shall we go, Miyuki?"

He'd be skipping student council duties in order to continue the search, but having come all the way to Class 2-A, he decided to at least escort his sister to the student council room.

"Yes!" Miyuki nodded to Tatsuya with a smile, then turned toward Masaki. "If you'll excuse us, Ichijou."

"Good luck with the student council work," he replied with a gentle smile.

For a moment, he watched Miyuki and Tatsuya go as they headed to the student council room.

Tatsuya felt Masaki's gaze linger on his back.

This time, he couldn't ignore what Masaki was thinking and feeling.

At exactly 6:00 PM, Tatsuya entered the restaurant where Katsuto was waiting, and at 7:00 PM, he left.

Today, Katsuto, Mayumi, and Tatsuya all had no progress to report. Tatsuya had already shared information about the situation in Kamakura during the day—to the extent that he could talk about it, of course. Tonight's meeting, then, was over once Masaki had been brought up to speed on the current state of the search. Once that was done, they quickly concluded.

Afterward, Katsuto, Mayumi, and Masaki decided to get something to eat, but Tatsuya demurred and went home. He'd been invited, but after he'd refused once, they didn't press the matter. Katsuto and Mayumi both seemed to take notice of Tatsuya and Masaki's adversarial relationship vis-à-vis Miyuki.

Inside the cabinet whisking him home, Tatsuya thought about his sister. Her forced smile when he'd stopped by her classroom had lingered in the corner of his mind.

It wasn't like he'd only noticed it today. He'd seen her do it several times, ever since they'd returned from the main Yotsuba house after the New Year, and each time it had bothered him. But Miyuki seemed to not want him to notice, so Tatsuya had thus far not pressed the matter.

But seeing her like that today, it had started to feel untenable. It was increasingly obvious that she was forcing herself to keep up appearances for some reason. Tatsuya felt a need to at least talk to her about it before she crumpled under whatever burden she was carrying.

Even after he transferred from a cabinet to a commuter and got closer to home, Tatsuya continued to mull over the problem of how to delicately broach the subject.

Forcing the matter would be a bad move—hurting Miyuki in the process of asking her what was wrong would be totally counterproductive. That said, he doubted she would willingly open up to him. Leading questions were little better than using force. It wasn't like interrogating a prisoner—getting her to talk wasn't the real goal.

In the end, Tatsuya found himself standing in front of his house without a surefire plan. As he reached his hand out to open the gate, his movements were a mite slower than usual.

Normally, he would have opened the gate already and have been standing in front of the door when Miyuki opened it, but instead his hand was still on the gate's handle when she came out to greet him.

"Welcome home, Tatsuya! —Oh, what's the matter? Are you not feeling well?" she said, looking suddenly pale at the mere thought.

"No, I was just thinking about something. Anyway, glad to be home, Miyuki."

Tatsuya scolded himself—what was the point of trying to figure out what to do if he was just going to make Miyuki worry more?

\* \* \*

He hadn't completely deflated, but nevertheless Tatsuya finished a late dinner with Miyuki without bringing the subject up.

He turned down her offer of after-dinner tea and took a bath, and upon feeling refreshed, he resolved again to talk to her.

Instead of retiring to his room, Tatsuya headed for the living room, where Miyuki was waiting for him in a lacy, classically shaped knee-length dress. She had removed the apron she'd been wearing previously.

"I'll make some coffee for you, Tatsuya, so please feel free to have a seat," Miyuki said, standing before Tatsuya could get a word out of his mouth.

She was so brisk, he wondered if she was being evasive.

Tatsuya got the feeling that she somehow had seen through what he was going to ask her, and she was already dreading the question.

But that also had to mean that Miyuki was aware that Tatsuya was feeling apprehensive. Unlike Tatsuya, however, who had only a vague unease that he didn't understand, what Miyuki was carrying something within herself that she understood all too well.

Still, from Tatsuya's perspective, he had no idea what was causing her such anguish and was still grappling with how to best phrase the question when Miyuki returned to the living room carrying a tray. "Here you are."

Deep in thought, Tatsuya had lost track of time, and he couldn't help but look up and glance at the clock.

Miyuki placed a saucer with a coffee cup on it on the table, peering at Tatsuya's face with a concerned expression. "Um, Tatsuya…are you absolutely sure that you're not overly tired? You've been rather distracted ever since you came home."

Tatsuya wanted to scold himself for his thoughtlessness. He'd made Miyuki worry about him again. *This is no time to be spacing out, mulling things over*, he chided himself.

"Miyuki, could you have a seat?"

"Yes, but...?"

This was his chance. He didn't relish it, but at least here, Miyuki couldn't run away or evade the subject.

"The person I'm worried about is you, Miyuki."

Up until last year, Miyuki would've been overjoyed to hear these words.

But now, her eyes flicked this way and that to avoid Tatsuya's gaze.

No matter how Tatsuya tried, his sister would not look him in the eye. Regardless, he pushed onward.

"What are you so upset about?"

"I'm not upset..."

Miyuki's reply was utterly unconvincing. As though aware of this, she turned her head away, not just averting her eyes.

"Please talk to me, Miyuki."

In profile, she blinked rapidly. Her eyes flickered back and forth uncertainly.

If Tatsuya had stared at her for ten more seconds, she probably would have spilled her worries out without omitting a single thing. But capricious fate intervened to save her—or perhaps deviously stole her chance to unburden herself.

Miyuki stood suddenly at the sound of the visiphone's ring. She could have taken the call at the table's wireless console, but instead she hurried to the wall panel with such speed that her skirt fluttered behind her.

When she saw the caller name that was displayed there, she exclaimed, "Oh! It's Aunt Maya!"

"Put her through," Tatsuya said, already standing and moving to the camera's field of view.

Miyuki pressed the ANSWER button on the panel.

Maya's form appeared on the visiphone's screen. *"Good evening, Tatsuya. Have I caught you at a bad moment?"*

It wasn't as obvious as it would have been if she had been meeting them in person, but Maya's gaze did land on the coffee cup on the table. "No, it's fine. What can I do for you today?"

It was a fairly strained answer for Tatsuya, but Maya made no move to pounce on it. *"Gu Jie got away from us last Saturday. We've figured out why, so I thought I'd let you know."*

Tatsuya immediately wondered why that was something the head of the Yotsuba family had to directly tell him, but:

*"Apparently, our communications have been intercepted."*

"I was under the impression that Yotsuba family communications were thoroughly encrypted."

*"We use military-strength encryption that cycles hourly, but it appears it's been broken."*

Just as Maya said, the Yotsuba family encryption keys changed every hour.

Every month, Tatsuya had to go to the Magic Association in person and receive a storage media from a courier containing sixty days' worth of encryption keys (the extra thirty days being a safety margin for unforeseen circumstances). The encryption device that Ayako had given to Balance contained 43,200 keys, and the device itself had been hardened against theft and unauthorized access of that data to the full extent of what was currently possible technologically.

It was far-fetched to imagine that all this effort had been for naught.

But no matter how far-fetched a theory was, so long as it could not be thoroughly disproven, it had to be acknowledged and treated as if it was truth.

"Does that mean we should assume that this conversation is being intercepted as well?"

*"Yes. From now on, leads pertaining to this case will be delivered by physical correspondence only."*

"Understood."

Maya had used the word *correspondence*, but Tatsuya didn't think that she was referring to mail delivered by the postal service.

There was another thing. Maya's phone call this evening had to mean that a new lead had been uncovered today and that she planned to inform him about it tomorrow.

"*I think that's all I had to say. Although—I just remembered, Tatsuya, are things going well with Mr. Juumonji and the young lady from the Saegusa family? I believe the Ichijou scion was supposed to be getting involved today.*"

Tatsuya wasn't sure what she meant by this sudden question. "If you're talking about the meetings, they're proceeding apace," he answered without giving the matter much thought.

"*Is that so? Well, keep your wits about you. Don't get too friendly with any of them.*"

Tatsuya regarded Maya dubiously.

Seemingly amused by his expression, Maya laughed. "*Oh, goodness, hadn't you noticed? It wasn't the Juumonji family who asked that Ms. Saegusa be included in the meetings, it was Mr. Saegusa. He's hoping you and she will go on some dates; for him, the meetings are nothing more than a pretext.*"

Tatsuya was instantly appalled that Maya would say this right in front of Miyuki, but he didn't let that show. "So there's an ulterior motive, then. I'll be on my guard," he said with a deliberately obvious frown.

"*Yes, you do that. Good night, then—to you, too, Miyuki.*"

"Thank you very much." Tatsuya bowed.

"Good night, Aunt Maya."

The call ended. Miyuki and Tatsuya stood there facing the dark display.

As Tatsuya had predicted, Miyuki was displeased.

But it was impossible to tell by only looking at her face.

Instead, a powerful feeling of discomfort assailed Tatsuya. At the same time, he got the feeling he knew what its true identity was:

Jealousy.

He took no pleasure in his sister's jealousy. He had never once wanted her to pursue him aggressively or sulk over him, though he'd never found it bothersome or annoying.

There was no need for her to contain herself and her emotions around him, Tatsuya felt. But he also thought that her doing so now was proof that she was maturing, or at least trying to.

Some might venture that the depth of someone's jealousy was equal to the depth of their love. But jealousy was not a virtue. Tatsuya's intuition told him that Miyuki's change was not a desirable one, but his common sense decided that it was a natural reaction for a young lady to have.

All that being said, Tatsuya found it impossible to plainly tell Miyuki that she could be every bit as jealous as her heart told her to be.

The next morning, February 12, saw a dusting of light snow.

Thanks to the heavy cloud cover, it was still very dark despite the approaching dawn.

Tatsuya rode down the hill at close to sixty kilometers per hour on his way home from Yakumo's temple.

Given the darkness, it ought to have been difficult to make out the faces of anybody he happened to ride past. But you didn't have to be Tatsuya to recognize *her*.

She was unmistakable, after all.

Tatsuya did not, strictly speaking, recognize her face—since she wore a newsboy cap on her head, large sunglasses over her eyes, and a muffler covering her mouth and chin.

Despite the steep angle of descent, Tatsuya came to a quick stop, halting directly in front of Yoshimi.

"Good morning, Miss Yoshimi."

Yoshimi responded to Tatsuya's greeting with a neat bow. She then produced an envelope from her coat pocket and thrust it at him.

She was Maya's messenger.

"Package received," Tatsuya said as he accepted the envelope, at which Yoshimi's head bobbed down and up in a faint nod. He couldn't even tell whether she was actually looking at him through her dark sunglasses.

After failing to ascertain her expression, Tatsuya again regarded Yoshimi. She struck him as odd. Her efforts to hide her face were so obvious that she was practically broadcasting *Look, I'm a suspicious person.*

It wasn't so odd to be wearing a muffler over one's face during the height of winter, and a newsboy cap was a plausible fashion choice. The combination of the two wasn't even that odd. The problem really was the—

"Miss Yoshimi, I think your outfit is making you stand out. Maybe you should take off those sunglasses?" Tatsuya suggested, even though he knew the advice would almost certainly be unwelcome.

Wordlessly, Yoshimi shook her head back and forth twice.

Upon returning home and taking a shower, Tatsuya opened the envelope in the living room before eating breakfast.

"Breakfast is ready," Miyuki called as she came from the dining room. She soon hit upon what the letter Tatsuya was reading had to be. "Oh, is that what Aunt Maya talked about last night…?"

"It is," he replied, standing. Having finished it, he handed the letter to Miyuki.

Miyuki took the paper hesitantly, and as her eyes followed the writing on it, they widened. When she looked back up to Tatsuya, those same eyes were filled with dismay.

The letter suggested that the National Defense Force might have been involved in Gu Jie's escape.

"No organization is totally free of corruption. The NDF is no exception. I'd like to believe that only one section is rotten, though," Tatsuya stated, taking the letter back from Miyuki and slipping it back into its envelope. "That said, it might be time to stop dwelling on the mistakes of the past. Regardless of whether or not they wish to, if they're actively hindering us, this is not the time for us to hold back."

"Tatsuya..." Miyuki murmured, looking up at her brother with a worried expression.

Tatsuya smiled and stroked her hair, then headed toward the dining room to attend to breakfast.

Class 2-A's first period was practical studies. Today's subject was the definition of a magic program's termination condition.

No magic continued forever. The effective duration was always limited. However, if the termination conditions of a magic program weren't clearly defined, it could end up continuing without any clear indication of when its effects would end.

One magic program could not interfere with another. Unless a special technique like program demolition or dispersion were used, an active piece of magic could not be undone. All you could do was overwrite it.

Overwriting one kind of magic into another required event interference strength that exceeded the currently running magic—even if all you were trying to do was restore something that had been altered by magic to its previous state. Thus, the ability to define termination conditions for a program factored heavily into the overall skill of a magician.

Magic program termination definitions fell into two broad categories. One was to define the active duration at the time of casting. This method's effectiveness had recently gained a great deal of traction thanks to developments in Taurus Silver's flight magic.

The other was to define the outcome condition of the magic

program, which would instruct the program to continue until some specified change or state was reached, at which point the program would end. This method tended to be used more often in practice.

The subject of the day's practice was specifying a program's termination condition using duration as the variable. The practice itself consisted of changing the color of a white plastic ball to red, green, and blue in turn, completing ten sets within thirty seconds. The duration and repetition count varied depending on the specific practice routine, but the average of one change per second was always the same.

If the timing wasn't specified precisely, the program would either take too long or go too fast. It was also not uncommon to see cases where, as the required interference strength rose with the need to activate one program before the previous one finished, students would be unable to complete the specified number of repetitions. There wasn't any particular requirement to keep the activation time to an average of one second, but getting to the end and having to make adjustments was considerably more difficult if you didn't.

Since today was simply a practice day, not an evaluation day, students were paired up to take turns drilling together, with the non-caster acting as timekeeper. The last time they'd trained like this, the practice room had been filled with pairs of students, one busy with the sequential casting while the other stared at an analog stopwatch summoned on their portable terminal in order to keep careful track of time.

The problem that had come up last time was that there was an odd number of students in Class 2-A. Rather than sticking three people in one of the groups, a certain student had been asked to tackle the exercise solo. And that student had been Miyuki.

The fact was that every student, boy or girl, had raised their hand in offering to be paired up with Miyuki. However, none of them had approached her before they'd paired up with somebody else—all these classmates suddenly volunteering to pair up with her already had partners. Thus, Miyuki had been left as the remainder.

Yesterday had been a classroom study and laboratory day, so the pair problem hadn't come up, but today, like the previous week, ought to have seen Class 2-A in the same awkward situation. Except today, Masaki had transferred in.

After receiving an explanation of the day's activities, Masaki immediately walked up to Miyuki. "Would you mind pairing up with me, Shiba?" he asked, counting himself fortunate that nobody else had asked her yet.

A murmur ran through the practice room. Muttered regrets and imprecations spilled from the lips of the class's boys in particular. But it was too late for that.

"Yes, with pleasure. Thank you very much, Ichijou."

Miyuki herself must have been quite tired of practicing alone—the smile she met Masaki's request with was brighter than it had to be.

Upon hearing the explanation of the drill, Masaki had thought, *Oh, that's easy*, although he avoided saying it out loud.

The junior students at Third High were currently practicing how to direct magic toward a target placed on the other side of a wall. It went without saying that this was training for learning how to hit opponents with magic attacks even when they were hidden behind cover.

Compared with the practical combat-oriented training at Third High, this drill seemed like little more than a cheap trick.

As he watched Miyuki do the drill first, that impression only deepened. She changed the ball's color exactly once per second, completing three sets of ten in thirty seconds without so much as a tenth of a second's discrepancy. Masaki found the brilliance of the color she changed the balls to even more impressive than the accuracy of her sense of timing, because it showed how strong her interference ability was.

"Thirty seconds on the dot. I'd expect no less, Shiba,"

"Thank you. Now, whenever you're ready, Ichijou."

Masaki had praised her out of politeness, but at the lovely girl's encouragement, he found himself surprisingly motivated. All notion of sandbagging left his mind, and he concentrated on the magic as though it were a combat drill.

"How would you like me to count? Shall I let you know every time ten seconds passes?" asked Miyuki

Masaki was about to reply that there was no need, but he thought better of it. "How about you count down the final ten seconds, then?" The idea of Miyuki counting down for him was strangely appealing.

"Understood," she stated.

The sound of her bright voice almost made Masaki smile in spite of himself. He hastily assumed a stern face. "On your signal," he said.

He concentrated his willpower anew on the magic. His spirit prepared for battle.

"All right, three, two, one, begin!"

As he set the completion time in his mental clock, Masaki began casting.

Red… Green… Blue.

Red… Green… Blue.

His colors were no less vivid than Miyuki's

Masaki felt a certain satisfaction at this evidence that he was just as strong as her.

Red… Green… Blue.

Red… Green… —Blue.

His rhythm started to falter, perhaps owing to the intrusion of idle thoughts.

Red—Green… Blue.

His sense of timing was functioning normally.

Red… Green—Blue.

But the sequence had unmistakably ended up shortened.

Red… —Green… —Blue.

Masaki compensated by introducing a termination condition longer than one second.

Red… Green… Blue.

Then he returned the interval to normal. He decided to use the final ten-second countdown to make any further adjustments.

Miyuki began her countdown. "Ten, nine, eight…"

His drift was now under a second.

Masaki decided to use the very last casting to sync back up with the allotted time.

"Three, two…"

Red, green…

"One."

"Blue."

The plastic ball's color returned to white.

"Done." Just a moment later, Miyuki announced the exercise was over. "Your extra time was 0.7 seconds. With that score, it's very hard to believe this was your first try, Ichijou," she said, smiling at him.

Masaki returned her smile, managing to hold back a grimace.

The pass-fail line for this drill was a drift of no more than one second, without the aid of an external count. While he'd managed the time portion well enough, that had come with Miyuki's countdown. When he thought about how Miyuki had hit the time perfectly without his help, it was impossible for him to be happy about his own result.

"Thirty seconds on the nose. Nailed it, Honoka."

Honoka giggled. "This kind of thing is my specialty."

The voice Masaki heard from somewhere nearby only made him feel worse.

After using the practice session's entire hour, Masaki finally crossed the pass-fail line.

Morning classes had ended.

It had taken Masaki all of second period to recover from the surprisingly arduous battle that he'd weathered through first period. A female student addressed him from his side.

"Hi, Ichijou."

Masaki turned in the direction of the voice. He had the excellent memory that was typical of magicians, so the name Honoka came to his mind with very little effort.

"Um, you're Mitsui, right?"

He knew her name not from the introductions the previous day, nor because he'd asked around about her, but rather because her name had lingered in his memory as the winner of the Mirage Bat event at the Nine School Competition.

"Yes, Honoka Mitsui," Honoka said, nodding with a content smile. This wasn't because she had a crush on him—it was simply because remembering names made interpersonal relationships go that much more smoothly. It was an obvious reaction to have.

Masaki filed Honoka's smile under the category of politeness—which was why her next statement took him by surprise.

"So, Ichijou, would you like to go to the dining hall with us?"

"Who, me?"

"That's right. With us." Honoka looked back over her shoulder. Behind her stood Shizuku and Miyuki.

When Shizuku met Masaki's eyes, she nodded, her expression unchanging. No—the ambiguous gesture might have been a bow.

Miyuki flashed an impenetrable smile; it was impossible to tell what she was thinking. He had no idea whether he was actually being welcomed or whether his presence would be bothersome.

"…You really won't mind if I accompany you?" Masaki asked, suddenly polite despite himself.

Miyuki correctly noticed that Masaki was primarily addressing her, and her expression softened, albeit somewhat ruefully. Her polite smile became a genuine one. "Yes, by all means," she answered.

"In that case—I'd be happy to!" Masaki rose to his feet energetically.

When they all arrived in the dining hall a bit late, it was Erika who raised her voice. "Huh?"

She had been the one who'd acted surprised at Masaki's actions the previous day, saying *I was sure he'd just stick to Miyuki*. But now that he was doing what she'd expected he would do all along, she seemed to find it puzzling.

The reaction wasn't limited to Erika, either—Leo and Mikihiko also regarded Masaki dubiously.

"Er, Tatsuya, is it all right if Ichijou sits with us?" Miyuki asked.

"Of course." Tatsuya shrugged, unconcerned.

If anything, it was Masaki who was the most flustered.

As he stood here unmoving, Tatsuya spoke to him in a brusque—although not unfamiliar—tone. "You know how to order, right, Ichijou? The dining hall and purchase system here should work the same way you're used to."

"Er, yeah. No problem."

"Let's go, Ichijou," Miyuki said, and at her invitation, they headed toward the ordering console. Honoka and Shizuku watched them go.

Miyuki returned with her lunch and sat next to Tatsuya.

Masaki sat directly across from her.

Honoka sat next to Masaki, across from Tatsuya.

That was where Erika normally sat, so she moved to sit next to Miyuki. After she deliberately made her way around to the other side of the table, she looked at Masaki, who sat diagonally across from her, and suddenly addressed him.

"So, Ichijou, how's the investigation going?"

Ichijou almost choked on the soup he'd just started drinking. He'd met Erika before, in Kyoto, so it wasn't her overfamiliar attitude that surprised him. Rather, it was her broaching his mission—which fell in a legal gray area—out in the open here, where there was no telling who might overhear.

To Masaki's surprise, as he was struggling to come up with a response, it was Tatsuya who came to his rescue. "Erika, he just arrived in Tokyo. No matter how outstandingly talented a magician he is, he's not going to come to the table with hard results after a single day."

"Yeah, I guess not."

"That's right, Erika. You shouldn't put people on the spot like that," chided Miyuki, then turned to Masaki and bowed. "I'm sorry about that, Ichijou."

"Ah, er, no, you don't need to apologize…"

Miyuki gave the now deeply flustered Masaki an open, genuine smile. She seemed to find his innocent honesty rather refreshing. "In any case, Ichijou, I must say I'm rather envious of you."

"Huh? Um, why?" Masaki's composure eroded more and more under Miyuki's bright smile.

"My brother just called you an 'outstandingly talented magician.' He's surprisingly hard to impress, you know." There was something aggressive in Miyuki's eyes as she smiled. No—not so much aggressive as jealous.

Her comment was clearly meant as a joke, but it made the last vestiges of Masaki's composure crumble, and he was no longer able to think of anything. His misgivings about the way Miyuki talked about her brother, too, went flying off into oblivion.

Tatsuya spoke up. "That's not true," he said. Whether he said it to pull Miyuki's gaze away from Masaki or to scold her for teasing him so obviously, in any case it was clear that he was trying to throw him a rope.

But his attempt was cut off by Honoka. "So, Tatsuya, you really *do* think Ichijou is just that good, don't you?" she said, as though covering for Miyuki. "That makes it like a manly rivalry kinda thing, right?"

Tatsuya couldn't just defer to Miyuki when Honoka addressed him so directly. No sooner had he looked to Miyuki next to him than he returned his gaze to the person sitting opposite him. "You say 'rivals,' but Ichijou's magic strength is far above mine."

"But aren't the drills we did today the kind of thing you specialize in?"

Tatsuya acknowledged Honoka's statement without excessive modesty. "I suppose, but only because the exercise is more about accuracy than speed or strength."

Masaki wasn't particularly relieved to hear this, but then Mizuki interjected. "Tatsuya perfectly nailed the one-second pace right from the start," she said proudly, almost as though she were boasting about herself.

"Is that true?! Tatsuya, that's amazing!"

Masaki glumly took the damage that hearing Mizuki and Honoka's chatter inflicted. Sitting across from him, Miyuki attempted to comfort him instead of leaving him to fend for himself. "I mean, I can usually finish more or less on time, but I always drift a little slow or fast in the middle."

But Honoka was sitting next to Masaki, which put her closer to him that Miyuki was. She didn't even glance in his direction. "So, Tatsuya, do you have any tips for the rest of us?" she asked, taking advantage of Miyuki being occupied with Masaki and attempting to draw his attention to her.

From Honoka's perspective, it was all proceeding just as she'd planned.

Honoka had been the one who'd invited Masaki to their table. She'd pushed Masaki at Miyuki and was using the opening to get closer to Tatsuya.

It would have been all too unfair to Honoka to call this sinister.

"The rules of fair play do not apply in love and war"—the famous saying appeared in a tragicomedy written by a seventeenth-century English playwright. Of course, in the modern era, there were multinational agreements that outlawed certain methods of warfare, so these words weren't quite unconditionally true.

Likewise, it couldn't really be claimed that *anything* was allowed in romance. For example, coercive methods like breaking up with one's lover and saying *I'm pregnant with your child* would be criticized as a fraudulent, morally unacceptable act.

But Honoka's actions were nothing so deceptive and were well within bounds for anyone pursuing a romantic interest. It probably wasn't the kind of thing you'd normally do to your friend, but that was just proof of how serious Honoka's feelings really were.

Tatsuya left Miyuki at school and returned home, then climbed on his trusty motorcycle and headed to Tsuchiura. His destination, it went without saying, was the base of the National Defense Force 101ˢᵗ Brigade, the headquarters of the Independent Magic Battalion.

Tatsuya was casually dressed in pleather and a generously cut jacket, but at the base's gate, his ID card spoke louder than his outfit. All he had to do was remove his helmet and he was let into the base without incident.

He parked his bike in front of battalion headquarters and looked up at the building, which had three floors aboveground and three floors below. It was a heavy gaze, weighed down by the negotiation he was about to undertake.

Nevertheless, the issue could not be left unaddressed. The Ten Master Clans' pursuit of Gu Jie, the mastermind of the Hakone terrorist attack, was in part a public-facing pose meant to assuage rising anti-magician sentiment.

Having seen Gu Jie's methods in person, Tatsuya was resolved to deal with this ancient magician from the continent as quickly as possible. Not because Maya had ordered him to but on his own conviction.

Gu's use of humans as literal tools was in direct opposition to Tatsuya's desire to offer magicians a life outside of being living weapons for the military.

They were mortal enemies. For Tatsuya to bring about the future he envisioned, he could not allow the man to live.

Gu had to die. To accomplish this, it would be impossible to avoid killing some of the people he'd made into his tools.

Tatsuya shook his head lightly and composed himself, then entered the building and registered his arrival—although he'd already called ahead to confirm Kazama's availability. He would've preferred to avoid such a thing, but he knew he couldn't very well show up unannounced.

Five minutes remained until the agreed-upon time, but Tatsuya was waved in anyway. He didn't pass anyone on the way to the commander's office; they seemed to be as understaffed as ever.

"Specialist Ooguro here, sir," said Tatsuya as he faced the office and knocked at the door. The person inside wasn't actually hearing his voice through the door; instead, there was a microphone in the door that filtered incoming voices before relaying them to the interior.

"Come." This voice, too, was reproduced by a speaker in the door. Advancements in technology had allowed things like this to be largely invisible to their users.

After hearing the locks disengage, Tatsuya opened the door.

Kazama sat behind a desk; today he was alone. A touchscreen terminal occupied much of the desk's surface. Apparently, he'd had been reviewing plans and reports until Tatsuya's arrival. Undoubtedly, his promotion had resulted in an increase in approval duties.

Tatsuya approached the desk and saluted.

Kazama stood and returned the salute but then immediately sat back down. Tatsuya continued to stand since he hadn't been invited to take a seat.

"At ease, Specialist. So what're you in such a rush about today?" Kazama wasn't angry. His voice was pleasant as he asked the question.

"Given the risk of having our communication intercepted, I thought I should come speak with you personally."

"Huh… Are you saying there's a chance the battalion's encryption has been compromised?"

Tatsuya played one of his opening cards. "Affirmative, sir. I've been warned that there's a high probability that the Yotsuba family's encryption has been broken."

Kazama's eyebrows rose fractionally. "I would imagine that our encryption is stronger than the Yotsuba's."

"I believe so as well, sir. But I decided caution was warranted."

Tatsuya didn't explain why, but Kazama did not demand elaboration. "…I see. Well, Specialist, let's hear what you've got to say."

"There is a possibility that the special forces training camp at Zama base has been compromised by hostile foreign agents."

*Special forces* was a euphemism for the soldiers at said special forces training camp who'd been subjected to enhancement that included procedures to strengthen their magic ability. It was called a training camp, but in reality, it was one of the military's facilities for the confinement of the subjects of human experimentation. When it came to subjects like this, the military had a large vocabulary of terms it used to justify their imprisonment.

That information alone, if leaked, would be enough to force the minister of defense to resign, but there was something even more problematic about the special forces training facility at Zama: It was the site of joint research with the USNA.

While it had occurred during the high international tensions that led up to the Global War Outbreak, the fact that Japanese citizens had been provided as test subjects for foreign experimentation was a shameful betrayal of the highest order.

This was the terrible legacy the military inherited from before the war, and it was one that could never be allowed to come to light. And Tatsuya was saying that this facility, which ought to have been managed with the utmost diligence, had been at least partially compromised by hostile foreign elements.

"…What happened?" asked Kazama. He didn't say *What?* or *Are you serious?* nor did he ask Tatsuya what his basis for the statement was.

What he wanted to know was what Tatsuya had encountered that led to this revelation.

"Early this past Saturday, while in pursuit of the culprit behind the Hakone attack, I engaged magicians who specialized in combustion magic. They were enhanced soldiers who were supposed to be stationed at Zama."

The special forces training facility at Zama base housed enhanced magicians whose psychic-like combustion and explosion abilities made them particularly useful for combat. Yoshimi's analysis of the three magicians who'd been turned into Generators that Tatsuya had dispatched at Kamakura early Saturday morning revealed that they were from the Zama training facility.

"Are you telling me that the terrorists' reach extends to Zama base?"

"Affirmative, sir."

Kazama murmured ominously as he folded his arms and scowled. It had been a bad enough scandal when Gongjin Zhou had hidden away at the Uji base, but the geopolitical significance of Zama made this situation even more serious.

This was a stone's throw from Tokyo, the nation's capital. It involved a facility that existed solely to keep the truth about human experimentation from the world, a comfortable cage for combatants whose destructive ability rivaled heavy weaponry.

The escape of experimental subjects alone would have already constituted a major problem. If the fact that those subjects had become pawns of an anti-Japanese terrorist was to become public, the buck would not stop with the National Defense Force.

"Who knows about this?" Kazama asked, his eyes closed.

"This has all been kept within the Yotsuba family."

In other words, the information hadn't leaked to the rest of the Ten Master Clans. Tatsuya thought he saw Kazama's expression soften slightly. But his brows were still deeply furrowed and his arms still folded. "Do you plan to strike Zama base, Specialist?"

"No, Colonel." Tatsuya's tone shifted subtly. "I don't believe that Gu Jie is hiding at Zama base the way Gongjin Zhou took refuge at Uji base."

"So our puppet master's name is Gu Jie, eh?" muttered Kazama, as though trying to burn the name into his memory, then uncrossed his arms and looked up at Tatsuya. "But you said experimental subjects from Zama base ended up as this Gu person's pawns?"

"There is no doubt about it. However, the fact that he used magicians from the special forces training facility as Generators doesn't mean that we can immediately conclude that he's infiltrated the base."

"Meaning you suspect that Gu had a collaborator inside the base who let them out, then?"

"Affirmative, sir."

"Hmm... I suppose that is more plausible than an unknown foreigner being allowed to enter the base. But how?"

"I expect he turned one of the base staff into a puppet. He probably has techniques that can rob someone of their free will without resorting to the drastic move of turning them into a Generator."

Kazama placed his elbows on his desk and folded his hands together, sinking wordlessly into thought. "...Do we know the identities of the subjects who were turned into Generators?"

"Here, sir."

Tatsuya offered Kazama an unsealed envelope. From within it, Kazama produced three folded sheets of paper, on each of which was printed the photograph and physical attributes of one of the Generators.

"Once we inform Zama base of this, they'll probably identify the puppet within a day or two. But, Specialist, I get the sense that you're not here to ask me for cooperation with your investigation."

Still sitting, Kazama looked Tatsuya in the eye. It wasn't overstatement to call the piercing gaze a glare.

Tatsuya played his second card.

"The truth is that we already know where Gu Jie is hiding. But it happens to be just next door to Zama base."

"...So you're worried about combat erupting on the base when you go after him?"

Tatsuya answered Kazama's low, heavy question quickly and affirmatively. "There's a significant chance of that. The enhanced soldiers kept there, including the ones at the special forces training facility, undoubtedly harbor considerable hostility toward the Ten Master Clans, so if any of them were incited to attack, they would enter the confrontation with the resolve to be killed."

Kazama could not refute Tatsuya's prediction. The facility had been built with the express purpose of confining the subjects of forced experimentation. Given the circumstances, they would not let their charges go easily. But there were in fact escape incidents every year, and the Ten Master Clans assisted with the *cleanup* that inevitably followed.

It sounded inhumane, but from the military's perspective, disposal of escapees was both cheaper and safer than continuing to detain them. For as long as the experimental subjects lived, considerable effort had to be expended to keep them a secret. Likewise, if they died, they left no evidence behind. With the power of the state available, it wasn't difficult to bury the truth. At the very least, it didn't incur the cost of allowing them to continue to live.

If clandestine combat broke out near Zama base and the base command learned that the Yotsuba family was involved, it was entirely possible that the facility overseers would deliberately release the experimental subjects in order to foist the task of their disposal off on the Yotsubas.

"You'll need the general's assistance if you want a guarantee to not interfere from Zama base."

"In that case, there won't be time. Gu Jie will escape."

"…You really want to settle this, Specialist?"

"I plan to do everything I possibly can to avoid combat with our military. But if inadvertent combat is unavoidable, I will erase all traces of evidence."

Tatsuya was saying that he would use the classified Mist Dispersion technique against friendly forces.

"It'll be unavoidable." Kazama's smile was bitter, but there was no hesitation in his voice as he authorized use of Mist Dispersion.

Tatsuya took care of various errands on his way from Tsuchiura base to the Zama base area, and by the time he arrived at his destination, it was 8:00 PM.

He had told neither Katsuto nor Mayumi that he was coming here, and obviously not Masaki. He'd settled on only Yotsuba family personnel to accompany him.

The other members of the operation seemed to have already arrived. Tatsuya left his bike in the park's parking lot and approached an unmarked van that was waiting in the same lot.

Once he was close enough that he could address them in a relatively quiet voice, Tatsuya greeted his second cousins next to the van, who, like him, were keeping a low profile. "Fumiya, Ayako, I'm glad you could make it on a weekend."

"Tatsuya!" Fumiya, like Tatsuya, kept his voice low, but he couldn't hide the shock in it. "I didn't notice you at all. You're getting better and better at staying stealthy."

"Good evening, Tatsuya. I understand that it's unavoidable given the circumstances, but I don't appreciate having things sprung on me, so in the future please be more careful," quipped Ayako nastily, in sharp contrast to Fumiya's delighted compliment. Ever since the announcement of Miyuki and Tatsuya's engagement, her attitude toward Tatsuya had changed slightly.

She was less reserved when she interacted with him now, and if anything, the distance between them felt smaller than ever. But that was the proof that Ayako was doing her best to accept reality.

"You nearly made poor Yoshimi pass out from shock."

Next to Ayako was Yoshimi, wearing her usual identity-obscuring outfit. She shook her head rapidly.

"You don't have to put on a brave face, Yoshimi. For such a sensible person, Tatsuya is obliviousness incarnate, so you're honestly doing him a favor to tell him these things." Ayako's barbed comment here was less due to her being less reserved around Tatsuya and more that she was letting her guard down to Yoshimi.

"It's fine. This isn't enough to bother me."

"Huh…? I don't know—you seemed pretty alarmed."

"No, I wasn't. I'm an adult." Yoshimi was more talkative with Ayako, maybe because she didn't feel a need to be as cautious with her cousins.

Tatsuya was Yoshimi and Ayako's second cousin on their fathers' side.

Yoshimi was Ayako's mother's older brother's daughter. In other words, a maternal cousin.

Her full name was Yoshimi Shinonome. She was twenty-one years old, but she wasn't attending college. For high school, in order to keep her time free, she had studied via correspondence instead of attending magic high school in person, and even then, her investigation duties took priority.

In that sense, she ought to have been considered Ayako's senior and an older sister figure, but between the two of them, Ayako seemed to hold the reins. This wasn't because she was the eldest daughter of the Kuroba family but rather a simple matter of personalities. Or at least that's what Tatsuya thought, looking at them from the outside.

"Tatsuya, would you change clothes in the van?" Fumiya asked, ignoring his sister and cousin clowning around. They'd brought close-quarters combat gear in the van.

Meanwhile, Fumiya was wearing his usual combat disguise. His makeup was heavier than before—maybe he was leaning into the sexiness of it.

"I'll do that," said Tatsuya, and without commenting on Fumiya's pretty-girl costume, he climbed into the van.

\* \* \*

The combat suit the Yotsuba family had provided looked quite similar to what Tatsuya had arrived wearing, with the obvious difference being that the liner of the jacket was a full jumpsuit. But in terms of its performance, it approached the level of the Independent Magic Battalion's MOVAL suits.

Today Tatsuya was armed not with the gun-style Silverhorn but rather Silver Torus, a set of thought-actuated bracelets. Concealed under his jacket he carried a sidearm and combat knife rather than a CAD. If they were caught by the police, they wouldn't get off with a simple questioning. This was another reason why they were taking the trouble to change clothes here.

Tatsuya flipped up the face guard of his gas mask–equipped helmet and addressed Fumiya, who was gazing at the dashing figure Tatsuya now cut, and Ayako, whose minidress was densely dotted with decorative buttons (each of which was either a flash-bang or a gas capsule). "Let's go."

Fumiya, who was already looking at Tatsuya, quickly nodded.

At some point, Ayako had started an argument with Yoshimi over which of them was dressed the least appropriately for the mission, but she then turned to Tatsuya and bowed faintly.

Tatsuya began walking.

Behind him followed Fumiya and Ayako—and a number of black-suited agents.

Suddenly surrounded herself by several shadowy figures, Yoshimi watched the three of them go.

"Looks like security's extremely tight," said Ayako in a worried tone as she looked through a pair of sensor-equipped binoculars that were sensitive to electromagnetic radiation down to the infrared level.

Tatsuya, Ayako, and Fumiya were observing their target building from within an invisibility field Ayako had set up. This was Gu

Jie's new safe house, the location of which Yoshimi had read from the corpse of one of the dead Generators. Superficially, it appeared to be a three-story private hospital, but in reality it was a secret research facility that performed illegal procedures at the military's behest. They'd expected a tight perimeter.

"It won't be too difficult to infiltrate the building, but with this level of security, I can't imagine they haven't prepared for that possibility," Ayako murmured.

"You're thinking this is an ambush, aren't you?"

"Yes."

Tatsuya confirmed the security situation with his own magical vision. Given its use as a facility that performed procedures for the military, it had to be fully prepared for mental intrusion.

The hospital's owner had probably already had his mind rewritten. He might already be dead.

Surely, Tatsuya wasn't the only one who had come to that deduction, and with all that in mind, he continued examining the interior and exterior of the building.

The security equipment in place was undoubtedly high-grade, but it wasn't anything beyond what was commercially available. It wasn't quite as sophisticated as the sensor net deployed for the Cross-Country Steeplechase course during the Nine School Competition, for instance.

He could sense nine people within the building.

There were five humans with normal structural information. He surmised that those were the on-duty doctors and nurses.

There was one person whose cranial region's structural information was corrupted by noise. That was probably the puppeted hospital chief.

There were two people with structural information distorted in a way he recognized. Definitely Generators.

And then one person with very strange structural information: It was much closer to what a baseline human would have than the Generators, but the age data was decidedly weird.

People who looked physically younger than they actually were still had a singular source of age data, which would record their actual age. Meanwhile, the factors that made someone look physically younger or older were recorded as health data.

But in the eidos Tatsuya was currently observing, there were two separate instances of the data that showed physical age.

*I feel like I've seen something like this before...but where and when?* Tatsuya dug through the troves of data in his mind to produce the memory. *That's right... It was Gongjin Zhou.*

He'd had to concentrate to discern the location information that the Qimen Dunjia technique had falsified, so he hadn't noticed the abnormal structural information at the time. But he'd never forgotten the strange unease he'd felt then.

"Found him. That's probably Gu Jie himself," Tatsuya whispered to Fumiya and Ayako.

They immediately tensed.

"Let's get a move on."

The three pushed toward the front of the hospital. Thanks to the obfuscation magic provided by the supporting agents, they encountered no one along their route. When the military's intervention materialized, they might be seen, but they probably wouldn't be spotted by residents of the neighborhood, at least.

"Tatsuya."

He nodded at Ayako's voice, then pressed a button on a transmitter he held.

The lights illuminating the hospital gate went dark. Another group of operatives had cut the power lines leading to the building. Underground cables could naturally be cut without excavation if magic was an option.

Of course, even a private hospital was still a hospital. The assumption was that it would have backup generators on-site.

After confirming the security systems had been cut, Tatsuya gave Ayako a hand signal.

Ayako's Pseudo-Teleportation magic jumped all three of them to the hospital roof.

The lights still hadn't come back on.

"Let's move just like we planned."

Per the plan, Ayako would secure their exfiltration here. Fumiya would guard her.

Tatsuya would proceed alone to secure Gu Jie.

Fumiya and Ayako had both strongly objected to this plan of action, but neither of them were so foolish as to dispute it now, while it was being carried out.

"Take care of yourself," said the cousins, who together looked like a beautiful set of sisters.

The lights came back on almost exactly as Tatsuya entered the building from the roof.

He remained calm. The timing of the power's restoration more or less matched what they had estimated during planning, and it didn't even really qualify as a close shave.

However, he couldn't afford to waste time, either. Possibly alerted to their movements because of the power outage, the eidos Tatsuya identified as Gu Jie had moved from a hospital room on the third floor and was heading down an emergency staircase.

It was convenient that he'd left a room and entered the stairs—this lowered the risk of the on-duty staff getting involved.

Tatsuya sprinted toward the emergency exit, coming to a sudden stop just before the last room of the hallway.

A hail of bullets came through the door, peppering the opposite wall.

Tatsuya shifted his vision from the emergency staircase to the room he was next to, focusing on the ambushers' guns.

He dismantled the weapons and rendered a combustion magic program inert using Program Dispersion.

Another Generator approaching him from behind brandished a gun, which Tatsuya disassembled into parts.

The room door slammed open, and the enhanced magician-turned-Generator charged at him.

The magician who'd provided the material for this Generator had more than just his magic strength enhanced at the military research facility. He drew a knife and slashed at Tatsuya with speed and strength far beyond that of an ordinary human.

But not only were Tatsuya's magic skills a product of old Lab Four, he'd also undergone intensive training as a close-quarters combat magician. If anything, his training had emphasized physical proficiency over magical strength, and he'd been thoroughly drilled in the specifics of controlling the movement of opponents using something much more primitive than psions—brute strength.

He hadn't been biochemically enhanced, but by reinforcing the structural information of his own body, Tatsuya had made it virtually impossible to be injured even when bearing loads that exceeded the theoretical limit of his spinal column.

Facing Tatsuya, the Generator loosed combustion magic at him. The fact that he didn't use a CAD was proof that he'd been forcibly reverted into a psychic.

Again, Tatsuya nullified the magic using Program Dispersion. Simultaneously, he drew his own knife from within his jacket and intercepted the Generator's blade.

They clashed for an instant.

Tatsuya relaxed in an attempt to parry his opponent's knife just as the Generator pulled back.

Tatsuya's attempt to collapse his opponent's stance ended without success. But in exchange, he'd opened up enough space between them to put himself out of knife range.

Tatsuya turned his back on the attacker in front of him.

As though looking over his shoulder, he threw his knife at the Generator approaching from behind.

Taken off guard, the other attacker stopped and swatted the knife aside with his own blade.

For an instant, his eyes flicked away from Tatsuya.

By the time his gaze returned to Tatsuya—

—he was staring down the barrel of Tatsuya's gun.

Fitted with a suppressor, the sidearm's report was muted.

The Generator had been expecting Tatsuya to use magic, but instead he'd taken a bullet at close range.

The low-velocity, high-caliber bullet slammed into the Generator—who was about Tatsuya's size and build. He fell backward, but there was no blood visible, which was proof that he was wearing considerable body armor.

Tatsuya turned around again.

He caught a horizontal knife slash coming at him from the left by grabbing his assailant by the wrist. His magic-calculation region quickly dismantled the Ignition and Combustion programs the Generator was about to unleash.

The Generator's casting speed was more than a match for a psychic. In sacrificing flexibility, his enhancements let him regain such speed at warping phenomena that he could activate it with a mere word. And after having been made into a Generator, the mental resources that had formerly been used for self-awareness were overwritten and redirected, accelerating those abilities further.

But even then, Tatsuya's dismantling was faster. As fast as the Generator's ability could execute magic, Tatsuya could dismantle that magic faster.

Tatsuya twisted the right arm of the knife-wielding Generator, collapsing his body. Then he fired his gun.

Even without the ability to feel pain, the degradation of the Generator's physical condition became noise that interfered with his ability to activate magic.

The other Generator that Tatsuya had knocked down had gotten back onto his feet, but his casting speed was still considerably impaired.

Having cleared away all his enemy's magic, Tatsuya's magic-calculation region was now free to conduct a counterattack.

He activated Partial Dismantle.

Holes opened up in both of his opponents' chests.

Even without their hearts, the Generators feebly tried to continue fighting, but their futile death throes soon ended.

After confirming their total lack of psionic activity, Tatsuya continued to the emergency stairs.

The eidos he identified as Gu Jie had already reached the first floor.

Tatsuya jumped from the stairs.

Using slight inertial control, he eliminated the injury that would've resulted and fixed his sights on the ambulance that Gu Jie was trying to get into.

Why did a hospital that didn't take urgent patients have an ambulance? And why did that ambulance have bulletproof, heat-resistant armor?

Tatsuya set aside such questions for the time being.

The psionic noise that emanated from the ambulance to jam his casting was also an obstacle he wasn't concerned about.

The several high-powered rifle rounds that were fired in rapid succession at him out of nowhere, though, *were* an obstacle he couldn't ignore.

That day, a large USNA military VTOL transport was scheduled for a flight to Zama base. Zama had been designated as a joint USNA-Japan base, so while it was fairly uncommon for American aircraft to land there, it also wasn't particularly surprising. Thanks to their historical understanding, the USNA knew about the existence of a special forces training facility that needed to be kept a secret. Their aircraft could not be denied landing privileges without a good reason.

After the transport hit the tarmac, the base commander received a request for a meeting from the transport captain. This was not particularly unusual, either. It saved the commander the trouble of asking what the reason for the visit was.

The transport captain introduced himself as Major Benjamin Lowes. The base commander got the impression of a formidable officer, clean-cut and intelligent—a man who extended his courtesy not just because he was addressing a fellow service member of an allied nation but as a matter of personal character.

But that didn't mean the base commander let his guard down. He knew the man he was addressing was a high-level magician the moment he walked into the building.

As a facility built to keep enhanced magicians under confinement, it was equipped with instruments that measured magical ability. Those instruments' readings had been skillfully garbled, which paradoxically proved that Major Lowes was a magician of considerable ability.

Once they'd finished exchanging diplomatic pleasantries, Major Lowes made an astonishing statement. "I'm extremely embarrassed to say that I've come to take a deserter into custody."

"A deserter?" said the astonished base commander, only narrowly avoiding adding *Again?* He was one of the few officers in the National Defense Force who knew that the previous year's vampire incidents had been caused by a deserter from the American military. This, too, was thanks to his position of responsibility over the special forces training facility.

"You may already know this, Commander, but in December of last year, some of our soldiers escaped and became fugitives here in Japan. We've confirmed that most of them are now deceased but haven't accounted for all of them yet."

Major Lowes—Benjamin Canopus, the commander of the first Stars unit—lied, having guessed exactly what the base commander was thinking. And because the commander had incomplete knowledge, he didn't question the lie.

"We don't know what his goal is, but we've discovered that one of the deserters who's continued to elude us is planning to abduct a doctor attached to this base who's responsible for medical treatment of your magicians. He'll be attacking tonight."

"...Thank you for sharing this intelligence, Major."

"I presume you already know what I'm going to ask, Commander."

The commander expected that this favor was for the base security detail to deal with this attack themselves. It was happening right at their own base, and the target was a civilian who was working for them so would be the obvious course of action.

But Canopus was one step ahead of him and preempted that guess. "We've heard that your Ten Master Clans have also been tracking our deserters. It would be an undesirable outcome for both Japan and the USNA if the magicians on standby at this base were to be disturbed."

His teeth bitterly clenched, the base commander held back the words that instinctually rose up in his throat.

"What I am asking for is your discretion, Commander. Would you be willing to overlook the actions of my unit as we deal with this threat?"

"...That oversteps my authority. I'll need permission from central command."

"Commander, this is a matter of urgency. The deserter plans to strike within a few hours. If you're unable to let us handle it, then I'm also willing to cooperate with your forces in order to thwart the attack." Here Canopus played his card: "Perhaps you could lend us some of the troops stationed here at the training facility. I think numbers twenty-four, twenty-six, twenty-nine, thirty-seven, and forty-one would be suitable."

These were the administrative numbers of the enhanced magicians that Gu Jie had "stolen."

"...Very well, we'll cooperate with you. But I expect a full debriefing!" spat the base commander.

Canopus met this demand with a pleasant expression and a salute.

This conversation took place three hours before Tatsuya and his unit commenced their operation.

◇ ◇ ◇

Tatsuya instinctively ducked, but it wasn't enough for a perfect dodge. The first bullet tore into his left arm, and while he dropped into a roll, he dismantled the second shot. By the time his body touched the ground during his evasive roll, the wound in his left shoulder was already gone thanks to his regeneration.

Unexpectedly, the sniper descended to the ground, situating himself between Tatsuya and Gu Jie's position—although given the speed of his descent, *fall* might have been a better term to describe it.

There was no shadow from a chopper or other aircraft. It was like he'd been shot here from a cannon.

As Tatsuya read the sniper's physical information using Elemental Sight, he couldn't suppress his shock. *What is the American military doing here?!*

Zama was a joint Japanese-American base. The fact that American troops were present wasn't in and of itself strange.

But why were American troops trying to aid Gu Jie's escape?

Even as he processed this new development, Tatsuya's training as a combat magician almost automatically kept his mind focused on the neutralization of his opponent.

He dismantled the high-powered rifle into its basic components and forcibly stripped the sniper of his equipment, body armor included.

If it had been a Japanese soldier, Tatsuya would've deleted him, destroying all evidence and leaving no body behind.

But this American soldier was completely outside his expectations, and he couldn't decide how to deal with him.

*Deleting him—bad idea*, Tatsuya concluded upon neutralizing him. He was engaged in a clandestine mission himself, after all. If he gave the American military a pretext to object that their soldier had been captured, it would only be added trouble.

The sniper was standing there stunned, not comprehending how or why his gear had come undone. Tatsuya fired several rounds into him, then vaporized the body armor, reconstituted the sniper rifle using regeneration, and left it there. This would disguise the corpse, making it impossible to tell what sort of magic Tatsuya had used on it.

He then resumed his search for his target. The ambulance carrying Gu Jie had already sped away.

Tatsuya expanded his sensory field and searched for Gu Jie's location.

However, he was unable to find the man. He'd noticed a much higher-priority situation developing, and it was one he couldn't ignore.

Fumiya and Ayako were fighting for their lives.

Tatsuya sprinted back inside the building.

Fumiya had taken immediate action against the soldier who descended onto the roof.

He'd used Direct Pain, a magic technique that directly stimulated the nervous system's pain response, to rob the soldier of strength in both his hands, causing him to drop his sniper rifle. However, this wouldn't help him and his sister against the grenade that came arcing in behind them.

Ayako quickly threw up an anti-material barrier to deal with any shrapnel that the explosion might send their way. But the grenade didn't have an explosive anti-personnel charge; it was a smoke bomb.

The rapidly expanding cloud of smoke made the already poor visibility worse.

Fumiya could aim his magic without relying on physical sight, but he wasn't as good at it as Tatsuya. His Direct Pain technique acted on the consciousness of the target. One would think that the inability to see the target would therefore have little bearing on its effectiveness.

But in reality, it was the opposite. Consciousness itself did not have a physical presence in the world. It did not have a location that could be searched for. As such, to aim the magic, you needed some kind of a physical marker that was connected to the consciousness that was the target.

Within the smoke, Fumiya and Ayako found themselves enveloped in a soundless noise, a vibration like shattering glass.

"Cast Jamming?" Fumiya asked.

"No," Ayako replied. "It's not. But what…?" She didn't seem at all comforted by the fact that it wasn't Cast Jamming, her face tense as she looked around for the source of the noise.

Meanwhile, Fumiya concluded that as long as the psionic noise wasn't interfering with their magic, they could afford not to locate its source right away. The immediate priority was pushing back the unknown enemy attacking them.

With his left hand, Fumiya activated his CAD, attempting to call up a movement program that would circulate the air and blow the smoke away. However, the CAD didn't work correctly. The resulting program was corrupted and unusable.

The CAD he'd just tried to use, a portable terminal-type multipurpose unit, was just as familiar to him as his specialized knuckle-duster CAD. There was no way a magician of Fumiya's level would make a mistake in using it.

A series of high-powered rounds pierced the smoke and impacted the anti-material barrier.

"Yami, pour more psions into your CAD!" shouted Ayako as she turned toward Fumiya, using her own CAD to strengthen the barrier by pumping more psionic energy into it.

Fumiya tried using his CAD again, this time doing as Ayako said and using about twice the usual amount of psions.

As long as the activation program was the same, the signal strength that came back from the CAD was roughly proportional to the amount of psions injected. The resulting activation program was noisy, but Fumiya was skilled enough to filter the noise and forcibly activate an airflow program.

The smoke cleared.

The number of enemies had increased to five. Three carried sniper rifles, and two—including the one affected by Fumiya's attack, whose arms were shaking uncontrollably—pointed flashlight-like devices with flared trumpetlike ends at Fumiya and Ayako.

Fumiya and Ayako both immediately intuited that those horn-shaped devices were responsible for scrambling their CADs.

They were Cast Jammers, CAD interference mechanisms—a breakthrough by the USNA that put them ahead of the rest of the world. The two of them hadn't known of the existence of such a device, but they cleverly deduced what it had to be from the adverse effect it had on their CADs.

"Sis, you should get clear," Fumiya told Ayako. "I'll contact you, so come get me when I do!"

"—All right!" Ayako was about to object, but she quickly thought better of it and nodded. She was well aware that her strengths didn't lie in direct combat.

But the decision came too late.

Fumiya suddenly turned to face the enemy. He leaped, his long skirt fluttering as he loosed a kick.

The soldier attempting to attack Ayako from behind her in midair went flying.

But Fumiya didn't come away entirely unscathed.

"Yami, are you hurt?!"

His thick tights were split, and blood dripped from his leg. The soldier he'd kicked had managed to slash him with a knife.

The material of Fumiya's outfit wasn't ordinary fabric. Even if it wasn't as robust as the bullet- and blade-resistant armor of Tatsuya's combat suit, it still offered a high degree of protection. The knives the American soldiers were carrying couldn't have been made with ordinary metals.

"I'm okay!" said Fumiya, reassuring Ayako as he landed on one foot. But the fact that he was careful not to land on his injured leg made it clear that the wound was anything but minor. And with their hands full handling the next wave that came down from above, there wasn't going to be a chance to heal the wound.

Ayako snapped a decorative button off her outfit and tossed it behind Fumiya.

There was a blinding flash of light, and the enemies advancing on Fumiya were stopped in their tracks for a moment.

They then crumpled to the ground at Fumiya's magic.

Meanwhile, a hail of bullets rained down on the two.

Ayako had no opportunity to maneuver away from their position, either. She had to keep the shield up in order to protect Fumiya from the high-powered rifle rounds.

If it hadn't had been for the Cast Jammer interference, it would have been simple for her to use Pseudo-Teleportation to escape in the gap between bursts of rifle fire. Fumiya was in a similar situation—normally, he would have been able to drop this number of targets simultaneously, but as it was, he was reduced to using Direct Pain on one individual soldier at a time. Neither of them had room to wonder how or why their enemies seemed to keep appearing, one after the other.

The enemy was deliberately sending reinforcements only to replace their losses.

If they'd thrown the same number of troops at the pair simultaneously, the battle would have been much harder.

But neither Fumiya nor Ayako noticed this.

The enhanced soldiers weren't even magicians, and Fumiya was struggling against them. Ayako couldn't make her escape because she had to keep the barrier against the rifle fire up. Before she could even think about doing anything else, someone would have to deal with those rifles.

Just as Fumiya was about to make a foolhardy gamble to break this deadlock, the situation changed.

He heard two shots.

The noise interfering with his CAD suddenly vanished.

"Tatsuya!" Ayako shouted despite herself.

There in the doorway to the roof exit stood Tatsuya, his face

hidden by his helmet. His gun was pointed at the soldiers who'd been operating the Cast Jammers.

Tatsuya took an interior route to the roof to avoid exposing himself to sniper fire, but he also took the opportunity to release knockout gas throughout the first and second floors. He'd given up on the possibility of fully concealing the commotion of the operation, but he still needed to keep the civilian doctors and nurses from getting caught in the crossfire.

Given how long that detour had taken, Tatsuya had ended up cutting it pretty close, but he'd still managed to make it in time. At the very least, he'd stopped Fumiya from trying a reckless attack.

The moment gunfire rang out, the two Cast Jammers snapped in half.

The rounds Tatsuya had fired off had been for show. He'd simultaneously used dismantling magic to destroy the Cast Jammers.

Sniper rifles were immediately trained on him.

Tatsuya didn't dismantle them.

High-powered rounds shot forth from the distant barrels. Tatsuya calculated their trajectories back to their origins and held his hand up.

This was the trick he'd entered in the 2095 thesis competition, but here its effect was devastating.

The soldiers froze at the illusion that Tatsuya had caught the bullets with his hand.

Tatsuya, however, did not waste the moment.

Using Dismantle, he put holes in their body armor and the vulnerable flesh beneath. Both the soldiers armed with rifles and the ones carrying Cast Jammers collapsed, viscera pouring from their midsections.

On the opposite side of the roof, Fumiya mopped up the rest of them with Direct Pain.

"Are you two hurt?" Tatsuya asked, his expression tense behind his helmet's visor.

He turned his left palm toward Fumiya's injured leg. The knife wound vanished in an instant, and the slash in his tights also closed up, returning to its original state.

After confirming that the two hadn't sustained any other injuries, Tatsuya shot his gun into each of the five holes he'd put in the enemy soldiers' body armor.

"Um, what are you doing...?" Ayako asked uncomfortably, her face pale.

"I want to make it seem like they were shot. Anybody watching will see right through it, of course, but..." Tatsuya answered with a wry smile. Next, he set about using his knife to stab every soldier that Fumiya had felled. "I'm not killing them. If they're treated quickly, they'll live," he added from within his helmet.

His excuse wasn't particularly convincing, but he wasn't trying to justify his actions—he just wanted to obtain Fumiya and Ayako's understanding.

"...Are we going to leave them?" Likewise, Fumiya wasn't criticizing Tatsuya—it was an honest question.

"These are American soldiers. Capturing them would have political consequences, and they won't have any information we need anyway."

"Understood," Fumiya replied, though he wasn't completely convinced. Even if they were foreign soldiers, he was certain that the fact they'd disrupted the mission would mean they would have clues.

But he also understood that openly inviting conflict with the USNA military was a terrifying prospect.

"All right, let's go collect the enemies you took down inside the hospital."

Tatsuya nodded at Fumiya's suggestion. "There are Generator bodies we need to take a look at on the third floor. I'll lead the way," he said, and the three reentered the building.

◇ ◇ ◇

Meanwhile, a conversation was taking place inside the large VTOL transport that was landing at Zama base.

"Major Canopus, the interference unit has been completely wiped out."

"Wait to exfiltrate them until the Yotsuba people have pulled out."

"Understood, sir."

"Did the car with Hague in it escape successfully?"

"There are no vehicles in pursuit."

"Good. Keep it under satellite observation."

"Yes, sir."

In the race to get Gide Hague, also known as Gu Jie, Canopus was currently a step ahead of the Yotsuba hunting party. He had an advantage: As part of their security measures against foreign and stateless magicians, the USNA intelligence agency had recorded Gu Jie's psionic wave signature.

They also had a short-range radar that was capable of tracking a given psionic wave signature—a technology that Japan had not yet developed. Given this, Gu Jie was as good as in the USNA's hands.

But Canopus was not moving to bring him in. He was following to the letter the orders Colonel Balance had given him.

The only question on his mind was how to interfere with the pursuit of the Japanese magicians while somehow leading Gu Jie back out to international waters.

# [9]

There had been little progress in the investigation ever since the American military had interfered in the hunt for Gu Jie two days earlier, and thinking on the events of that night gave Tatsuya a terrible feeling of futility. His enthusiasm for the mission only made the disappointment that much worse. The only good thing to come out of all this was that he'd been spared having to fire on troops from his own country's military. Thanks to how everything had developed, Tatsuya's motivation was extremely low, and he was not particularly inclined to put much effort into his duties.

As far as the USNA's aiding of Gu Jie's escape went, he'd given reports to both Maya and Kazama. He'd also requested that Kazama look into the background of the incident. But a full day later, nothing had come of it.

Of course, neither Katsuto, Mayumi, nor Masaki had come up with anything, either. Nothing promising came from the meeting Katsuto held. Nobody had anything to add to the redacted report Tatsuya gave, aside from witness reports coming from Zama.

Masaki, who'd gone so far as to temporarily move, was feeling pressured enough that he was also considering skipping school in order to fully devote himself to the investigation. Doing so, however, would fly in the face of both his father and Ms. Maeda, the principal of Third High, after all they had done to make his unusual arrangement a possibility, so Masaki decided to grit his teeth and be patient.

During practical magic studies, any distraction could lead to serious injuries, so he managed to suppress his ever-present anxiety about his mission and simply apply himself to his studies for a few hours, but during academic classes, it was impossible for him to focus. Feeling ashamed of what he'd been reduced to, he stood and headed for the dining hall once lunchtime rolled around.

For the last two days, Masaki had been invited *by Honoka* to sit with her and Miyuki at their lunch table. For him, this had been an unexpected and delightful way to spend his time. Rather than Miyuki being super-close to Tatsuya, she seemed to go out of her way to talk to Masaki, chatting more with him than she did Tatsuya.

But today, he didn't particularly want to show his dejected face to the girl he liked.

So the moment the class period ended, Masaki stood and tried to head for the dining hall alone.

But before he could escape the classroom, a girl's voice called out to him. Two girls, actually—and not Honoka, Shizuku, or Miyuki, but two random girls from his class.

"Ichijou!"

"Please take this!"

Before Masaki could reply, two small ribbon-wrapped boxes were thrust into his chest.

He reflexively accepted the boxes, but he didn't even have time to ask what they were before the two girls ran off, squealing.

"Aw, they got the drop on us!"

"Fine, I'm next!"

Even as Masaki continued to fail to grasp the situation, other girls from the class began to swarm around him. There were five total. Like the first two, they foisted their prettily wrapped little boxes off on him before hurrying away from the classroom themselves.

"My, Ichijou, *you're* certainly popular."

Masaki turned at the amused voice that came from behind him.

There was the usual trio, with Honoka in front, and Shizuku and Miyuki behind her.

Miyuki smiled serenely at the many boxes Masaki was still holding.

Masaki suddenly felt unaccountably nervous. There was no reason for this to be happening, he thought—but this was his misunderstanding. "What the heck is…?"

Shizuku made an incredulous face at Masaki's continuing incomprehension—a surprisingly easy-to-read expression, coming from her. "Today is Valentine's Day."

Masaki froze. He slowly looked down; he was holding seven boxes. There was no way to hide them, even if he'd tried. There would've been no point in trying, but Masaki was too alarmed even to realize that.

"If you've already got this many, you'll probably get even more before the day is out," Miyuki stated casually, striking Masaki another blow.

Masaki borrowed a shopping bag from a male classmate who'd had one on hand for whatever reason—no one pressed him as to why—and after filling it with the boxes he'd received from the girls, he left it next to his desk and, mourning the loss of his resolve to eat alone, was marched by Honoka to the dining hall.

It was here that Masaki finally noticed the restless atmosphere that was spreading throughout the school. A pall had fallen over the hearts of the student body thanks to the worldwide increase in anti-magician sentiment, and everyone was generally gloomier than average. And yet, it was undeniable that a certain agitated anticipation was suddenly present as well.

"Ah, *there* he is," Erika said with a grin as she caught sight of Masaki.

"C'mon, Erika, knock it off," Mikihiko chided with an uneasy smile, but she was having none of it.

"What? What's the matter? It's not like *you* have any reason to envy anybody, Miki."

Still not understanding what was going on, Masaki brought his lunch tray to his seat, whereupon Erika immediately pounced.

"So, Ichijou, how many chocolates have you gotten so far?"

Masaki counted himself lucky that he hadn't taken a bite of his lunch yet. If he'd had anything in his mouth, he was sure he'd have spit it out. "Chiba, what are you…?"

"What do you mean, 'what?' If I'm asking about your Valentine's chocolate haul today, what else could I possibly mean?"

There was nothing to say to Erika's comeback other than that it was absolutely correct, and Masaki was at a loss for words.

"So what's the number? My money's on you being in double digits."

"Money?"

"Uh, whoops." Erika pretended to clamp her mouth shut at the scandalized look Masaki shot her. But the delight in her eyes made it clear she didn't harbor a shred of guilt.

"I'm surprised you found someone willing to take that bet, Erika. Who was it?" Tatsuya asked slyly.

"I couldn't say."

"I'm not on the disciplinary committee anymore."

"Sure, but the chief of said committee's right there," Erika replied, her finger pointing at Mikihiko, who was leaning his elbow on the table and propping up his head. He heaved a deep sigh.

"Tatsuya, Erika…that's the jurisdiction of a student council member."

"Oh, is it? Well, I'm still not talking." Erika sounded like she was about to stick her tongue out. She turned back to Masaki. "So how many?"

"Does it matter?" Masaki grumbled, sounding quite resentful.

He seemed to have figured out there was no need to be formal and reserved around Erika.

In any case, he didn't want to linger on this topic for long. Even if Miyuki didn't think anything of it—the fact that he'd been given chocolate, that is—it still gave Masaki the uncomfortable sensation that he was being unfaithful.

But his hope that this would end the conversation was cruelly dashed.

"Seven."

"Seven, I think."

The answer came nearly simultaneously from Shizuku and Honoka.

"Seven, huh...? Well, I guess it's only lunchtime. You'll definitely hit double digits before you go home."

Masaki wanted to change the subject as quickly as possible, but Erika wasn't the only one who'd taken an interest in it.

"Seven? That's pretty impressive for someone who only just transferred here," Leo said with an exaggerated nod.

He didn't seem to have any ulterior motive, but it wasn't like a simple lack of malice would let Masaki just laugh it off. "I didn't transfer. And how many did *you* get, Saijou?"

"Me? A big fat zero."

And yet, it wasn't as though Masaki was genuinely irritated at the Valentine's situation. He wasn't so petty a man as that. So when he heard Leo's unexpected answer, he was suddenly and awkwardly at a loss for what to say.

"You're acting pretty calm about that, Leo."

"I've still got my club coming up, so I'm not worried."

So *that* was the situation. Masaki breathed a sigh of relief at hearing Tatsuya and Leo's exchange.

"Ha, they're just going to be obligatory chocolates anyway."

"I don't wanna hear that from a girl who doesn't even have anybody to give obligatory chocolate to."

"Sucks to be you—I just don't care, that's all."

"Say whatever you want; it amounts to the same thing."

"All this wishful thinking coming out of your mouth."

Erika had switched her attention from Masaki to Leo, but it just ended up making Masaki uneasy for a different reason.

"Cut it out, you two," Mikihiko interrupted them, already sounding tired. In that moment, Masaki felt a kind of kinship with him.

Class ended, and Tatsuya headed for the front gate. He was missing student council duties again today, thanks to the Gu Jie search.

That said, it wasn't like Tatsuya himself was going to personally interview witnesses. His job was to follow up on the analyses provided by magicians like Yoshimi who had perception-enhancing abilities, as well as the leads provided (illegally) by cooperative intelligence agencies. So long as there wasn't any new information, he would remain on standby.

Ever since the intervention from the American military two days earlier, they hadn't discovered any useful leads. Tatsuya knew that the more time passed, the more difficult apprehending their target became, but flailing aimlessly would only waste energy. There was no meaning in such action. If today hadn't been Valentine's Day, he probably would've attended the student council meeting.

Tatsuya was trudging toward the school gate when he heard the sound of running footsteps approaching from behind.

"Tatsuya!" Honoka called out, just as Tatsuya turned.

Behind Honoka stood Shizuku. Tatsuya was relieved that Honoka hadn't come alone. He felt bad for her, but Tatsuya really didn't want to deal with her today.

"Could you spare a bit of time?" Honoka's voice was nervous, but the look in her eyes spoke of her determination.

"Should we go somewhere else?" Tatsuya suggested, instead of just agreeing.

"No, er, here is fine," she said, then from her vintage bag—a century earlier, it would have been called a schoolbag—she produced a beautifully wrapped box. "Please accept this!"

They were right in the middle of the broad walkway that led out through the school's front gate. Tatsuya and the two girls were not the only students there. Several passersby slowed their pace and peered curiously at the developing scene.

It wasn't that Honoka was too nervous to notice her surroundings but the opposite. She was showing her resolve by choosing to do this where so many other students could see.

"Thanks." Tatsuya didn't reject her, but what he did reply with might have been crueler than simple rejection. "But is this really okay with you? I'm engaged to Miyuki."

However, Honoka's resolve was not so fragile as to collapse at this expected obstacle. "It's fine," she said. "I know. But I would still be very pleased if you would accept it."

"…I see. In that case, I will." Tatsuya had nothing more than that to add, given Honoka's feelings. "See you tomorrow."

"Wait," called out Shizuku, just as Tatsuya had taken the chocolates and was turning to leave. "Use this," she said, thrusting a stylish carrying bag at him. It was made of artificial leather in a black-and-white pattern and used a tote bag design, with an airtight closure to keep water out.

Since Tatsuya hadn't brought a bag that day, he didn't have anywhere to put the chocolate he'd received. He was honestly grateful for Shizuku's offer. "I'll take you up on that. Thanks."

Accepting the second gift, Tatsuya noticed that it was a bit heavier than he'd expected it to be, and he furrowed his brow slightly. When he went to put the box inside the already-open bag, he realized there was another box already in there.

"Don't worry—you can have it," Shizuku said with perfect timing as Tatsuya looked up. "It's obligatory," she added with a faintly mischievous smile. "Oh, and you don't have to give the bag back."

She then quickly looked away, bashfully.

A faint smile colored Tatsuya's face. The anxiety between him and Honoka relaxed into something more pleasant. If it had ended there, the encounter would have felt like a lovely, youthful interlude.

But then another actor leaped onto the stage, delaying the curtain's fall.

"And from me, too!"

"Amy?!"

Ignoring Honoka's vaguely indignant cry of her nickname, Amy trotted up to Tatsuya. "Here, have some obligatory chocolate!"

Tatsuya found himself presented with a little box, small enough to easily fit in the palm of his hand. "Uh, sure." Having just accepted Shizuku's "obligation chocolate," he didn't have any excuse not to accept this one.

"Amy, what about Tomitsuka?!" Honoka demanded.

"I was just on my way to give him his," she said without looking particularly guilty or embarrassed. "But it looked like Shiba was heading home, and obligation or not, if you don't hand out your chocolate on Valentine's Day, then what's the point?"

She was entirely nonchalant about it.

Subaru appeared out from under the shadows of the trees lining the path. "And here's some from me," she said, offering Tatsuya not a box but a small pouch. "Ah, and I'm sure you can guess, but this is strictly obligatory."

"Naturally," Tatsuya responded smoothly with a faint smile, accepting the pouch.

Honoka didn't seem inclined to protest this.

Just as Tatsuya thought the encounter was over—

"Shiba!"

A freshman student called out to him. It was the girl who'd been paired up with Minami during the Shields Down event at the Nine School Competition. She had her classmates in tow, and when all was said and done, the bag Shizuku had given Tatsuya was so full that he couldn't keep it closed with just one hand.

◇ ◇ ◇

When Tatsuya returned home after the meeting with Katsuto ended, Miyuki was waiting for him just inside the threshold of the entryway, sitting in a formal kneel with both her hands resting in her lap.

"Welcome home, Tatsuya."

"Miyuki… What's going on?"

Miyuki was wearing a frilly apron over a long, flared dress, but the way she greeted him made it seem like a traditional kimono would've been more fitting. The feeling he got that she was deliberately blocking his way into the house had to be his imagination.

"Is something strange?"

"No… Not strange, but…"

Miyuki wasn't moving, so Tatsuya stayed where he was in the entryway.

"Incidentally, Tatsuya, are you carrying anything? I'll be happy to take it for you."

"As you can see, I'm not… Why do you ask?"

Miyuki looked away, breaking eye contact. "I…simply heard that you had become rather loaded down on your way home from school."

With this explanation, Tatsuya understood what had gotten Miyuki bent out of shape.

"I didn't get anything from Saegusa. Although she does enjoy her pranks," he said, recalling the previous year—and that exceedingly bitter chocolate—but he avoided derailing the conversation by mentioning it explicitly. "And you didn't even give obligatory chocolate to Ichijou, right?"

In fact, Miyuki didn't give such a thing to *any* of her classmates or seniors. The fuss it would raise was more trouble than it was worth. But that wasn't the only reason why she'd avoided Masaki. If she'd given him chocolate today, she knew there was every chance it wouldn't be perceived as ordinary chocolate for a friendly acquaintance. Remembering that, Miyuki understood what Tatsuya was getting at.

"When I received chocolate from Honoka, I made sure to very clearly tell her that you and I were engaged. She said that she still wanted me to accept hers, so I didn't refuse."

Miyuki looked hastily up. Her eyes were wide. "Tatsuya! That's just so…"

"…Hard to watch?"

Miyuki looked down again. It was the same motion as before, but the mood in the entryway was very different. Her charmingly prickly demeanor was all but gone. A heavy tension now lingered in the space between them.

"Honoka probably noticed I felt sorry for her. Maybe I should've flatly refused her, for her own sake, but…"

Miyuki stood, her gaze still averted. "You haven't had any dinner yet, right? I'll get it ready, so please go ahead and wait in the dining room." Without responding to Tatsuya's moment of introspection, she turned her back to him.

Since Tatsuya had informed them that he'd be having dinner after he got home, neither Miyuki nor Minami had eaten yet. This had become a fairly common pattern recently.

The conversation around the dinner table that evening was halting, and dinner concluded amid a rather awkward mood.

"Thank you for the food," Tatsuya said. Once everyone had finished eating, he stood, thinking it would be good to give everybody some time to cool their heads. He collected his dishes and started to head for the kitchen.

But Miyuki stopped him short. "I'm sorry, Tatsuya, but could you stay for a moment?"

Tatsuya nodded and sat back down.

At a glance from Miyuki, Minami quickly cleared the dishes from the table.

Miyuki took a silver platter covered by a cake dome out of the refrigerator and carried it back to the table.

"I'm not sure if your accepting Honoka's chocolates was the right thing to do or if it was a mistake." Miyuki looked evenly into Tatsuya's eyes. "Honestly, I'm still not sure, so I decided to stop thinking about it. Maybe that makes me a heartless girl, but I have other things to think about."

Miyuki took a breath, less in preparation for what she was about to say next and more to calm her racing heart.

"After seeing you so preoccupied with Honoka's feelings, I almost decided not to do this, but...I didn't want it to go to waste."

Miyuki set the cake down. An indescribably bitter scent wafted across the table, tickling Tatsuya's nose mischievously.

It was a simple dark-chocolate cake, without cream or fruit topping of any kind.

But its surface was glassily smooth and reflective, and its perfectly round shape was clearly not something an amateur could have made.

"Since I went to the trouble of making it, I'd like for you to have some, Tatsuya. Will you accept my Valentine's chocolate?"

Miyuki set a dessert plate with a knife and fork on it in front of Tatsuya.

Tatsuya picked the knife up, as though he'd been waiting for this moment, and sliced into the cake with it.

Slicing a sixth out of the whole, he then used his fork to transfer it to his plate.

"The truth is, I was looking forward to this," said Tatsuya, locking eyes with Miyuki with a smile.

"I'll go make some coffee!" his sister said, quickly rising to her feet and hurrying to the kitchen.

With her back turned to Tatsuya as she worked the hand-crank coffee mill, Miyuki's cheeks were faintly flushed, and she couldn't help the little smile that played about her lips.

# [ 10 ]

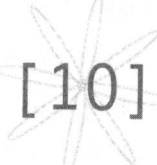

Amid a constant stream of bad press for magicians, Valentine's Day had been the rare day during which the students of magic high school and Magic University could laugh and cry over harmless trivialities.

But their enjoyment lasted only a single day.

Friday, February 15, 2097: What anyone involved with magic—high school student, college student, and adult alike—dreaded most finally came to pass.

Though, perhaps *began* was a better word.

The location was the main gate of Magic University. The time, 11:00 AM. A group of protesters organized by an anti-magician group clashed with police as they tried to force their way onto the campus.

Given the large amount of classified defense information that was stored and used at the university, entry of anyone who wasn't affiliated with the institution was strictly regulated. The police blocked the protesters not because they sided with the magicians but because it was simply government policy.

But those who'd come to demonstrate against magicians didn't see it that way. Or perhaps they did understand, but chose to willfully misinterpret the situation. Some of the protesters resorted to force—nay, violence.

At first it was merely a shoving match between the two sides.

Pushed back by the police, the protesters would deliberately fall, pretending to be the victims of unreasonable force. From then on, the outcome was a foregone conclusion.

"Well damn, they've really gone and done it now," groaned Leo, exasperated, as he watched the news play on the large display in the dining hall.

"Man, this is terrible." Whether it was deliberate or not, the radical protesters that had started swinging their signs around as weapons had encouraged others to start throwing rocks at the police line. Mikihiko's brow furrowed as he watched the developments on the screen.

*There aren't any loose rocks around the entrance to the university, so the protesters must have thrown gravel that was holding down garden fabric under the city trees that grow along the streets they took to get there…*

As the police in the recorded footage started to tackle and subdue the more violent protesters, the broadcast switched to a live feed.

"…Twenty-four arrested, huh? Is that a lot? Or hardly any?" asked Masaki, who by now had thoroughly integrated into Tatsuya's lunch group, since he didn't really know what the ballpark population of the metro area was.

"This is much calmer than the anti-war protests, but as far as recent history goes, it's a lot," Tatsuya answered succinctly.

"But—it looked like there were easily double that many people throwing rocks," Honoka cut in. These past several days she had become much more proactive.

"There weren't enough police to arrest that many people."

"And even if they don't arrest them in the act, they've got traffic camera footage. They don't have to rush; they can arrest as many as they have to," Erika added, who had a detective in her family as well as several police officers as fellow disciples.

"Hmm? Erika, isn't that your brother?" wondered Leo, who was still absorbed in watching the news, his gaze not leaving the screen.

But the moment everybody's gaze turned to the display, the news cut back to the studio.

"I mean, he is a detective…and he does deal with magician-related cases, so I'm sure he'd get borrowed for anti-riot duty," nonchalantly replied Erika, who'd noticed him in the footage long before.

Mikihiko changed the subject, and not necessarily out of caution toward the siblings' bad relationship. "How many protesters do you think there were, in total?"

"Neither the police nor the media have reported any numbers, so…"

As Mizuki said, the authorities had long since stopped reporting the number of participants at protests. If the major media outlets had wanted to analyze their aerial photography to get rough estimates of protest sizes, they certainly could have done so, but out of consideration for the police, they didn't publish those figures. And of course, nobody trusted the reports of the protest organizers themselves.

"There were about two hundred in the shot the TV showed," Tatsuya offered.

Masaki took that figure and estimated the scale of the protest. "So three or four hundred total…maybe even over five," he said with a sigh. "People are free to think what they want, but that said, it's pretty discouraging when you're on the side being vilified."

"It's true," murmured Miyuki in response to Masaki's grumble.

Suddenly, Erika let out an enraged "Huh?!"

There on the screen, a lawyer was contending that the police had carried out too many arrests.

"'An infringement on their right to freedom of speech?!' 'Freedom of assembly must be respected as freedom of association?!' My ass! We're talking about attempted forcible trespassing and resisting police orders here!"

"I agree with what Erika's saying, but…I bet there are a lot of people who are gonna use the same reasoning as that lawyer."

Nobody argued with Mikihiko's gloomy prediction.

◇ ◇ ◇

"Inagaki, are you okay?" Toshikazu asked clinically.

"Yeah, I'm fine," Inagaki answered brusquely.

There had, in fact, been a scene that was deliberately omitted from the news broadcasts.

The recorded footage had showed the police restraining the protesters who'd begun using their signs as weapons. But at the height of the chaos, there had been one violent protester who'd used a blunt weapon to try to beat his way past the police perimeter that had been set up to keep onlookers out of the road.

That violent protester had been apprehended by a plainclothes detective—Inagaki—who had been keeping a low profile in the crowd of onlookers.

Owing to the magic Inagaki had used to subdue him, the protester was not yet in any condition to be questioned. As a result, his connection to the protest group was still unknown. It seemed very likely that he was one of them, but they couldn't be sure.

The footage hadn't been aired out of concern for the protesters—they didn't want the public to immediately assume the man was connected to the nonviolent demonstration. At the same time, the media didn't want that notion circulating *even if it was true.*

The officer who'd been about to be struck had avoided injury thanks to Inagaki's quick action. But in protecting him, Inagaki had gotten a terrible bruise that made it clear he was very lucky not to have a broken arm—although bruises like that were an everyday occurrence at the Chiba dojo.

And Inagaki was a master, a man who had been given the trust of a future family head. He might have taken a hit in the process of protecting a police officer and the civilians around him from a blunt weapon, but he'd done so without sustaining any serious injury. It was clear that Toshikazu understood this as he looked at the bruise.

Inagaki put his hand to his forehead and frowned, and Toshikazu regarded him dubiously. "Hmm? Inagaki, was your head hit, too?"

The thug had only struck him on his arms. It was hard to imagine a man of Inagaki's caliber not realizing he'd sustained an injury somewhere else.

"No, I just get the worst headaches when I listen to you talk, Inspector."

"Okay, buddy... Inagaki, I think you need to go back to the academy and learn how to respect the rank," Toshikazu teased. Then he added, "If you're not feeling well, you can go home," before giving him some space.

He'd seen Inagaki putting his hand to his head like that quite a bit recently. Toshikazu was teasing him about it just now, but the truth was he was quite worried about the man.

The evening news featured a rather heated debate on the events of the day. This wasn't because there was any programming that specifically included a debate between pro- and anti-magician figures. Rather, considerably differing views were being pushed on each channel.

On one channel whose history went all the way to the analog era, representative Kanda—a member of the opposition party and famously anti-magician—was strongly condemning the approach the police had taken.

*"...Even if some of the protesters went a bit too far, the police clearly overreacted in arresting whoever they could lay their hands on. The police went out fully geared up in shields, helmets, and body armor. And in fact, not a single police officer was injured while confronting the protesters.*

*"Now in fairness, one plainclothes officer did sustain light injuries. He didn't even break any bones, but in retaliation for the mild bruise he accidentally received, he attacked a civilian with magic. Given the natural power to inflict harm that these magicians possess, that was clearly excessive.*

"When it comes to the police's exercise of magic, I believe we must demand even more caution than we require for the use of firearms. I plan to introduce legislation calling for stronger limitations on the use of—and consequences for the misuse of—magic in every aspect of law enforcement. The use of magic must require prior approval, and it must come from a higher authority than the magician themselves."

Meanwhile, on CulNet—Culture Communication Network—a cable TV network where cable news and newswire reports were more prominent, representative Kouzuke was calmly answering a question from a newscaster. Kouzuke was a member of the ruling party, which largely defended magicians' rights.

"Magic University isn't open to the public in the first place, and the entry of nonaffiliated individuals is strictly limited. This is because of the many crucial research projects our nation has entrusted to the university, many of which are important elements of national defense. The protesters weren't singled out for harsh treatment simply because of their anti-magician positions.

"The protesters weren't just swinging around their metal signs; they'd also started throwing rocks. If the situation had been allowed to spin out of control, there is every chance it would've put not only university students in danger but innocent passersby as well. For the police not to intervene then would have been a complete dereliction of their duty to the public.

"As far as the use of magic goes, there are already strict rules in place, and the detective who arrested the violent criminal during this incident followed these rules to the letter. Further tying the hands of our men and women in the field with needless regulation would only hinder their ability to ensure the safety of the public and, by extension, could be considered actively harmful to the public.

"Magic-based restraint has been scientifically proven to be safer than incapacitating gas, stun guns, or flash-bang rounds. It would be a great loss to our society to make the art of magic into our enemy."

Kouichi, watching the broadcast with Mayumi, wore an

expression like a teacher who'd just finished grading a test from a completely average, unremarkable pupil.

"Representative Kanda's tone was surprisingly calm. I was sure he'd make more extreme demands."

"Don't you think it's going to upstage Mr. Kouzuke's argument?" Mayumi grumbled. Her presence here had been compelled, and she wasn't bothering to hide her displeasure.

Behind the slight tint of his glasses, Kouichi's eyes swiveled to regard his eldest daughter with a look of interest. "Representative Kanda is a clown, but the world is full of rubes perfectly willing to take a clown's hyperbole literally. It's tempting to dismiss rhetoric that uses appeals to emotion as nothing more than the childish ranting of a self-proclaimed expert, but the masses can be easily manipulated if you tempt them with empty empathy and comfortable ignorance. This kind of malicious reasoning is easier to deal with from the inside."

"Don't you think Mr. Kouzuke is a little lackluster when it comes to playing to the crowd like that, though?"

"I want him to douse the flames, not fan them. De-escalating statements will work on both sides."

Mayumi's scowl made her loathing for her father's casual misanthropy crystal clear. "Well then, Father. What comes next?"

"For the moment, we watch and wait. I'm surprised to see CulNet coming so clearly down on our side... I may give that actress a call soon."

"Actress? Don't tell me you're talking about Maki Sawamura?"

Mayumi had never heard anything about her father backing someone in the entertainment industry. The only actress she could think of with any kind of individual connection to him was Maki Sawamura, who'd visited their home the previous April.

"That's right. I'm surprised you guessed correctly."

"I didn't—she's just the only one I could think of. So...why her?"

"She's the daughter of the CEO of Culture Communication Network."

"You don't say," Mayumi replied with a disinterested hum.

Takuma was watching the same broadcast, and the instant Representative Kouzuke's segment on the news was over, he called Maki.

*"Why, hello, Takuma. What's up?"* Maki affected surprise at receiving the call.

A year earlier, Takuma would've been annoyed at her playing dumb, but now he didn't care whether she was misdirecting him or being sincere.

"Sorry to call at this hour. I just wanted to thank you, Maki."

*"Thank me?"* Behind her curious voice, Takuma could hear a faint commotion of some kind.

"Are you at work? If you are—"

"We're taking a break from shooting—it's fine. So what's this about?"

Maki laughed, but Takuma kept things short, not wanting to trouble her any more if he could help it. "I saw Representative Kouzuke on your family's cable channel. The news anchor was pretty favorable toward magicians, too. You arranged that, didn't you? Seriously, thank you."

*"Oh, is that all?"* Maki giggled, sounding almost disappointed. *"Well, I did tell my dad that it wasn't a good idea to be too sympathetic to the anti-magic people, but not just because you asked me to help. We're an upstart network, so there's no profit for us in just following the lead of the old guard. My dad just made a business calculation. Now, Mr. Kouzuke owes us a favor, too, so you really don't have to go out of your way to thank me for this."*

"Still, it really helped. Thank you."

*"It did? In that case, I look forward to being* repaid *for the favor."*

"Yeah, anything you need, just say it."

Takuma apologized again for interrupting her during work and then ended the call.

Perhaps unsurprisingly, many people were displeased that the mass media was not united in embracing anti-magician sentiment.

Gu Jie, still on the run, was not only displeased but impatient.

The goal of his terrorist attack had been to incite outrage toward magicians by laying the deaths of ordinary civilians at the feet of the Ten Master Clans. He'd expected that the magicians of Japan would use the Ten Master Clans as a scapegoat in order to placate the rising swell of anger and dismay. The negative feedback loop was supposed to culminate in the downfall of the Clans and, in particular, his true goal: the social destruction of the Yotsuba family.

Yes, both internal divisions among magicians and discontent with the Ten Master Clans momentum were definitely increasing. But at this rate, Gu Jie suspected it would peter out before achieving anything decisive.

"There is no meaning in that. This cannot end until those who stole my vengeance from me taste the same bitter regret I did so long ago."

Forty-three years earlier, Gu Jie had failed and fled his country. He'd achieved renown as a practitioner of ancient magic, only to lose everything and become dead to the world.

And with a mind warped by the indignity, Gu Jie had sworn revenge.

He would inflict his own miserable circumstances on the modern magicians of the Kunlun Institute who'd driven him out, and he would laugh at their suffering and resentment.

He could think of no other way to soothe the bitterness in his heart.

But his revenge became impossible. The Yotsuba clan had wiped out the very object of his vengeance.

With nowhere else to go, his embittered mind turned toward the ones who'd robbed him of his satisfaction.

And just as his former self had once done, he set himself to the task of masterminding the destruction of the Yotsuba clan.

"—I won't kill them. I won't give them sweet release of death. They can live on in misery, writhing in mud."

The suicide terrorist bombing had been his last measure to that end. With the repudiation of their utility and contribution to society, he was sure it was only a matter of time before the magicians of Japan would find themselves stripped of their position, prestige, pride, and place in society by their fellow Japanese citizens.

If he could just see that with his own eyes, the only thing left to do would be to find a place suitable for a quiet death. But if his goal wouldn't be fulfilled, he would have to come up with another ploy. He had no intention of rotting away before accomplishing his revenge.

In any case, his immediate goal was getting out of the country. If he was going to plan another attack, he couldn't afford to take his time. Gu Jie could feel the noose tightening.

The network of connections that Gongjin Zhou had built mostly lay in ruins, but there were still a few here and there left alive in Japan, and they were what allowed Gu Jie to remain a free man.

Losing access to Hlidskjalf had been a blow, but he'd always known that it was dangerous to rely too much on that tool. Friends sworn in blood were more reliable than such an unknowable implement, Gu Jie realized anew.

In order to get out of the country quickly without taking the time to cover his tracks, he needed powerful pawns. He needed to find components with greater potential than even the enhanced magicians he'd stolen from the military.

Having concluded as much, Gu Jie remembered that one of his

friends had told him he'd carved a mark into a promising student from a powerful magic family.

*This student's talent didn't seem too impressive, but anyone from that family ought to make an excellent puppet.*

With the marked student as bait, he would hook and land the master. Gu Jie set about planning his next move.

Saturday, February 16. There was another anti-magician protest but not at Magic University. They marched from the central government district to the National Diet Building, and unlike the previous day, there was no violence.

However, that didn't mean there were no problems. There was an incident four hundred kilometers west of Tokyo, in Nishinomiya's Second High School. A junior student on her way home from school was attacked by anti-magician activists.

"Tatsuya?"

"Um, Tatsuya?"

Tatsuya had heard about the incident on his own way home and then promptly turned around and headed back to school, where Miyuki and Honoka met him, uncertainty in their voices.

"I heard about the Second High incident and came back," Tatsuya answered before they had to ask. "Do we have any details?"

"A female student on her way home was attacked by several violent protesters, but another student quickly came to her aid, so she wasn't hurt. However, in the process of fighting them off, apparently they made a mistake in limiting their magic, so the attackers sustained significant injuries. Minami's setting up a conference call with Second High right now."

Just as Miyuki finished her explanation to Tatsuya, Minami announced, "We're connected."

Miyuki nodded to Minami and leaned toward the mic. "This is

Miyuki Shiba, president of the First High student council. Can you hear me, Second High?"

"This is Minoru Kudou, vice president of the Second High student council. You're coming through loud and clear."

The voice coming through the speaker was Minoru Kudou, who'd cooperated with them the previous fall in Nara and Kyoto.

"Oh, Minoru, you're the vice president at Second High?"

"Yes, although I'm more like the vice vice president. By the way, Miyuki, would you mind if we switched to a video call?"

"No, not a bit."

They hadn't started with a video call out of good manners. Both sides were familiar with the embarrassment of seeing something they didn't particularly want seen in the corner of a display when a camera was connected.

Once a voice connection was made, it was quick to switch. In less than a second, Minoru's face appeared on the large screen in the student council room.

Several quiet gulps were audible in the room.

The student council members who hadn't gone to Kyoto still knew Minoru's face from the thesis competition. But seeing a clearly masculine face that was nonetheless just as beautiful as Miyuki's was still more than enough to overwhelm all the girls present except Miyuki.

Minoru's eyes widened slightly at seeing Tatsuya among the members of First High's student council. Minoru had heard from conversation around his house that Tatsuya had been put on the search for the terrorist. But he knew better than to bring that up here, so he asked no questions.

"Getting right to the point, Vice President Kudou," began Miyuki in a briskly professional tone. "We'd like to hear about the attack on a student from your school in as much detail as possible."

"*Certainly, President Shiba,*" Minoru replied, his voice becoming similarly formal. "*About an hour ago, a freshman from Second High was* on her way to the station from school, when she was suddenly accosted by six men who appeared to be in their late teens or early twenties."

Hearing this, the entire First High student council, the president of the disciplinary committee, and a female member of the disciplinary committee all frowned.

"Facing the student, the men began shouting at her about the principles of humanism. 'Miracles are the purview of God alone, and twisting the order of God's creation is an act of the devil. Humans should live by only that power granted them'—all that stuff."

Hearing the humanist principles stated again, it was painfully clear how they had deliberately twisted existing religious thought into a cultish ideology.

"The student resolutely kept requesting, 'Please get out of my way,' but the men surrounding her refused to open up a path. When she tried to push the panic button on her portable terminal, one of the men grabbed her and started struggling with her for the terminal."

The panic button functionality included in portable terminals didn't just sound a loud alarm noise. It also transmitted location data to nearby emergency services. It was easy to imagine why men who'd ignored her clearly stated request would try to stop her from hitting it.

"Hearing the commotion, other students came running. There were three freshmen and one junior. The junior broke the ring of humanists surrounding the accosted student, and the freshmen pushed through, and it immediately devolved into a brawl. In addition to being physically larger than the students, they seemed to have some martial arts training, and when the junior was struck and knocked unconscious, a freshman girl used magic to disable the attackers."

"What's the situation with injuries?"

"The junior sustained fairly serious injuries—a broken nose, a burst eardrum, a cracked rib, and some internal bleeding. They also reportedly have some organ damage. One freshman boy has a broken collarbone, and another got a concussion. He sustained a vicious blow to the back of his head, so he's undergoing thorough testing. The other boy and the girl didn't have any serious injuries."

"And the men?"

"*The magic used was Spark and Press. Spark left one man with an irregular pulse and another with a cut inside his mouth from the impact to his face he took when he fell. Apparently, he also cracked a tooth. The others have scrapes and bruises from being forced down by Press.*"

"We've been hearing that the attackers sustained worse injuries, but it sounds like the junior got the worst of it," pointed out Miyuki.

Minoru smiled bitterly—although his appearance was so composed, it didn't show. "*Apparently, the irregular pulse was particularly severe immediately after the magic... Now we know that he has high blood pressure and is prone to arrhythmia, but until he was examined, it wasn't clear how bad the electrical injury actually was, so the story became that he was 'badly wounded.'*"

The First High students' reactions were split between those who looked relieved and those couldn't help their sarcastic smirks at hearing this. Miyuki was among the relieved, while Tatsuya was among the latter.

"So it sounds like the freshman student won't be accused of using excessive force in self-defense, then."

"*Our student council president and the other vice president are with the police right now, along with a teacher. We won't know anything specific about that until they get back, but it probably won't be a problem.*"

"I see. In that case, would you tell me how things went once your president gets back? A text is fine."

"*Understood. I'll message you when I know.*"

"I appreciate it, Vice President Kudou."

"*Certainly. President Shiba—ah, Miyuki—thank you for your time.*"

"Not at all, Minoru. Take care." Miyuki flipped the switch on the teleconference system and turned to Tatsuya. "Minoru seems quite certain, as you heard, but it sounds like the question of whether or not the use of magic will be deemed excessive force is very much up in the air."

"Even if it doesn't end up being ruled a crime this time around, the problem of proportionality remains," Tatsuya explained. "I think it's quite unlikely that clear criteria for what use of magic is allowed for what level of danger will be established. In the worst-case scenario, a judge might rule that magic-based resistance is never allowed until physical harm has been inflicted."

"But, Tatsuya, isn't that unreasonable? If that logic goes unchallenged, doesn't that lead to the conclusion that magicians don't have any right to self-defense at all?" Izumi objected.

"They may just tell us to defend ourselves with anything besides magic," Shizuku pointed out matter-of-factly.

Nobody, Izumi included, had anything to refute Shizuku's hypothesis.

"Because actual harm was inflicted, it was ruled as legitimate self-defense, huh?" Tatsuya asked.

He was sitting at the dinner table, after returning home from the now-routine daily meeting, when he heard his sister's answer.

"Yes… It wasn't spelled out in such clear terms, but I do have the feeling that your pessimistic prediction is coming true, Tatsuya."

Tatsuya and Miyuki were in agreement. So long as clear criteria weren't established somewhere, the risk remained that a judge somewhere might issue a ruling that banned any use of magic in self-defense on purely ideological grounds.

"We may as well try to send a request to clarify the legal right for magic-based self-defense through the Magic Association. Even if it gets approved, it'll take a considerable amount of time."

The case laws governing permissible use of magic were—outside of government employees going about their duties or private citizens acting in the capacity of a public servant—rather vague. The wording was deliberately broad, with phrases like *when there is an urgent need* and *in the service of the public good.*

This had its origin in the historical precedent of how magicians had come to be used as tools of state authority. In order to preserve public stability and prevent disaster, the administration at the time had been motivated to ensure that they could use magic as freely as possible, which was what had led to the current laws on the books.

But it was now very clear that these very laws were insufficient to protect individual magicians. The harmful consequences of treating magicians as nothing more than implements of national policy had finally surfaced.

"First High may very well be targeted next," Tatsuya stated. "Minami?"

"Yes, sir." She entered from the kitchen at the call.

"Minami, whenever I'm not able to be close to Miyuki, I want you to accompany her as much as is possible. Take even greater care now not to leave her side."

"Yes, sir."

"And so long as magic isn't being used to attack you, don't use any magic where there's the possibility of injuring your opponent. Avoid Reflector, too."

"But, sir—even Interruption will turn the energy of an attack back on its source. Moderating it with Deceleration will considerably shorten the amount of time I can maintain a shield."

Minami hesitated to object further, and Miyuki came to her rescue. "Tatsuya. Perhaps I should be the one in charge of Deceleration?"

But Tatsuya's response was not especially favorable. "No…your magic power would eat away at Minami's shield. With dividing your attention between that and my seal, it would be hard to maintain precise control, wouldn't it?"

"I…won't dispute that," Miyuki said carefully.

"Anyway, now that you've been publicly announced as the next head of the Yotsuba family, it wouldn't be a good idea for you to use magic against a civilian. Leave it to Minami unless things get truly dire."

Seeing his sister nod in assent, Tatsuya returned his gaze to Minami.

"If Miyuki is ever attacked, I'll come running, no matter where I am. You just have to hold out until I arrive."

"Understood. You can count on me, sir."

The truth was, Tatsuya's request was putting a considerable burden on Minami. But Miyuki's protection was more important to her than her work as a maid.

Minami gave Tatsuya a resolute nod.

—Why did her precious Sunday have to start out by meeting such a rotten guy?

Such were Erika's thoughts after she returned home from a fairly long training run. She'd run into her older brother Toshikazu at the front gate, who appeared to be just on his way out.

Toshikazu did not look as though he was going out for leisure. With his suit and overcoat, he was dressed for work. Erika didn't find this particularly odd, though. It was no overstatement to say that detectives didn't get to have weekends. At the very least, the magician detectives affiliated with the Chiba family all seemed to live life that way.

Erika had attempted to run right past Toshikazu without greeting him or making eye contact.

But as she'd expected, he stopped her short.

"Erika."

Erika hated her half brother by a different mother more than anyone in the world except her father. And her brother was, if anything, harder for her to deal with.

Memories of him beating her to the ground during their training as children still lingered in the corners of her mind.

The sneering things he used to say when teasing her were so grating that even at the time she would wonder why he had to go so far. The fact that his words always seemed to strike at things she'd hidden in her heart made them all the more infuriating.

She had no idea how many times she'd wished he would just ignore her. Since becoming a high school student, she'd given up on that, too, as futile.

"What?" Erika glared at him with as much ill temper as she could muster.

"There's something I want to ask you." His usual malice was absent.

"Well, what is it?" Erika snapped, wondering if something was wrong with him.

Toshikazu paid Erika's combative attitude no mind. He seemed unusually preoccupied. "Have you seen Inagaki?"

"Inagaki?" The question was so unexpected Erika found herself seriously thinking about it. "…Not recently, no. When was the last time you saw him?"

"Yesterday."

"Yesterday?" Erika frowned, not sure what her brother was getting at. Was it really worth worrying about an adult who hadn't been seen for just a day?

Toshikazu looked away from Erika, perhaps uncomfortable with the curious gaze she was giving him. "That bastard took yesterday off work without even checking in," he explained, still looking away, as though he needed to offer some excuse for his asking.

"Inagaki lives alone, right? Could he have gotten sick or something and wound up in a condition where he couldn't call in?"

"He's not at home. Where'd he wander off to anyway…?"

"…So you went all the way to his place, huh?"

Toshikazu turned his back at Erika's jab. "L-look, if you see him, tell him to call me immediately, okay? And tell the rest to do the

same." By "the rest," he was referring to the students of the Chiba dojo.

Toshikazu turned his back to Erika and strode off briskly. "Sure, whatever," she muttered and returned to her own quarters in the house.

A little while after showering and eating a solitary breakfast, she went into the dojo.

Neither her father nor her elder sister were there. Those were the times Erika aimed for to do her training in the dojo. Conveniently, her sister also avoided using the dojo when Erika was there. The two half sisters did not get along and had very skillfully divided the Chiba home between them.

Despite it being Sunday morning, the dojo was crowded with students. Men in their twenties predominated. There were also some students of Inagaki's age.

Remembering Toshikazu's request, something like a whim compelled Erika to ask them about it.

"Naitou, Kadota, do you have a second?" Erika called out to a man swinging a wooden practice sword and another who was standing next to him, giving him some pointers.

The two men stopped their work and turned to her.

"Oh, Miss Erika, good morning."

"Miss Erika, you trained today?"

"I just got here. So you two started at the school the same time as Inagaki, right?"

"Yes."

"Although Inagaki's older than we are."

"Not by much, though," Erika noted, spearing Kadota with a cold gaze when he tried to emphasize the two-year difference. She then decided she'd make no progress if she kept getting hung up on little details like that. "Anyway, apparently Inagaki has been missing since yesterday, and I was wondering if you two had heard anything."

"He's missing?" Naitou frowned; he was Inagaki's age and

probably the closest to him of anyone in the dojo. "That's odd. He doesn't seem like the type to take off without leaving a message, no matter what kind of emergency came up."

"Yeah, he's very methodical, unlike you, Naitou."

A fairly loud *bonk* rang out as a hand made contact with Kadota's head.

"...C'mon, I was just kidding around a little!"

"Be grateful I didn't use a wooden sword."

The whack that Naitou had given Kadota's head with his fist had looked forceful enough, but Kadota didn't seem particularly fazed.

"Okay, okay, save the horseplay for later," Erika said, an unamused look in her eyes. "So I take it you two don't have any idea where he might be?"

"We do not... Attention!" Naitou turned his head and shouted across the dojo. "Anyone who saw Inagaki yesterday or today, hands up!"

No hands rose.

"Does anyone know Inagaki's whereabouts?"

This time, two of the younger students raised their hands. "This was the evening of the day before yesterday, but we saw him near his home," said one. The other nodded.

"You two live in Kamakura, right?"

"Yes."

"It seemed like he was looking for something. We didn't say hello since we thought he might have been on duty."

"Did you notice anything else?"

"We only caught a glimpse of him... I'm sorry."

Naitou turned to Erika.

Erika nodded to him.

"Understood. Back to training!" Naitou barked.

With a chorus of "Yes, sir!" the students all returned to their individual training, and Naitou looked away from them and squared himself to Erika. "Well, you heard them. I'm sorry we couldn't be of more help."

"This comes from my brother Kazu, so you don't have to apologize to me. Make sure to tell Kazu all this, okay?" Erika said, then turned and left Naitou and Kadota.

Naitou knew very well that Erika didn't get along well with Toshikazu, so he smiled and promised to do as she asked.

After getting the message from Naitou, Toshikazu climbed into his unmarked patrol car without even making an appearance at the temporary investigation headquarters.

Hearing the word *Kamakura* had given him a flash of inspiration—and a clammy feeling of regret, too.

The ancient magician they'd visited to hear an explanation of corpse-manipulation magic lived in Kamakura.

Immediately beforehand, Toshikazu had gotten a warning from Fujibayashi that the magician in question was blacklisted by the Magic Association and that he was rumored to have connections with magicians from Dahan.

There had been other signs, too. After they'd talked with that magician, Inagaki had constantly been rubbing his forehead, as though he'd been suffering from a headache that wouldn't go away.

The magician—Kazukiyo Oumi, "the Dollmaker"—must have used some technique on him. Probably of the mind-controlling type.

Why hadn't he noticed that Inagaki had been exhibiting the exact symptoms Fujibayashi had described to him on the phone?

A shout almost escaped Toshikazu when he realized his lapse but he held back, stifling the urge and contenting himself with a mere grinding of teeth.

Parking the unmarked patrol car a block short of his destination, Toshikazu stealthily approached the Dollmaker's residence.

While he wasn't at the level of First High's counselor, Haruka Ono (alias Mizz Phantom), Toshikazu was a first-rate user of concealment magic. Making sure passersby didn't notice him carrying his sword cane was child's play. It wouldn't fool any technological observation, but he was confident in his ability not to be spotted by any human eyes.

As he continued to conceal himself, Toshikazu extended his extrasensory perception into the residence—not like a cloth blanketing his field of vision but rather countless threads extending outward from within it.

Contrary to his expectations, he found no obstacles barring his way. He detected no walls blocking his threads, nor traps turning them back against him. But he remained vigilant as he explored deeper and deeper into the residence.

He found Inagaki with unexpected ease.

It was so easy, in fact, that it put Toshikazu even more on his guard.

The sense of Inagaki that was coming down through the threads of Toshikazu's perception was very weak. He seemed on the verge of death. Even if he'd gone an entire day and night without eating or drinking, it didn't explain this level of debilitation. He required immediate medical attention.

There was no time for hesitation. Toshikazu quickly abandoned standard procedure.

*If I'm wrong, I'll submit my letter of resignation.*

He summoned his courage and decided to enter the residence.

He took the friendly approach to start, pressing the intercom button. He didn't think anyone would just let him inside, but it would at least give him an excuse for breaking the lock. Right as he was about to follow through with his plan of action—

"Ah, the officer from the other day. I've unlocked the door. Do come in."

The sudden response caught him off guard. His sense that he was in danger only increased, but in the end, he knew that this was no time for caution. He turned the doorknob.

It wasn't locked.

As Toshikazu stepped into the entryway, the lights automatically came on. Gimmicks like this and houses with few windows weren't particularly uncommon these days. And it was his second time visiting the place. Leaving his shoes on (it was the procedure for this house), he continued down the hallway.

A white-haired old man in a long, high-collared robe awaited him at the end of the hall. He appeared to be in his fifties or early sixties. His hair was completely white, but aside from slight wrinkles, his dark skin was free from any liver spots, sagging, or other signs of aging. Judging by his skin color and features, Toshikazu guessed he might be from the Indonesian Peninsula. In any case, this was not Kazukiyo Oumi.

"Dr. Oumi is out at the moment, but he left instructions that any police officers were to be allowed in," said the old man in slightly English-accented Japanese, bowing his head.

"Excuse me, but who are you?" Toshikazu asked the old man, aware that the wind was rapidly being taken out of his sails.

"I am Nguyen, an old friend of Dr. Oumi."

*Vietnam, then*, thought Toshikazu. *As long as that's not a false name*, he added to himself.

"Your acquaintance is this way."

"Do you mean Inagaki?" His adrenaline was down, but Toshikazu was still nervous as he put the question to Nguyen, careful not to let his caution show on his face.

"Yes, that's right, Mr. Inagaki. Dr. Oumi called him that as well," answered the old man without turning around as he continued to lead Toshikazu farther into the residence

The old man opened the door to a room.

Inagaki's prone form suddenly came into view. He was lying feebly on a bed, his breaths coming with great difficulty.

"Inagaki!"

Toshikazu burst into the room, only to suddenly realize that in doing so, he'd turned his back on the old man. He froze.

Seemingly paying Toshikazu's strange actions no mind, the old man walked up to the side of the bed where Inagaki lay.

Careful to keep both Inagaki and the old man in his field of view, Toshikazu approached the bed.

"What's going on here?" Toshikazu demanded as he looked down at them, not bothering to hide the fury in his voice.

"Your friend is suffering from a hex."

"A hecks?"

"Pardon me. I mean to say that a curse placed on him by someone is draining him of his life force."

"A curse…?" Toshikazu's confusion was not because this fact itself was unexpected. He'd suspected that Inagaki had been the victim of a magical attack from the Dollmaker. But this situation made it seem like the Dollmaker was actually trying to *heal* him.

"Dr. Oumi found your friend collapsed and brought him here to the residence where he has been receiving emergency treatment. That's why he's been unable to call you. The hex can also travel through the phone lines, you see."

The old man's story seemed to hold water, but there was absolutely no proof that it was true. All Toshikazu took away from this was that the old man was bothering to make sure it was consistent.

But he didn't want to start getting rough with someone who hadn't taken any hostile action at all. Toshikazu decided to return to his car and call for backup.

However, he didn't get the chance to carry out that decision.

"Inspector…"

Inagaki's weakened voice brought Toshikazu up short. "Inagaki, you're awake!" Toshikazu automatically placed his left hand on the bed frame. Still, his right hand remained free, out of caution toward the old man behind him.

Inagaki's right hand feebly grasped Toshikazu's left.

But the next instant, Inagaki's grip gained immense strength, immobilizing Toshikazu's wrist.

Toshikazu's mind reeled.

The power in man's grip was unthinkable. To be so weakened—to have lost so much vitality that he was easily mistakable for a corpse—it should have been impossible for him to summon such strength.

Inagaki's left hand sprang up from the mattress. In it, he held what looked like some kind of a pressurized hypodermic injector.

Reflexively, Toshikazu tried to defend himself.

But the next moment, Toshikazu was shocked from behind with what felt like a stun gun. He lacked the strength to turn around, and a shroud of blackness fell upon him.

Under the direction of the Ten Master Clans, magicians were putting all their talent toward the task of searching for the mastermind behind the Hakone attack, and law enforcement agencies were working around the clock on the terrorist investigation. Despite all this effort, by February 18, almost two weeks since the incident, they had yet to locate Gu Jie.

No new leads had been gleaned from the Generator corpses recovered at Zama. As a feeling of deadlock spread through all those involved in the investigation, Tatsuya decided to go take another look over the location where Gu Jie had previously hid.

However, as he rode alone to Kamakura, he was suddenly assailed by a sensation of danger. He wondered if this was what people meant by a "gut feeling." He stopped the bike and focused his vision, but he saw no elements that posed any danger to Miyuki. And he hadn't yet found a technique for seeing into the future.

Still, he respected the uneasy premonition and turned his bike toward Hachiouji.

There was still plenty of time left before she would have had to leave school for the day, but Miyuki was already at the nearby station.

"I'm very sorry for this, Miss Miyuki."

Beside her walked Minami, who was apologizing repeatedly.

"How many times do I have to tell you that it's fine? This is also part of my student council duties, and I have no intention of pushing it all off on you."

"We really wouldn't have minded going by ourselves, Miyuki." Izumi was also superficially apologetic, but she couldn't hide the fact that she was actually very pleased with how things had turned out.

Miyuki was accompanying Minami and Izumi to consult on gifts for the graduating students. Every year, commemorative items were ordered at a store near the station that had its own fabrication facilities. This was Miyuki's second time meeting at the store to decide on gifts, and she would have been just fine on her own, but she had brought along the other two to prepare them for next year.

"Hello, we're from the First High School student council."

"Ah, yes, welcome!" It was the owner's wife who emerged from within the shop to greet them.

Apparently, the shop, too, had learned quite a bit from their experience last year…

"That took quite a bit of time, didn't it, Miyuki?" murmured Izumi in a small voice as soon as they left the shop. Her refined voice didn't make it sound like she was complaining, but the sense that she was still annoyed somehow came off her in waves.

"I suppose so. But we got basically all the requirements worked out today, so let's call that a win," Miyuki announced with a comforting smile.

Izumi immediately perked up. "That's true! You really were a great negotiator, Miyuki. I mean, of course you were."

"I don't know if I was all *that* good, but…"

"No, you were! It's all thanks to you that we finished the meeting so fast." The fickle approach to life that let Izumi say "so fast" immediately after complaining about how long something had taken was her default setting—at least, with the proviso that she was with Miyuki. "And that reserved elegance you have is just wonderful."

Izumi was hitting all the usual things people talked about when singing Miyuki's praises. Miyuki was used to this sort of thing, so she just smiled and let the energetic girl say what she pleased.

It would soon be time to go home from school. Despite not needing notebooks or textbooks, the girls always had to bring various grooming and cosmetic accessories with them, so it wasn't as though they commuted to and from school empty-handed. So before they could go home for the day, they had to stop by the school first.

"Anyway, let's hurry back to school. We're not cutting it too close, but we don't have that much time to spare, either."

"All right."

"Yes, let's."

Izumi and Minami respectively both agreed with Miyuki's suggestion, and the trio made for First High.

But before the girls had been walking for even one minute, they were forced to stop.

On a side road one block off the path that led to school, they caught sight of a large group of well over a dozen men.

Not only were they tightly grouped together, but through the gaps between the men's feet, they could see the boots that First High's female students wore.

"Hey, you there, what are you doing?" shouted Izumi as soon as she realized the men were surrounding a girl from her school. She began to run toward them.

The men on the nearer side of the crowed looked over their shoulders, talking to one another. "Hey, she's from the Saegusa family," said one. "That's the First High student council president behind her!" added another. Both Izumi and Miyuki could hear them.

"Izumi, wait!" Miyuki quickly ran after Izumi, grabbing her shoulder and stopping her.

But Miyuki's intervention was too late

Or rather, the men were too quick.

Releasing the girl they'd been harassing, they quickly surrounded Miyuki and her two friends.

"What're you doing?!"

One of the men pointed.

"You there, daughter of a master of dark and sinful arts!" he called, sounding ham-fistedly theatrical. "Repent!"

Following the shout, the others chorused, "Repent!"

"What'd you say?!"

"Izumi, wait—" Miyuki held the sputtering, enraged Izumi back.

"The working of miracles is the sole providence of God. For any other than God to twist his divine creation is an act of evil!"

The man intoned a familiar statement in a booming voice, but Miyuki refused to take the bait. She turned her back to him. "Would you mind letting us pass?"

The men pierced by Miyuki's gaze flinched and hesitated, but rather than heeding her request, they just shouted again, "Repent!"

"Humans must live only by that which God has…"

Of course, Miyuki wasn't listening to *them*, either. "If you do not let us pass, you will be engaging in unlawful detention. Do you understand?" Miyuki insisted, ignoring the words that the leader almost seemed to be reading off a script and instead going for the attention of the one in front of her.

"Shut your mouth!" said a third man, standing next to her target.

Miyuki paid him no heed. "Minami."

"Yes, miss," she replied crisply. She'd already prepared her magic activation, and now she deployed a composite magic barrier that included both Insulation and Deceleration, with a radius that just barely avoided touching the men.

They didn't immediately understand what Minami had done.

Until Miyuki pulled out her portable terminal and pressed the panic button.

The man who'd been shouting at Miyuki reached out to grab her terminal, but his hand was blocked by Minami's barrier.

They realized they were on the other side of a barrier that stopped them from laying a hand on the three girls.

"Oh, so you think you can just use magic, huh?" shouted their assailants.

"We are merely protecting ourselves against an illegal attempt to restrict our movement," Miyuki stated in a clear, calm voice. "I also feel threatened as woman," she added with scorn.

Izumi eyed the leader coldly.

Those eyes were an unbearable provocation to someone with absolute faith in his own righteousness. Even if that wasn't what Izumi intended, it was how the leader felt.

"Let us punish these insolent women!" The leader raised his hand, then brought it forcefully down.

Four men, two on each side of him, advanced from behind, their right fists thrust forward. Each hand had a ring on the middle finger, which shone with a dull brass sheen.

"Is that antinite?!" Izumi shouted.

"This is divine retribution!"

At the leader's order, Miyuki, Izumi, and Minami were assailed with Cast Jamming noise.

Minami, maintaining the barrier, groaned in pain.

All around them, hands pushed through the barrier.

*(To be continued in Part III)*

# Afterword

And now this series has reached its eighteenth volume. At this point in the story, Tatsuya and Miyuki will soon be senior high school students. It feels like the finish line is getting close. I don't think that's necessarily the reason why, but in any case, I've started worrying more than usual about elements I didn't write enough about or didn't write about at all... Yeah, actually I think that *is* because the finish line is getting close.

Initially the Master Clans Council arc was going to be a two-parter, but it's ended up as three, because I kept thinking, *Oh, I should write about this. Right, gotta write about that, too.* For example, per the original outline, Raymond wasn't going to appear in Volume 18. But as I was writing, I started thinking that it would make sense to drop some hints that among the Seven Sages, his position was somewhat different from the other six. Kyouko Fujibayashi's and Toshikazu Chiba's roles were also steadily expanded the more I wrote. All these minor additions ended up adding another volume's worth of text.

Speaking of things I was worried about leaving unwritten, the incident on the flip side of the Steeplechase arc where Erica and Leo meet again is something that had always stuck in the back of my mind. I don't plan on writing a side story before I finish this arc, but once the

Master Clans Council arc is done, I'd like to write some extra material about Erika and Leo next.

That said, it's not entirely my decision. Currently, all that's certain about this series is that Volume 19 will conclude the Ten Master Clans arc.

I'll do my very best to get that conclusion to you all as soon as I possibly can. Thank you all very much.

*Tsutomu Sato*